Too Many Sisters

Nina Guilbeau

Visit my website at www.NinaGuilbeau.com
First Printing: August 2008

Thank you Mom
Thank you Dad

PROLOGUE

Paula forcefully nudged the sleeping, overweight passenger in the seat next to her. He jolted, released a slow hissing sound from between his teeth and then repositioned himself without ever waking up. He had fallen into a deep, relaxed asleep almost as soon as he sat down and that just made Paula mad. If she was uncomfortable, then he should be uncomfortable, too. He was already taking up more than his share of space in their cramped, little seats and Paula felt as if she could barely breathe. Plus he smelled odd, but he was no competition for the stench coming from the small bathroom directly behind them.

Paula was unlucky enough to get stuck in the back row of a bus full of people she hoped would never cross her path again.

Degenerate bus people- all of them.

She hated feeling packed in a like mule, but unfortunately, it was the only transportation her meager funds could afford for now anyway. She thought about the plan she would put in motion the moment her feet touched the ground at her destination. She still had a few hours left on her long ride, but the anticipation she felt was almost sexual.

She rummaged in her bag for her "inspiration" and locating it, held it up to the window. The glow of the moon illuminated the plastic cover. The uneven motion of the heavy bus jostled her and the trees lining the highway cast shadows across the front of it as they sped by, but Paula did not lose her focus. She stared at her sister's pretty face which graced the cover of the music CD she held in her hands.

Her sister looked happy but Paula envisioned her own happiness

5

that was sure to come soon. Of course, she held no such guarantees for the rest of her sisters. They would all be surprised to see her and even more surprised that she was going to stick around this time.

"See you soon, Callie," she said aloud.

The man beside her stirred, catching Paula's attention. He had opened his legs even wider and his giant belly pushed up against the seat in front of him. Paula eyed him with contempt before giving him another stiff elbow.

CHAPTER 1

Callie's head throbbed. It was the type of headache that she had grown accustomed to over the last few months. She had gotten drunk again and now she was paying for it. She couldn't quite focus on her own thoughts because of the echoes, which were getting louder and louder. Even though she was lying in a puddle of water, she thought it was strange how the wetness didn't bother her. The rhythm of the steady stream calmed her somehow. She just wanted to float away, and then all of her pain, anger and unhappiness would be gone forever.

Please, God, she thought, *if you make this hangover go away, I will never, ever drink again.*

"Get up!" the voice said.

Callie's eyes flew open, squinting against the spray of water aimed at her face.

"God, is that you?"

"No such luck, honey"

Callie continued to struggle through the fog in her mind as she tried to get her bearings. Little by little the realization of her state became clearer. She wasn't floating into a peaceful oblivion. She was lying on the hard, cold shower floor. The water was from the shower nozzle and the voice of God and echoes belonged to none other than her older sister, Alise.

"Sober up, Callie! This is ridiculous! You bein' passed out and it's not even one o'clock in the afternoon. I had to drag your heavy behind in here just to wake you up! I don't know why you picked today of all days to have one of your out of control moments!"

I didn't pick today, Callie thought. *You don't understand how this works, Alise.*

She tried to say it but she only managed a few grunts and mumbled dialogue. It didn't really matter what came out of her mouth. How could she explain this to anyone? She didn't completely understand it herself. No matter what she did or where she was physically, in her mind she always ended up back in Marlisa's condo to relive the scene from three month's earlier when she "caught" them in the act. Michael Armstrong, her husband, love of her life, and center of her whole world was in bed with her sister.

She wished she could get through this - grieve her marriage without having to see either one of them again but that was easier said than done. She had three children with Michael and she held joint ownership with Marlisa in their recording and music production studio, a thriving business that kept them both financially secure. The worst part of all of this, besides the obvious betrayal of both her husband and her sister, was that she knew Marlisa had set her up. She was *supposed* to catch them.

Callie had re-played her phone conversation with Marlisa in her head again and again. Marlisa had practically *begged* her to come by for a quick meeting regarding the launch party for a new artist. CM Music Productions had just signed an international distribution deal and would, for the first time, be acting not just as a production company but also a record label. The new artist had already achieved local celebrity status through recent radio play of one cut from the CD. Callie named the song she had written a long time ago for Michael 'Soul Mate'. It was their special song.

Everything was perfect for Callie: her job, her family and her marriage. Maybe that's why she didn't think twice about how unusual it was for Marlisa to ask her to come to her condo for a meeting. "I'm flying out of town and I'll be packing and just running around like crazy!" Marlisa had said. "Don't forget your emergency key. I'll be so busy taking care of things I may not even be home when you come by. Just let yourself in."

"Why don't you just stop by the office when you're done? That way we could -"

"No, no," Marlisa had cut Callie off. "Just come by my place around one o'clock. See you then!"

Callie closed her eyes tighter and shook her head in fierce denial. The memories were coming back stronger as she sobered on the shower floor. She could see the look on Marlisa's face when she had walked into the bedroom. In the split second before she feigned surprise they had locked eyes. What was that she saw in Marlisa's? Was it satisfaction? Hatred? Both?

The water spray ended and a towel landed across Callie's face. Alise grabbed Callie's hand and yanked her to her feet.

"Today of all days," she said while wiping Callie's face with the towel before vigorously rubbing her hair with it.

"Ow, my head," Callie managed to whimper in a tiny voice as she grabbed her temples.

"Here, take this." Alise offered Callie two Excedrin's and a glass of water. "You should have a headache with your hung over self!" Alise continued to chide. "I found three empty wine bottles on your nightstand! Three! And you passed out on the floor like an ol' drunk. Callie you know it's Ashley's sweet sixteen party tonight! She's been talking about it since last year! And look at you!"

Callie looked past Alise into the large bathroom mirror directly in front of her. Usually the reflection was that of a beautiful black woman with bronze skin, large hazel eyes and full lips that turned easily into a wide, bright smile. What she saw now should have frightened her. She barely recognized the woman in the mirror who stood soaking wet in yesterday's clothes. She had hollow, distant, dull eyes complete with dark circles. Her shoulder length hair looked like a tangle of frizzy weeds. She had lost a great deal of weight; skipping

9

meals had taken its toll. She looked as if she had aged twenty years in just the last three months. The only more frightening than the complete deterioration of her physical appearance was her sadness. Her sorrow was so overpowering that you could *feel* it just by being in the same room. Alise felt it. The burden of her sister's pain hurt her more that Callie would ever know.

"Michael's going to be here," Alise voice softened. "Honey, he has to be here. He's her father. His relatives will be here. *Our* relatives will be here. None of them really knows what happened. You don't have to be hostess to anyone. I'll do that. You just have to get through this one night, for Ashley. Michael moving out and all of this divorce talk have hit her really hard. You can't let your feelings towards Michael, Marlisa and what happened take over. Do you understand?"

Callie looked away from herself in the mirror and back at her sister. Expressionless, she turned and walked out of the master bathroom, down the short hallway into her dressing room. Moments later she re-appeared wearing a thick blue terry cloth robe, walked to the other side of the spacious bedroom and disappeared again through a doorway that led to the adjacent office.

Alise went into the dressing room to get the discarded wet clothes that lay, just as she suspected, in a pile in the middle of the floor. She picked them up and took them into the bathroom, dropping them into the tub. Grabbing another towel, she quickly wiped the puddles from the Italian tile floor and made a mental note to send Tess, the housekeeper, in to clean up properly. Alise slowly walked to the other side of the bedroom and stood at the office door.

This was Callie's haven. Her office. Callie had stylishly decorated it in warm browns and vibrant rust and gold accents. There was a beautiful, large mahogany desk and matching bookshelves and all the accessories that a functional office required. However, it also had a comfortable sitting area with a handsome deep-seated leather couch, a stereo, plasma TV, small refrigerator, coffee maker and a small private

10

bathroom. It was all very elegant but still relaxed and cozy, which is just what you would expect from Callie. The far wall had four giant floor to ceiling windows and a set of large French doors, which led out to a spacious balcony overlooking a serene lake and wooded area. Picture perfect on a beautiful day like today. It was Callie's most personal and special space in the large custom designed home.

This was where Callie came to think in peace. Where she worked tirelessly into the night and the place where she was the most creative. And it was off limits to everyone unless you were invited into her private sanctuary and that included Alise. Going into the office was Callie's way of saying, "go away".

Alise heart broke as she watched Callie sitting in a lounge chair on the balcony and staring at the lake. The only time she could remember seeing Callie this sad was when Daddy died. It took a long time to make her smile again.

Alise flinched when Callie reached for the bottle of wine she had removed from the office refrigerator that was now sitting on the small table beside her lounge chair. She poured herself a glass of wine and just stared at it in her hand. She held the glass by the stem and twirled it slowly in her hands before setting it down on the table and pushing both the glass and the wine bottle to the far end. That one gesture gave Alise hope that she had gotten through to her.

Wine had become Callie's new best friend over the last few months. Wine didn't judge you. It didn't drag you into the shower and give you lectures and tell you to get yourself together. It was a good listener, it gave you comfort and it helped you forget the pain – not remember it. What other friend can do that? Certainly not Alise. That's why wine had slowly but surely pushed Alise into a distant second in the friendship category. Alise couldn't help but feel a twinge of hurt knowing that Callie was pushing her away again even now. She sighed and walked over to pick up her purse from the bed before walking out of the bedroom.

"Maybe I got through to her," Alise thought as she walked down

11

the stairs. But even as she said it to herself she didn't believe it.

Callie heard a car start at the front of the house and looked back towards the office door and her bedroom. Alise was gone. Callie thought about Alise. She loved her sister a lot. She has been her protector ever since she could remember. Their mother had suffered from depression and their father traveled almost nine months of the year, so many times she and Marlisa had to depend on Alise to take care of them. She knew Alise felt helpless watching her younger sister suffer, but Callie felt powerless, too. She never knew loving a man could control her life like this. And she loved Michael more than she had ever imagined.

He betrayed her, but Callie knew he loved her even now and that made it so much harder for her to pick up the pieces. He has been fighting against their break up - first the separation and now the impending divorce. Not a day goes by when he doesn't tell her in one way or another that he loves her and wants her back. Callie snubs his every attempt, scared to death that it will be his last. She loves him with all her heart, but she also hates him with that same heart. One day she'll have to come to terms with her battling heart, but for now it took all that she had just to deal with the anger. As long as she had her anger she didn't feel the hurt so much.

And the anger boiled with such intensity that it should have frightened Callie rather than comforted her. She wasn't just angry with Michael and his choice to destroy her and their family, but her rage was directed at Marlisa too.

Her baby sister and good friend had obviously played her for a fool. They were only one year apart and had been inseparable ever since Callie could remember. They had taken baths together and dressed alike and had stayed awake in the bedroom that they shared whispering and giggling late into the night. They had shared a lot of little girl secrets, the kind of secrets too childish to tell Alise who was so much older. Marlisa had been so sweet and so easy going that Callie could remember more than once rolling up her sleeves to fight

12

on her behalf. Callie was determined that no one would ever hurt Marlisa and over the years Marlisa begin to rely on her as the big sister rather than Alise. Alise was Callie's protector and she, in turn, had become Marlisa's. Callie was more than aware that Marlisa was not just a part of *her life,* she was a part of *her being.* That's why the hatred she felt for Marlisa was tearing her apart.

Michael and Marlisa. It was hard to accept that two people so close to her heart could get together and conspire against her.

But when Callie found herself teetering dangerously on the emotional edge, she would force herself to remember all the good things she still had in her life. She had three beautiful, healthy daughters. She had her very own successful business. She was living in an affluent suburb of Washington, D.C. and she knew financially, she could do just about anything she wanted. She knew what it was like to be in love. Some women never experience that. And she had big sister Alise, her very best friend.

"You need to count your blessings, Callie," she said before grabbing the bottle of White Zinfandel and putting it up to her lips.

CHAPTER 2

Alise walked briskly into Callie's house and immediately began surveying the progress. She was carrying a garment bag that held her dark blue silk dress. It was cut low enough in the front to get a man's attention, but still respectable enough to wear at her niece's Sweet Sixteen affair. It flattered her generous shape and it was a shape that had taken some getting used to, if the truth be told. She had always been rail thin until the babies came. Now some thirteen years after the last child, she's still forty pounds heavier than she was before and she loves it! A little "junk in the trunk" can be a good thing.

Secretly Alise wondered if her ex-husband Terrence would come tonight. For the most part, he was still on good terms with the family and Ashley had asked her if it was okay to invite him. She also knew that when Ashley invited him it was with the stipulation that he comes without a date. There would be no "other women" drama at this family affair. Alise by no means still wanted that man or anything from him including his name. She had changed her last name from Scott back to Elliot before the ink was dry on the divorce papers. He had cheated on her all through the marriage. But she had to admit that she wanted *him* to want *her*. She wanted him to suffer knowing that he had made a terrible mistake ruining what he had with her and the boys for the single life. She knew none too well how lonely the single life could be and she hoped, no she prayed, with everything she had that that man was miserable.

Alise hung her garment bag in the hall closet and looked in the

14

mirror hanging above the foyer table. Her thick black hair was cut in a short bob, which fit her round face and enhanced her large almond shaped eyes. Her skin was a little too pale for her liking but that was to be expected coming out of the winter months. She couldn't wait for an opportunity to bake in the sun in order to achieve a beautiful golden brown color. Summer couldn't get here fast enough because right now she looked like a ghost. Sometimes she hated her fair skin.

Alise looked around the downstairs area and was very approving of the décor. The formal dining room table had been set with the fine china used only for special occasions. The table could only seat sixteen, so Ashley decided to use it to for the hors d'oeuvre. Incoming guest could socialize there before being led to the entertainment room to be seated for dinner.

The entertainment room was the equivalent of a small ballroom and the caterers had set up round dinning tables with white tablecloths and folding chairs for the guests. Ashley had insisted the folding chairs have seat cushions to match her color theme of peach and ivory. Each table had a small crystal vase with peach and ivory roses as the centerpiece. As a matter of fact, there were fresh cut peach or ivory roses in crystal vases set out throughout the entire downstairs.

Ashley's dress was a beautiful peach, too. She had picked her own color scheme and had been involved with every detail of her party from the beginning. There was classical music playing softly through the downstairs intercom. Another one of Ashley's ideas. They were expecting sixty people in formal attire for what Ashley called 'The classiest affair of the decade'.

Callie had been suspicious when she first saw the original guest list and with good reason.

"I know my daughter," she had said to Alise, "and only eighty people, mostly relatives, for a sweet sixteen party is making my "spidey senses" tingle."

"She wanted it to be elegant and simple," Alise had said smiling.

"Uh-huh," Callie had said narrowing her eyes as she looked at

15

Alise. "I'm waiting for the other shoe to drop."

They both knew there was more to come. From the time Ashley had been old enough to understand the concept of a birthday party, she had been extravagant. Her special day could easily last a week, as she would sweetly request a birthday dinner at her favorite restaurant, in addition to the party she was already having. Then the birthday party would turn into a sleep over and somehow they would all end up at the beach or some other weekend destination. Simple, no matter how elegant, was never a part of her plans.

The other shoe came in the form of a second guest list of 400 of her closest friends in the largest ballroom of the JW Marriott in DC. Not to mention, Michael was put in charge of booking a Grammy award winning rapper (someone Michael had never heard of) and Callie was in charge of securing Johnny Depp to make an appearance to personally wish Ashley the happiest of birthdays. He was supposed to seal it with a kiss on the custom built stage where everyone could see and therefore envy her forever. Immediately following this sensational party would be a weekend trip to the Bahamas with ten of her BFFs to complete the birthday festivities.

The Bahamas weekend was an absolute no, however Callie was willing to negotiate on the other plans. The eighty guests for the home party became sixty.

"Unless they are close friends, only one party per guest." Callie had told Ashley when she noticed names that were on both guest lists (not hers or Michael's name of course). The four hundred guest became two hundred, any Grammy winners performing would be via music videos running while their songs played and Johnny Depp, or rather the life-sized cardboard cutout, would be available on stage whenever she was ready for the big kiss.

"He can't wish you a happy birthday, but you can smooch with him a much as you like," Callie had told Ashley.

"You're not funny, Mom," Ashley had replied rolling her eyes and getting up from the kitchen table.

"I'm a little funny," Callie had said aloud to the empty kitchen.

After Callie tweaked the birthday plans to line up with how things were really done on planet earth, Ashley sulked a few days, but finally came around. One other condition Callie had if Ashley wanted two parties was that she would have to plan one of them with the budget Callie gave her. Ashley had chosen to handle the gathering at home and by what Alise could see, she had done a brilliant job so far. The party should go on without a hitch.

Michael's parents had pushed for it to be held at their country club, a club where they were only one of three black families. Of course, if you had enough money and looked white enough they would quietly and begrudgingly accept you. And Michael's parents were both rich and looked white, right down to the processed hair. Alise was sure his parents hoped that his marrying the very brown Callie was a sign of rebellion that Michael would tire of quickly. Even after nineteen years of marriage Alise believed they still had hope that Michael would come to his senses, leave Callie and come go back to the light side. Take the light skinned children, too. Alise had no doubt that if Ashley wasn't a fair complexioned beauty with long hair, they would not even bother to show up, much less push for it to be at their esteemed country club. Alise knew what Michael's family thought of hers. They thought that Michael Armstrong, their only beloved light skinned son, was too good for Callie and her family.

That's why Alise needed Callie to hold it together tonight. *Do it for Ashley and for your own family. We're just as good as the Armstrongs,* Alise thought.

She wished she could be more like Callie when it came to Michael's family. Callie loved Michael and could care less what his parents and other family members thought. She was just comfortable in the fact that Michael openly dismissed their bourgeois attitude. But Alise couldn't help how she felt. She didn't want her family to be put down by anybody.

"We gotta represent girl!" Alise said aloud.

17

"Who are you talkin' to, Aunt Al?" eight year old Maya said as she bounded down the stairs in a pink robe covering the toffee colored gown which was peeking out from underneath.

"Nobody. Oh, my, you do look gorgeous! Look at your hair!" Alise exclaimed.

Maya twirled. "You want to see my dress? I got this robe on because I'm scared it's gonna get dirty before it's supposed to."

"Before it's *supposed to*? You mean to tell me you have a *plan* for gettin' your dress dirty?"

"No, no, Aunt Al!" Maya giggled. "You know what I mean! I gotta stay looking nice until at least everyone is here!" Maya took her robe off and twirled around again.

"You do look beautiful, but I have an idea. Why don't you take the dress off for right now? You can get comfortable and then just put it back on later."

"Cause Grandma sent the hairdresser over early for me and this dress pulls over my head. I can't take it off now or all that stinkin' work goes down the drain." Maya put the robe back on making sure to completely cover her dress. "It's ok, really. I was just watching TV in my room and got a little hungry. Smelling all that food is making my mouth water!"

"Mine too. Smells like the caterers are doing a fantastic job in there." Maya shook her head in agreement and flashed Alise a mischievous smile.

"Now Maya, don't you go getting all in their way scrounging around that kitchen for a hand out."

"I won't" Maya yelled as she raced towards the kitchen.

"Maya!" Alise yelled but Maya had already disappeared through the double doors leading into the kitchen.

"Oh, well." Alise said as she began to climb the stairs. "I got bigger fish to fry - like your mother. Lord, please let that girl be up and getting ready and looking gorgeous. And if not gorgeous I'll settle for her just looking like she's alive."

Alise knocked on Callie's bedroom door. When she didn't get an answer, she turned the doorknob and went in. The room was cool and quiet. Too quiet. Alise checked the bathroom and the dressing room. Everything looked just as it had three hours ago when Alise had left. It was 4:30 now and guest would begin arriving for dinner at 6:30. Where was Callie?

Alise walked back to the office and looked in. No Callie. She was about to turn around when she spotted the blue bathrobe slumped down in a lounge chair on the balcony. Alise rushed over to the chair and stood over Callie. She had an empty tissue box in her lap and there were used tissues everywhere - on her lap, on the ground, on the table. Next to Callie lay a wine bottle that Alise picked up. Empty. Not again Callie. Alise grabbed Callie preparing herself for "the shower part two" when Callie jerked awake.

"Huh, Wha...? What are you doing, Alise?"

"I'm getting ready to give you another cold shower. If this is the way you want to play it, suit yourself, honey." Alise tugged on Callie's arm.

"Wait Alise! I'm not drunk!"

"Well, somebody is! I sure found another empty wine bottom laying around!" Alise picked up the bottom and shook it at Callie.

"It must have fallen over or something but I didn't drink it. I mean... I drank some but not the whole bottle!"

Alise eyed Callie suspiciously. She looked down at the balcony's natural stone flooring. Alise was sure that if all that wine had pored out there would still be some evidence of it left. The floor was as clean as ever.

Callie eyes followed Alise's to the tiled floor. "Well, I know what you're thinking and I can't explain it either. But I just fell asleep. I didn't pass out. I'm not drunk. Well, no more drunk than I was when you last saw me."

It was then that Callie spotted her black Labrador snoring loudly in the corner.

"There's the culprit, right there. Sleeping it off in the corner!" Callie yelled pointing. Alise looked over at the dog and back at Callie.

"You see what kind of an influence you are."

They both looked back at Jasmine who had turned on her back and now had all four legs in the air and her mouth open still snoring. She began flailing all four legs in the air and twisting her body as if she was desperately trying to scratch a very persistent itch. Then, just as suddenly as she began, she stopped and with all four legs frozen in the air she began to snore again, this time even louder than before.

Callie and Alise looked at each other and then burst out laughing at the same time. Finally when she could catch her breath, Alise called downstairs for her oldest son Jamal to come and get the dog.

"Take her and put her in the back yard," Callie told him still laughing. They followed Jamal through the office and into the bedroom as he carried a sleepy Jasmine in his arms.

"Labs have very sensitive stomachs and she's going to be feeling pretty sick very soon." Callie continued, "Gotta learn how to hold your liquor if you wanna run with the big dogs, right Jasmine?"

As if on cue, Jasmine raised her head from Jamal's shoulder and burped. Jamal turned up his nose at the smell, "Ugh!"

That set Callie and Alise off into another fit of uncontrollable laughter. Jamal frowned and shook his head not understanding the humor as he looked at his mother and aunt laughing loudly. Then adjusting the big dog in his arms he walked out the bedroom mumbling about not understanding "old folks".

"Drunk dog coming through!" They could hear Jamal shout as he walked down the stairs.

"Do you remember Tuffy?" Alise asked still laughing.

"You mean that three-legged dog that you hid in our house for a week, talking 'bout we gotta save him from the dog catcher?"

"He wasn't three legged! He just had a bad limp. Couldn't run fast. That's why he needed our help."

"*Our* help? It wasn't my idea!"

20

"But remember," Alise giggled before continuing, "you fed him your Halloween candy and he got sick and threw up and when Mama saw it, you pretended it was *you* that was sick and had threw up?"

"I had to think quick, otherwise we were both gonna be in trouble!" Callie was laughing again too.

"You fell to the ground grabbing your stomach and Mama grabbed you to pick you up and smelled your breath! Oooh, girl! You had ..." Alise was now laughing so hard could hardly catch her breath.

"I know, I know, I know! I picked that day to get my first taste of Daddy's beer. I had taken a can and drank some of it and Mama thought I was sick because I was drunk!"

Callie and Alise were both laughing hysterically at the memory.

"You got to walking around like you were dizzy and stuff! Stumbling! Everybody got in trouble that day!"

"All because you wanted to save some dog! That's you Alise. Always trying' to save the world," Callie said wiping the tears caused by the laughter from her eyes. "I just hope I'm not the new three legged dog that you're trying to save."

Alise grinned at Callie and shrugged.

"What if you are?"

Becoming serious, Callie walked over to her sister and put her arms around her.

"Then you can't let them get me." She hugged her sister tightly and whispered, "Alise, please don't let them get me."

"I won't," Alise said softly. "You just get through tonight, honey and I'll help you do that. Now the first thing we need to do is get you in the shower."

Callie rolled her eyes and mumbled "not again," as Alise pushed her in the direction of the bathroom.

Callie took a deep breath before opening the door to her bedroom and stepping into the hallway. She was still feeling a little hung over and not quite like herself. But she hadn't felt like herself since that fateful day when her marriage ended - at least in her mind it had ended on that very day. And soon it would be over legally no matter what Michael wanted.

Callie closed the door to her bedroom and smoothed her dress down. She had showered and dressed quickly, expertly doing her hair and make-up. Her fingers self-consciously patted the puffiness under her eyes. She was aware of the dark circles and large bags or "suitcases" that were still visible under her eyes even after applying what seemed to be a ton of eye cream and concealer. She had done the best that she could with the make up and although she was good, this was a big job and she wasn't kidding herself – she was no miracle worker.

If she was careful, she could stay in soft lighting. Callie smiled as she imagined herself darting from one dark corner to the next. The kitchen, with its bright recess lighting, should be completely of limits. But since it was the best place to hide at a function like this, Callie knew it would be hard to resist. It's a good thing Alise would be playing hostess so she could concentrate on looking and acting like her normal self. She reminded herself of Alise's words - *Just get through tonight.*

"The dress looks really good on you." Callie startled at the voice as she looked up into the eyes of its owner; her daughter Ashley. She looked down at her dress before smiling and saying

"What, this old thing?"

Ashley smiled too. The dress was a beautiful antique ivory dress that Ashley had picked out for just for this occasion. It was an off the shoulder design with tiny rhinestones trimming the entire neckline. The form fitting lace design played peek-a-boo with Callie's smooth caramel skin and lay flat across her stomach and thighs before ending just below her knees. Callie wore a thin rhinestone anklet that was an exact match for the tennis bracelet and earring set she also wore. As a finishing touch, Callie had put on a hint of body shimmer across her shoulders and at her cleavage. Ashley, completely unaware of Callie's tumultuous start, thought she looked beyond beautiful.

22

It had taken Ashley more than four months to find just the right dress for tonight. She had wanted her and her mother to match the color scheme of peach and ivory. She had wanted them to be connected tonight; a team and she wanted everyone to know it. But that was back then. Back before the anger and hurt feeling had come between them. Back when they were as close as mother and daughter could be and when Ashley seemingly worshiped the ground Callie walked on. It almost felt like it used to as they stood smiling at each other in the hallway. But then Callie felt the wall come up between them. She could see the hostile look in Ashley's eyes. Now what began as a happy, memorable moment had suddenly turned awkward.

Ashley couldn't seem to forgive Callie for not being able to forgive Michael. She was old enough to put all the pieces together and had figured out Michael had betrayed her mother. She only recently found out about the very last piece – the woman in question was Aunt Marlisa. The realization had crushed Ashley.

Aunt Marlisa was the fun aunt who wore young, funky clothes. She used to come and get Ashley on the weekends and let her stay up all night if she wanted to. Ashley remembered the "sugar comas" she would fall into after pulling all nighters of cookies, candy and ice cream with Aunt Marlisa. She knew her Mom would have had a fit if she knew just how far her aunt let her go on so many things. But that's what made Aunt Marlisa so great. She didn't treat her like a baby. She bothered to ask Ashley what she thought and what she wanted and then she *listened*.

Of course, Aunt Marlisa would always make her promise never to tell anyone, especially Callie. And Ashley never did. Not Callie, not Michael or her other sisters. She knew Callie didn't approve of a lot of things her Aunt Marlisa did, but she also knew that Aunt Marlisa trusted her, little Ashley, with so many of her secrets. She understood Aunt Marlisa in a way that no one else did. Maya was too young and Vanessa, who was only a year and a half older than Ashley, was too judgmental.

23

Vanessa had just started college and wanted to be a psychiatrist, which was fitting since she was always analyzing people and making conclusions about their behavior. She thought Aunt Marlisa just did things to get attention. Like when she upholstered her car seats in leopard print. Obviously, that was a ploy to get people to notice her, not to mention ghetto. Ashley thought it was stylish and bold. She really liked her aunt and that's why it hurt her so much that she would do this to her mother.

Even so, Ashley thought Callie should give Michael another chance and not send her father out of their life. Michael had moved out and she hadn't seen him as much these last few months. He spoke to her every day on the phone and was able to pick her up on the weekends, but Callie wouldn't see him. He was not even allowed to come in the house and Callie never came to the phone when he called for her. Ashley knew her father was trying very hard to make them a family again, but her mother wouldn't even speak to him. If she loved him and if she loved her children, why wouldn't she try to make it work?

Ashley knew Aunt Marlisa may have been the reason that they separated in the first place, but she believed Callie is the reason that they're still apart. Her mother simply didn't love them enough to get past this one mistake. That's what Aunt Marlisa had said. She had also told Ashley how sorry she was for everything and how hard she was trying to fix things even though Callie wouldn't let her. Aunt Marlisa had said that Callie had everything, but was willing to throw it all away because she was selfish. Ashley agreed.

She loved her mother, but she trusted and believed her aunt. Aunt Marlisa had never lied to her before, unlike Callie who wouldn't even tell her the truth about why her Dad left. She still wanted to treat her like a child and like she couldn't understand grown up things. She was sixteen and not a baby. Aunt Marlisa understood that and she wanted to fix what had gone wrong in their family. Why didn't her own mother care about her as much as her aunt did?

24

Ashley's eyes clouded with tears as she stood and looked at her mother in the hallway. She missed her Dad a lot but she missed her Mom even more. She wanted to run to her mother and hug her just to feel safe and loved like she used to. But that's what a child would do and Ashley reminder herself again that she was no longer a little girl.

Callie needed to realize that as long as she refused to make them a happy family again, then everything that happened to unravel the family now was her fault. If she didn't love her family enough, then Ashley would no longer love her the way she used to.

After the party, she was going to ask to live with her Dad. That would be a blow to her mother and she knew Callie would try to talk her out of it. Maybe then her mother would see how much the family was splitting apart and would allow her Dad back in the house. It was worth a try.

Ashley's smile had long faded from her face when she averted her eyes and walked past her mother down the stairs. Callie watched her with a heavy heart. She desperately wanted to reach out to her, to hug her, love her and do whatever she could to make things good again, but that would take the kind of energy that Callie no longer had. She was an emotional wreck and couldn't help anyone, not even herself. In her current state, trying to make Ashley understand and trying to be strong for her would only make things worse. Callie closed her eyes and took a deep breath and whispered, "Just get through tonight".

Callie walked downstairs into a hub of activity. It appeared that all of the invited guests had arrived as well as some uninvited guests. Michael's parents Ursula and Monroe had taken it upon themselves to invite a few of their country club friends and they were all seated front and center at the table reserved for the immediate family. Callie saw her nameplate on the floor next to the toe of one of Ursula's satin shoes. It was just as well. She hadn't planned on sitting any where near Michael anyway. Let the great Armstrongs take over. Alise, however, was not as accommodating. She grabbed Callie's arm and pulled her into the kitchen and started fussing before Callie could even

25

protest.

"Girl, do you see what's going on out there! I told that damn Ursula that that table was reserved for Ashley and y'all. I told her immediate family – that means mother, father, sisters, and brothers! I even pointed out the nametags and everything! Next thing I know, Shannon come walkin' by me talkin' 'bout 'Oh Mother, over here, over here. This is the family table'" Alise had imitated Shannon by changing her voice to a falsetto, sticking her nose in the air and waving her hands in a beckoning motion.

"Then I look up and they all sitting down at the table. Hell, except for some of Ashley's friends, we *all* family here tonight! And aunts ain't never meant immediate family. Shannon so educated with all her college degrees, but she didn't know that? And then on top of that, they have the nerve to have some people that are strangers, complete *strangers* at the table!" Alise eyes had grown large as if to emphasize the outrageousness of it all.

"Alise, I really don't have the strength to go off on nobody right now so-"

"Well, I got plenty of strength," Alise cut in. "Girl, I'm strong enough for the both of us and I'm going out there and *correct* this situation."

Alise stormed to the kitchen door and turned and wagged a finger at Callie. "If you hear the sound of fisticuffs and then a body getting' slammed across the table, just rest assured I won't be on the receiving end of any of that!"

Alise pushed through the door as Callie calmly watched. Then pangs of hunger surprised her as she stood alone in the kitchen

"No wonder, "she said as she looked around the kitchen and saw all the delicious food waiting to be served. Callie had not eaten since the previous evening and she suddenly realized she was famished. She picked up a stuffed pastry of some kind and took a bite.

Oh, heaven, Callie thought as she munched on the seafood pastry. The only thing that would make this better was a glass of wine.

26

Callie was quick to spot the uncorked wine bottle sitting next to a silver platter of wine glasses. She grabbed both the wine bottle and a glass and walked over to lean up against the sink. She poured the wine, took a sip and looked out the window into the garden.

This was always a calming view for Callie. It was not yet officially spring, but the flowers were already so colorful and beautiful. The weather had been unseasonably warm for the time of year and everything was in a rush to bloom. It all looked so fresh and new. She could see the water falling gracefully from the fountain and immediately felt at peace. She opened the small window so that she could hear the sound of the water, hear the birds and smell the flowers.

"Aw, peace, quiet, serenity," she said before taking another sip of wine, this time closing her eyes to savor the taste, sounds and smells. She heard before seeing her eldest daughter enter the kitchen.

"Mom, you have to come get Aunt Alise! I think she's going to kill Grandma Ursula!"

Callie slowly took another sip of wine before calmly saying, "Well, if you can get past the whole *murder thing*, I mean, getting rid of her is not necessarily a *bad* idea."

"Oh, Lord! Where's Dad? I need somebody sane!" said an exasperated Vanessa as she ran out the kitchen.

Callie was on her third hors d'oeuvre when the kitchen door flung open again. It was a red faced Ursula, clearly enraged

"Where's my son!" she screamed at Callie.

Callie continued looking out the window and immediately thought of the singsong children's retort that was one of her favorites when growing up.

"In his skin

Drinkin' gin

He jump out

You jump in"

27

"You are so classless," Ursula said haughtily. "Not only are you drinking, but you're *singing* about drinking when you're probably already *drunk* at your daughter's affair. I cannot imagine how low my son had to stoop to pick you up to marry."

"Yeah, and I wonder how low he's gonna have to stoop to pick you up off the floor. You just keep talkin', Ursula."

"You have no respect to threaten me that way!"

"Ursula, I'm just trying to mind my own business in my own house. If you don't like it you can -"

"Mom!" Vanessa yelled coming up from behind with Maya following closely. "You're not helping anything," she said just as Ursula grabbed her chest.

"My heart!" she squealed nearly collapsing in Vanessa's arms as Maya pushed a chair under her grandmother.

"Call 911!" Vanessa yelled to her mother.

"Why?"

"Mom! She could be having a heart attack!"

"Yeah, right. She's had more heart attacks than Fred Sanford. She's quite talented actually. As a matter of fact, I saw her first performance when Michael introduced us. It was good, not great," Callie took a sip of wine and looked pensively off into the distance while Ursula moaned, "but then I was only his girlfriend. Now I have to admit she put on a *spectacular* performance when your father announced that we were getting married. Can you believe that? She would rather have a heart attack than say congratulations. If I hadn't been preoccupied with rating the styling of her presentation, I would have *really....been... insulted!*"

"Mom, *please*! Can you at least try to help?" Vanessa pleaded while placing a damp linen napkin to her Grandmother's forehead.

"Help how? Clap? I'm not falling for-"

"Mommy, she might be dying!" Maya cried.

Callie looked in the fearful eyes of her youngest daughter and then at Vanessa who was clearly afraid for their grandmother. Ursula was

28

slumped in the chair with her eyes closed gasping for air.

"Ok, don't worry girls. I'll get Michael- oh, there he is. He just walked by."

With that Ursula sprung up and stormed out the kitchen yelling for her son. Stunned, Vanessa and Maya looked after her with mouths open and eyes stretched wide before looking at each other in complete disbelief.

"What the f -"

Vanessa quickly covered Maya's mouth. "Hold that thought, Missy!" she said grinning.

Now it was Callie's turn to be surprised. She stood with her mouth open looking at her youngest daughter feeling something between shock and amusement. Callie then looked at Vanessa who began backing towards the kitchen door with her hand still clamped down over Maya's mouth.

"We'll just go find Dad. Which way did he go?"

"I don't know. I didn't see Michael," Callie said with a sly smile.

"*Ohhh*," Vanessa said still backing up as the realization of her mother's ploy dawned on her. She looked down at Maya's eyes above her hand as they darted back and forth between her sister and her mother in confusion.

"We're just going to find Dad anyway," Vanessa said and still grinning, she dashed out the kitchen door with Maya in tow.

Callie shook her head and laughed softly to herself. She would have to have a talk with Maya a little later. Right now all she wanted to do was to relax. After pouring another glass of wine, she reached for another delicious stuffed pastry to munch.

So far this party is pretty good, Callie thought pleasantly. Maybe, just maybe she could get away with hiding in the kitchen all night. After all, she had everything she needed to make this a perfect evening - good food, good drink and no company. Callie began to dance the waltz when her Aunt Mattie walked through the door.

"I have to warm up my tea. Those waiters are terrible out there.

29

Besides, I had to get away from your crazy ol' Aunt."

Callie knew her Aunt Mattie was actually referring to her own sister Harriet.

"You know what she said to me?" Aunt Mattie said while putting her cup of lukewarm tea in the microwave. "Callie, how do you turn this thing on?" Callie set the microwave timer and turned it on while Aunt Mattie continued speaking.

"That woman, that woman is gonna make me slap the taste out of her mouth. She always gotta get her digs in. She asking why my kids ain't here at yet *another* family function. Then talking 'bout how we, as black people, need to learn how to support each other, especially family. I know she don't want to get me started 'cause I'm tired of keeping' my mouth shut. I've held my tongue too long. I remember the way she used to treat Momma. Cussing her out over the phone and hanging up. Momma used to cry and I didn't say nothing then, but I have held everything in too long! I promised myself…"

Callie drifted off. Trained to say 'uh huh' at the right moments. She watched an ant crawl up the window screen until it reached the top and was out of sight. Then she looked at the clock above the kitchen table for a moment and watched the second hand moving before studying the numbers on its giant face. Whose bright idea was it to keep track of every miserable second of a person's miserable life?

Callie let her eyes drift around the kitchen as her Aunt Mattie continued to talk, frowning while she thought of Michael. Why hasn't he come looking for her? He apparently hadn't noticed that she wasn't at her own daughter's sweet sixteen. He apparently hadn't noticed a lot of things, like how much he really hurt her or how much she cried over him or how much she still loved him and missed him and wanted him back, but didn't know what to do about it.

Callie wondered if she fixed herself a plate and snuck up the back stairs if her Aunt Mattie, who continued to talk, would even notice she was gone. She just liked to hear the sound of her own voice because she told the same stories over and over. Plus they all seemed to go on forever – present story included. This must have been how the people who followed Moses into the wilderness felt. First a little chat about the Promised Land and the next thing you know it's forty years later. Finally Callie heard the familiar beeping sound.

"Oh, a minute's up already?" Aunt Mattie said opening the microwave. She took her cup of tea out and walked toward the kitchen door that led into the dinning room.

"For your sake Callie, and for respect for your family, I'm gonna try my best to hold it together. But I can't promise you like I want to 'cause I might have to pull that heifer's hair out before I leave here tonight." And with that she was out of the door.

"Just get through tonight. Just get through tonight. Just get through tonight." Callie said it over and over again until she thought she felt sure of herself again. She put her wine glass down and went out the kitchen door but what she saw on the other side of her dining room table stopped her in her tracks. Marlisa.

Alise grabbed her by the shoulders pushing her back into the kitchen.

"Please Callie, don't do anything. Please. I'll get rid of her. Just stay here, *please Callie.* Are you listening to me?"

Alise was more than a little nervous now. Callie had "the look". When joking, Alise called that look in Callie's eyes the "high beams". Her eyes were somehow bright and dark at the same time. Piercing. Angry. Scary. Callie was eerily calm. She flicked her "high beams" at Alise and said quietly, "Move."

Alise knew she had no chance with Callie, but maybe she could still do damage control. She ran out of the kitchen ahead of Callie pointing to Marlisa

"You need to leave right now," she said.

"I have a right to be here. My niece invited me and I-"

Alise didn't see the shoe but she heard it whiz past her ear right before popping Marlisa in the mouth. Marlisa's hand flew up to her mouth. Her eyes, already wide in disbelief, grew even larger when she

31

removed her hand and saw the blood. The party had turned silent and everyone seemed to have moved into the dinning room to find out what was causing the commotion. Marlisa dabbed at the blood flowing from her lip with a napkin.

"You're crazy!" Marlisa began to shout, more for the sake of her new audience than to Callie. "You're acting crazy at your own daughter's party!"

"Leave now," Callie said in a tense but surprisingly controlled voice. She was oblivious to her audience and was focusing intently on Marlisa. Alise pointed towards the door, afraid to say anything for fear it would set Callie off. Everyone else stood in silent shock with mouths ajar. You could feel the tension crackling throughout the room.

"Why are you doing this, Callie? I'm not going -"

"If you say another word, I'm on you," Callie warned.

"If Michael says-"

In the blink of an eye Callie tossed aside a dining room chair and climbed on the table. She half slid, half crawled across the table before crouching and launching herself at Marlisa, sending dishes smashing to the floor. Somehow in mid air she caught Marlisa by the throat on the other side of the table forcing her to fall backwards to the floor. Now the previously silent room was filled with shouts, gasps, people running to get out of the way of flying food and more dishes breaking. Someone was yelling 'call 911'and someone else was yelling 'She's killing her!'

Michael and Uncle Fred were trying to pull Callie off of Marlisa, while Jamal was desperately trying to pry Callie's fingers from around Marlisa's neck. Just then, one of the younger cousins came in yelling that the dog had gone crazy.

"The dog keeps running in circles! And...and she throw-did up!"

"The drunk dog got out!" Jamal looked up at his mother.

"You go get the dog; I'll take care of the choking!'

Jamal got up and ran out while Alise took over, finally removing

Callie's grip from her sister's throat.

Marlisa was helped to her feet rubbing her neck and crying. Callie, realizing Michael was still restraining her, forcefully twisted away from him.

"Don't touch me!" she yelled looking hatefully at Michael.

"That's why he came to me," Marlisa managed to say in a raspy voice still rubbing her throat. "Careful she got another shoe!" someone in the crowd yelled. Michael restrained Callie again, but not before she snagged a handful of Marlisa's hair and yanked her backwards, pulling out her clip on extensions. Marlisa set off a high pitch shriek as she and Uncle Fred struggled to release the rest of her hair from Callie's grasp. Callie managed a kick just as they were pulled apart, hitting Marlisa squarely in the chest. Uncle Fred ushered a hysterical Marlisa quickly out the room and to the front door.

Again Callie snatched herself away from Michael and tried to follow them to the front door, but Michael blocked her path. He then ushered her into the kitchen out of the eyesight of the gawking guests.

"She's gone, Callie," Alise said coming into the kitchen moments later. "I saw Uncle Fred put her in the car. She's gone."

Callie took a deep breath and seemed to deflate like a beach ball. She turned to go up the back stairs leading from the kitchen to the second floor, but a teary-eyed Ashley blocked her way.

What have I done? Callie thought, seeing the pain and embarrassment on her child's face. This should have been a happy occasion for her child, but instead Callie had turned it into a battleground. Whatever happened to "just get through tonight". Why couldn't she control herself?

"I hate you," Ashley told her mother.

Callie just looked at Ashley. She wanted to hug her and tell her she was sorry for the second time tonight. She knew Ashley would push her away and with good reason. What kind of mother can't comfort her own child? Callie, feeling like damaged goods, just looked at Ashley.

"I hate me, too," she finally said.

Ashley broke out in tears and ran up the stairs. Callie slowly walked up the stairs behind her.

Alise was true to her word as hostess. With Vanessa's help, she saw everyone out including the caterers, the company that had rented out the extra furniture and the cleaning crew hired to come in afterwards. The house was clean, quiet and back to normal, if only in appearance. Maya had been put to bed and even the dog was all settled.

"All in all, things went pretty well," Alise said examining her shoe with the broken heel and her torn dress. She looked at Vanessa who was sitting on the stairs with both dress and hair disheveled. Her niece's eye make-up was so smeared that she looked like a raccoon.

"Yep," Vanessa replied, "just another family function. Hey, did you see *your* cousin, 'cause he ain't no kin to me, stuffing shrimp in his pockets?"

"What? Don't tell me, let me guess, it was Ricky, wasn't it?"

"Sure was. This time he came prepared and was putting them in little plastic baggies. I guess he got tired of picking off the pocket lint and God knows what else from his last batch of smuggled shrimp. What gathering was that?"

"A holiday family reunion. Your mother's idea. She wanted the family to get together for something other than a funeral."

"Oh, yeah. Now, that was some party, too."

"Girl, don't get me started! But I think this one will go into the family hall of fame."

Alise and Vanessa laughed thinking about the party that would be the talk of the family for a long time.

"If there's no drama then it ain't our family involved," Alise said limping in her broken shoe as she gathered her things.

"I already told you, they ain't none of my people," Vanessa said grinning at her aunt hobbling around and then seeing for the first time

34

a few hors d'oeuvres hanging from the back of her hair.

After pointing out her unique hair ornaments, Vanessa gave her aunt a hug and watched her get into her car and drive away. Now Vanessa looked at the long staircase and sighed. What a day. Somehow she had to find a little more strength to make it up the stairs. She had to check on her mother and Ashley. She had to pretend for Ashley's sake that she wasn't so pissed off at Aunt Marlisa for having the audacity to show up at her mother's house, especially knowing her Dad would be there too.

Maybe if she explained things to Ashley she would understand why their mother reacted that way. They hadn't seen each other since that day in Aunt Marlisa's condo. She knew her mother took careful steps to make sure they wouldn't run into each other. For goodness sake, their mother didn't even go into her own office any more. Her assistant Marvin picked up the slack in the office. Vanessa was convinced that if Ashley knew, then she would understand why Callie had such a bad reaction to seeing the woman she had avoided all this time standing boldly in her own home. It violated and disrespected their mother all over again. Aunt Marlisa deserved everything she got tonight. It took all Vanessa had not to cheer her mother on. It was just unfortunate that it happened at Ashley's expense.

Vanessa quietly opened the door of Callie's room and peeked in to see her mother resting quietly in the dark. Vanessa knew better that to believe her mother was asleep. Her mother hardly ever slept any more. She closed the door and walked to the other end of the hall to Ashley's room. Vanessa knocked quietly.

"Who is it?"

"It's me, Vanessa"

"Come in."

Vanessa could tell by her voice that Ashley was still crying, but she wasn't quite prepared for the red eyed, make-up smeared mess that sat up in the bed.

"Wow, you look terrible. So, I guess asking you how you're doing

35

is a dumb question, huh?"

Ashley smiled thinly. Vanessa's weak attempt to lighten the mood seemed to have worked a little.

"How could she have done that, Nessa?"

"Well, maybe it's time you knew the whole story. I know Mom and Dad didn't think it was necessary for us to know all the details, but there's a reason Aunt Marlisa is not welcome in this house. Um, well it's like this, um…"

"Relax, I know the whole story, so you're off the hook."

"What do you mean you know the whole story?"

"I'm not a kid. I can put two and two together. I figured out there was another woman and I figured out she was Aunt Marlisa."

"You *knew!*" Vanessa eyes widened in disbelief, "and you still invited her!"

"I had already invited her, I just didn't *uninvite* her. It was my party and I should have been the one to decide who could come – not Mom!"

"How could you do that to Mom – and to Dad too?"

"Dad didn't go crazy, so don't put him in this! I talked to Aunt Marlisa after I found out and she said she was trying to make up with Mom, but Mom wouldn't let her. She said Mom was going to hold this one mistake against her for the rest of her life! She didn't want to loose me like she lost some of the other people in her family that turned against her!"

"People turned on her for good reason! She came here to stick it to Mom and she used you to do it! And you let her! She's just a selfish, jealous, petty 'ho!"

"Well, I like Aunt Marlisa and I've forgiven her so *I* wanted her at *my* party!"

"Well, then *you* can take responsibility for this mess tonight! I hope your party turned out the way you apparently wanted it to. Happy Sweet Sixteen, dumb ass!"

Vanessa slammed the door behind her and marched down the hall

36

back to her mother's door. She stood a moment to catch her breath. Not only did her mother have a back-stabber for a sister but she also had a back-stabber for a daughter. Aunt Marlisa had always been able to get to Ashley, but this was ridiculous. Ashley should know better.

Vanessa quietly opened the door and tip toed over to her mother's bed. She climbed in next to her mother and rested her head on her shoulder like she used to when she was a little girl. Instinctively Callie's arms went around Vanessa.

"Mom," Vanessa whispered

"Go to sleep, Vanessa."

"Ok, but Mom?"

"Yes, Vanessa."

"I love you, Mom. I don't hate you at all."

"I know, Vanessa."

"I'm on your side. I just wanted you to know that, but I'll be quiet now."

"Ok," Callie whispered and smiled sadly in the dark.

CHAPTER 3

Alise placed the breakfast plate in front of Callie along with a tall glass of orange juice.

"Eat. You're practically skin and bones," she said picking up a fork and putting it into Callie's hand.

"Alise, really, I'm not hungry."

"Too bad. You ain't leaving this kitchen until you eat something."

Callie looked at the stack of pancakes with maple syrup and sides of bacon, eggs and applesauce. This had always been her favorite breakfast growing up but it had no appeal for her now. Callie looked at her sister's face and saw how concerned she was for her. Callie had lost over thirty pounds and counting and she had admitted to Alise that the dark circles under her eyes were probably due to the lack of sleep.

Soon after Ashley's party, Alise began "dropping by" on her way to or from some errand, almost daily and coincidently always at mealtime. Callie had told her she was eating but Alise wanted to see for herself. And what she saw was a housekeeper that looked after Maya and the house, but no one looked after Callie. So Alise made it her mission to be the one to watch over Callie, making sure she ate daily.

After awhile she stopped making up excuses for being in the neighborhood. She made it part of her daily routine to come by to check up on her sister, always fixing her a meal or two. Callie appreciated the gesture, but coming by at seven in the morning and expecting her to eat a big breakfast was going beyond sisterly concern.

She would have to talk to Alise and convince her that this was no longer necessary. She was getting along fine now. Almost.

She looked up at Alise. Her eyes were pleading with Callie to eat. It was clear that she was more than just a little worried. Callie didn't think that now was the right time to discuss their routine. Squeezing the fork and picking up the knife, she began to cut her pancakes. It wasn't until she took her first mouthful that Alise let out an audible sigh and relaxed.

"How is it?" Alise asked, happy to see her sister eat.

"Mmm....it's good," Callie said between chews.

"Guess what?" Alise asked grinning. She continued talking before Callie had a chance to respond. "Tammy got arrested!"

"What! Why?" Callie questioned, surprised.

Tammy Benson was Alise's neighbor and friend. Callie knew her through her relationship with Alise, but she had become friendly with her too. After being divorced for fifteen years, Tammy had just starting dating again. Her children were grown and had all moved out of the house, so Tammy felt it was time for her to live her life to the fullest again. She had begun to go out nearly every Friday and Saturday night and she realized that she had a taste for younger men.

Apparently she had found more than her share of young men in their twenties who loved older and larger women. Tammy had taken to telling Alise the details of her escapades and Alise, in turn, would fill Callie in on them. Alise thought that sometimes Tammy gave her a little too much information, but she always managed to get a chuckle out her dates. Callie looked at Alise in anticipation. She had a feeling this latest update was going to be good.

"Well, she was out robbing the cradle again and found a really nice guy," Alise began. "They had gone out to dinner a couple of times and the other night he was ready to make his move. So they're making out, hot and heavy, rolling across the bed and stuff and then he asks her if she's ready to get a little freaky."

"Freaky?"

39

"Yeah," Alise was chuckling as she flipped another pancake. "So Tammy said 'ok'. Now you know Tammy used to be the biggest prude in the world, but she had him thinking she was a wild *thang*. A sexual beast, you know all hip and in the know. Anyway, he laid down across the bed on his stomach and told her to beat him."

"Oh, my goodness!" Callie said laughing. "What does she know about S&M?"

"Well apparently nothing. That's what got her arrested!" Alise said laughing

"Now, I know it's kinky but it's not against the law. Well, as far as I know."

"Not if you do it right. Girl, she beat him unconscious!" Callie and Alise howled with laughter. "Tammy said she didn't know what the heck he was talking about, so she just went to whaling on his head. They charged her with assault and battery!"

They continued to laugh as Callie drank her orange juice and Alise chattered on about Tammy and her choice of men. Callie knew she was good for maybe one or two more mouthfuls before she would have to push the food around on her plate. Hopefully she could keep Alise side tracked with enough conversation that she would not notice how little food she had actually eaten. However, when Alise sat down at the table with her own breakfast plate, she started a conversation that captured Callie's complete attention.

"I've been thinking. Now hear me out before making a decision, but I think this will be good for both of us." Alise leaned towards Callie with eyes twinkling. "Why don't you and me go into business together?"

Callie's smile faded and her eyes narrowed.

"What kind of business?"

"Restaurant and music! You know, a supper club!"

"Where did you get that idea? I don't know anything about running a restaurant."

"But I do! I've been managing one for years! I do practically

40

everything there but own the place. And I've been thinking about it for the last couple of years."

"Then do it. Why are you bringing me into this?"

"Because you know music. You sing, you write, you have your own studio and you've been involved in the music business in one way or another since you were a kid singing radio jingles."

"Wait, wait, wait. I still don't understand how I fit in."

"You know what a supper club is, don't you?"

"Yeah, I know what a supper club is, but people don't do that anymore."

"Sure they do! Maybe not so much anymore, but they miss it. I know I do."

"That's because you're old as dirt," Callie said with a smile. "This supper club thing went out of style with, as Mom would say, "high button shoes". It takes a lot of work to make it successful. I mean really, really successful as far as I know."

"Well, you don't know everything," Alise said and leaned back in her chair. "I've been doing marketing research on this. Don't forget I have a lot of knowledge and a lot of connections in the restaurant business."

Callie sighed. "I know you do, Alise. But I guess I'm back to my original question. What do you want with me?"

Alise smiled. "I want *you* to be my headliner."

"*What?*" Callie looked at Alise incredulously.

"This is the part where I want you to hear me out," Alise said quickly as Callie stared at her in disbelief. "In the last couple of months you've become a bit of a local celebrity. Those kinda of jazzy recordings that you made about a year ago have really paid off. You know, when you recorded them, especially the songs that you wrote, like *Soul Mate,* you had planned to promote yourself as an artist, remember?"

Callie nodded her head in agreement and Alise continued.

"And then Marlisa signed Marc as an artist. All of a sudden you

41

were knee deep in "all things Marc" because you had to try to keep all the promises that Marlisa had made to this guy. The good thing is it all worked out for the best. The not so good thing is that you never finished what you had started for yourself. But now you can."

"No, Alise, I can't. I'm still knee deep in "all things Marc". There are still a billion things to do. I may have missed the launch party, but there's still a long way to go. I can't afford to turn my attention to something as big as what you're talking about! I just can't! He's only had radio play for a couple months but that's nowhere near success."

Callie stood up and began clearing her breakfast dishes hoping Alise did not notice the amount of food still on her plate. "And by the way, *he's* the local celebrity, not me. I don't have a CD out to promote and owning a production company certainly doesn't make for celebrity status. Besides, I don't know how much of a drain becoming a record label will have on our resources, financial as well as human. We just signed that distribution deal a few months ago and I don't know if it was a good idea or not. We just have to wait and see, but I need to get…." Callie trailed off in mid-sentence looking at Alise. "Why are you looking at me like that?"

"Callie," Alise said softly, "You signed that distribution deal almost a year ago."

Silence fell over the kitchen. Callie put the dishes down slowly into the sink. "What…I mean…what are you saying, Alise?"

Alise spoke very softly and slowly as she got up and walked towards Callie standing at the sink. "I'm saying …that Marc's CD has been doing very well for months. I'm saying that …the distribution deal *was* a great move. I'm saying that …your CD was released on your own record label recently and locally it seems to be doing well too… I'm saying …I'm saying, Callie, that you should know all of this."

Alise reached out and slowly took a dumbfound Callie in her arms. "And I'm saying," Alise hugged her tighter, "that I'm sorry because I should have known you needed my help and not just to feed you a meal or two. I watched you practically disappear into yourself for the last eight months, but I didn't know it was this serious."

Callie slumped in her sister's arms. All of sudden she was felt dizzy. Eight months? Eight months put her back in Marlisa's condo discovering the betrayal. Time seemed to have stop for her the very moment she saw Michael touching Marlisa and she didn't even realize it until now. The days went by but her life didn't go on. She had never left that condo emotionally but *eight months*? Things had been happening all around her for eight months and she couldn't get out of that condo. How much had she neglected her children? She knew Ashley had moved out to live with Michael while she stood by not saying or doing anything. After the disastrous Sweet Sixteen party there was not much she could say or do to make Ashley feel better. She cared that Ashley was leaving, but truthfully, it had been better to just let her go. It was easier to let Ashley think that she didn't care, rather than try to get her to understand what was going on in her own heart and mind. Actually, Callie knew she couldn't explain it because she really didn't know herself.

And what about Maya, her youngest, her baby? She was supposed to car pool and volunteer with her Girl Scout troop, wasn't she? Didn't she promise Maya? She had obviously let her down, but why hadn't she realized it before? How could she do this to her own children?

It was a repeat of her own childhood when her mother wouldn't, or couldn't, even come out of her bedroom to take care of the house and children. Everybody thought her mother was crazy, and maybe she was. Callie remembered feeling abandoned by her mother and yet she was able to do the same thing to her own family. What kind of mother simply gives up like nothing mattered, not even her children? She wondered if her mother had begun to fall apart over a man, too.

Callie shuddered now feeling frightened as it dawned on her that she had completely lost control of her life. Her days all seemed to run together and she spent many of those days in bed. She couldn't even remember if she cared or not. She simply withdrew into herself. She couldn't stop that day from playing over and over in her mind and she acted as if nothing else mattered. Nothing, that is, except the overpowering emotions of anger towards Michael and pity for herself. She had "lost" months of her life because she couldn't cope. She painfully realized that if she didn't get herself together soon, one day it might be too late. She could lose everything in her life that *really* mattered. Is this what they meant by hitting rock bottom? What has been happening to her business? Her business with Marlisa! Callie's head flew up from Alise's shoulder.

"The company! Who's been…?"

"Don't worry," Alise said. "Marvin is working diligently with your best interest at heart."

A numb Callie turned away from Alise and went to sit back down at the kitchen table. She covered her face with her hands and began rubbing her temples.

"One of the best things about your assistant," Alise continued, "is that he can't stand Marlisa. He's been keeping a close eye on her, you know, just in case she tries something. He's the one that made sure your CD got released. His theory has always been that Marlisa surprised everyone by signing Marc because she wanted to sideline your project. He never trusted her."

Good old Marvin, Callie thought just before the rush of tears came.

CHAPTER 4

Callie buttoned the neatly pressed dark blue shirt and tucked it into her jeans. The weight loss was not as evident, but her jeans still were a bit too loose for her liking. She looked in the mirror and felt a surge of confidence that she hadn't felt in quite a while. There was a spark in her eyes again. She hadn't realized it was gone before, but now that it was back she was determined to keep it. No more pity parties.

Priorities, Callie thought, *my children, my livelihood and me!*

She still thought daily about Michael and her life "pre-betrayal," but she would never let it rule her like before. However, Callie wondered if the pain of the ten-second heartbreak would ever go away. That was the amount of time it took her each day to awake to full consciousness and realize that Michael was out of her life.

Michael had been her knight in shining armor. Talk about good looking! He was probably the most gorgeous man Callie had ever seen. He had big brown eyes with long eyelashes and beautiful curly, dark brown hair. He had a nicely trimmed moustache that was soft and never failed to tickle Callie when they kissed. Even now when Callie thought about it she couldn't help but smile. She had met him when he was a junior in college and she was making her rounds on the music circuit singing. He was tall with an athletic build and a brilliant mind. When they were together they would talk for hours about music and history and art. Callie was never sure what had impressed her most – his looks or his mind.

45

It was immediately clear that she wasn't the only one impressed. The women, co-eds of every race and color, swarmed around him like bees to honey. Their blatant flirtatious behavior irritated Callie, but she was careful not to show her displeasure. After all, it wasn't any of her business. They all wanted the sweet and handsome Michael Armstrong and many were determined to have him, but Callie never interfered. She had promised herself to stay out of the fray, but the friendlier she and Michael became, the more other women considered her a threat. Women who had set their sights on him confronted her on more than one occasion. It was difficult to be a woman friend of Michael Armstrong. Everyone thought there had to be something more going on between the two of them and, much to Callie's delight, Michael didn't seem to mind.

However, Callie was content to just keep their friendship. She began to look forward to their time together. After awhile, Callie reduced her time out of town and not long after that she stopped traveling all together. There were plenty of gigs available right in downtown DC. All that mattered to her was that Michael knew she wasn't like all the other women who were throwing themselves at him. She didn't even know he was from a wealthy family until much later in their relationship. Michael knew she was a true friend and seemed to be relieved to find someone that could see him for who he really was.

The funny thing was, with all that he had going for him he seemed to be oblivious to it. He ignored the fawning and would gently dismiss the many advances with the kindest eyes and gentlest smile. At first, Callie thought that this was part of his game: pretend that he was humble and down to earth. She restrained herself from falling for him romantically, secretly wishing that deep down he really *was* just another conceited jerk because that would make everything easier for her. However, soon she saw that this was no act. He was the real thing. Even though Callie loved everything about him, she couldn't bring herself to tell him how she felt. She was happy with the way things were. They were just friends that enjoyed each other's company and the more that she ignored any thoughts of romance, the closer they became as friends.

The friendship portion of their relationship was long and fun and wonderful, while the transition to lovers and then husband and wife happened in what felt like the blink of an eye. However, they both knew it was the mutual respect they had for each other that anchored their strong friendship -that and the fact that they genuinely *liked* each other. Even throughout all the years of marriage and children and getting their separate businesses off the ground, they managed to remain close friends. That's why Callie felt so lost without him. He wasn't just her husband and lover, but he was the best friend she could have ever hoped to have. It was truly a once in a lifetime love and friendship and nothing could replace what she had with Michael. Now it was all lost. Callie had decided to begin a new chapter in her life. One that she knew could only begin when she accepted the fact that Michael would not be by her side.

It had only been three weeks since she had taken Alise up on her offer of a partnership and they had a tight grand opening schedule to keep. Callie had never seen Alise so vibrant and focused. It not only made Callie feel happy, but inspired as well. The whole project was proving to be exciting and fun. Alise had already planned everything before she even approached Callie. It was mostly a matter of money that was the hold up. Callie was the financial, but not exactly silent partner, that Alise had wanted in order to get this venture off the ground. But Callie made sure to let all the final business decisions be made by Alise. She knew nothing about the running of a restaurant and was impressed with all that Alise knew.

This partnership could work and all Callie really had to do was what she did best - music. She would bring in the acts that would perform and she herself would do a few shows. Her CD was doing pretty good now so she would have to strike while the iron was hot. Callie hoped that performing at the restaurant for the grand opening

47

would give a boast to the restaurant as well as her CD.

Marvin had been ecstatic over the idea and Callie had promptly promoted him and given him additional duties that included music management within the restaurant. She and Marvin met every morning to discuss the status of everything going on at both businesses. He also thought of himself as a talent scout, so he frequented the nightlife scene and was happy to write off all the entertainment expenses he incurred on behalf of the companies. Callie was just happy to have him on her team. It gave her time to write music, put together a show and still spend quality time with her children.

She was able to pick Maya up from school everyday and have an afternoon snack with her, talking about their day, before helping her with homework. Ashley was still at Michael's, but they were at least talking. Callie made it a point to speak with her daily and see her at least three times a week. She was determined not to let the family fall completely apart because she failed as a mother. Michael's behavior ended her willingness to be a loving wife, but not a loving mother.

She knew that Michael still spoke with Marlisa and allowed her to be a part of Ashley's life. She felt a slow burn of anger rising as she thought about it. Michael's reasoning was that it would have been more harmful to Ashley to remove Marlisa completely from her life, especially since Ashley already felt so disconnected from the family.

"Callie, it's what's best for Ashley, and she has to be the priority for both of us!" Michael had yelled to a hysterical Callie one evening after she had dropped Ashley back to his house. Even if Michael's intentions were pure, Callie knew Marlisa's weren't. She was still coming between them and with Michael's blessing. Callie wondered if Michael had slept with Marlisa again. He swore nothing was going on between them, but she was convinced he would have told her that no matter what.

"The hell with both of them," Callie said and waved her hand in a dismissive gesture. She had things to do. Mainly meet with the owner of the advertising company that would handle the marketing for the new restaurant. Callie fished her keys out of her purse and took one last reassuring look in the mirror. She put her sunglasses on and began to hum "It's a Beautiful Morning" by the Rascals as she walked out to her black Lexus.

Alise had found what she said was the perfect location and renovations had begun immediately. This was one of those business decisions that Callie had left up to Alise. She had had her doubts and had voiced them in the not-so-silent partner way, but in the end Alise had addressed all of her concerns. As Callie stood and looked at the outside of the building and its surrounding area, she had to admit Alise seemed to be right on target. Callie's main concern was that this location had been a previous restaurant that had already gone out of business. Alise had insisted that the location was right, but their management had been all wrong. She then presented Callie with market research to back up her position. This was still a risky venture to Callie, so she was still a bit nervous, but she would just have to let Alise do her thing and have faith that it would all work out.

Callie walked inside the restaurant, took off her sunglasses and looked around. A lot of progress had been made since the first and only time she had been inside of the building. It looked good. A small stage had been built which was slightly elevated above the main floor, but designed so it could be used for extra dining space during the lunch service when there wasn't live entertainment.

It was Callie's idea to put up a series of large monitors to show videos of past shows and unsigned artists. There had been a flood of CDs arriving at CM Music Productions when they announced the need for new or unsigned artists to perform and have their music videos played at a hot new venue. It was a great source of free publicity since the artist could include information in their video such as a web address for CD purchases and a performance itinerary. Plus it got a buzz going about the restaurant.

Callie smiled as she continued to look around. It was really looking pretty good and she felt confident in her decision to back Alise. Opening day was still weeks away, but already she was feeling a little eager.

"Hey, whadda ya think!" Alise said as she twirled around with arms open wide. "Is it not fabulous?"

"It's fabulous. I'm impressed!"

"Well, wait 'til you see this!" Alise went behind the bar and hoisted a large box on top of it. She opened it and took out a handful of napkins waving them in the air.

"Look at these! They turned out great!"

Callie walked over, took a look at the napkins and broke out in a big grin. "Oh, my goodness! Look at that!"

She saw the name of their restaurant written in her own script. *Josephine's*. It was named after their grandmother who used to sing in the old juke joints in Louisiana that Callie and Alise had heard about from their father. She took a lot flack for her line of work, especially after their father was born. Everybody thought she was "fast", as they used to say in those days, but she didn't care. She was a single mother doing what she did best to make it. She was talented, like Besse Smith or Billie Holiday, and everyone said so, but she never made it out of Louisiana. It was hard enough as a black woman making it as a professional in the 1930s, but with a small child it was nearly impossible. However, she happily sang until the day she died. Music was her lifeblood - just as music was her son's lifeblood and now her granddaughter's. It was a fitting tribute and Callie and Alise grinned at each other feeling a swell of pride.

"Perfect," Callie said. "You know what else would be perfect?"

"What?" Alise asked.

"If this marketing genius shows up so this wonderful tribute doesn't become a disaster."

"He'll be here. He's running late."

"First day and late?"

"Don't start, Callie. I know what I'm doing. He's a great businessman and well sought after *and* within our budget."

"That's what I don't understand. If he's so well sought after, why so cheap?"

"He's not cheap. He just wanted to get in on the beginning of this type of venture and since it's his first time, he's selling himself cheap....er. Cheap*er* than most."

"It's his first time!" Callie's eyes grew wide. "Do you realize what's at stake and you've got some new-be working on this because he's within the budget?"

"Callie, for heaven's sake," Alise said exasperated. "I'm an industry insider. When are you going to trust me? I managed to get a great location at a great price, didn't I?"

"From a going out of business sale – the *restaurant* business!"

"I've got the best chef in town."

"Which you *stole* from your former employer!"

"The best kitchen service staff."

"Stole, stole, stole."

"The best decorator. Look at this place!"

"She was *my* decorator, Ms. Industry-Insider. Where did you get this guy's name from anyway? Don't tell me it was from your former employer, too?"

Alise looked away. Callie slapped her hand down on the bar. "Aw, Alise! How do you know they weren't setting you up by acting like they wanted him so badly? You took their chef and their kitchen staff and then you took the bait."

"You sound ridiculous, you know that, right? Why is everything a conspiracy to you?"

"Because I'm just a grassy knoll kinda girl! There *was* a second shooter. But don't change the subject. Marketing and advertising can make or break us. Why in the world would you want this guy?"

"Because she's a shrewd businesswoman."

Callie froze when she heard the deep voice coming from the

51

restaurant entrance. It was the strong, steady voice of a man who was obviously sure of himself.

"I thought you said she was a silent partner, Alise?"

The voice was closer now. Callie could detect a slight southern drawl. She listened to his footsteps and finally could feel his presence directly behind her- close behind her. Too close. Callie turned around and embarrassment made her avert her eyes to the ground. Cowboy boots? Is this guy kidding?

Callie took a breath and looked up into his eyes. Hazel. Sparkling hazel eyes. Familiar hazel eyes. His hair was sandy colored and wind blown making him look as if he hadn't a care in the world. He flashed a gorgeous smile and Callie thought he had the absolute whitest teeth that she had ever seen. Dazzling. But cowboy boots?

"Hi, I'm Stephen Russell," he said and held his hand out for Callie to shake.

"Oh, you gotta be *kidding* me," Callie said recognizing him now.

"So, you've heard of me?"

"Me and everyone else on the planet. You invest in businesses. There's always a happy ending, but not necessarily for the *original* business owner."

"You don't have to worry. I'm not interested in taking over your business. I just like the thrill of building a business from the ground up. Your restaurant is just starting and my new marketing company is just starting. Your success will be my success."

"Callie, shake the man's hand, for goodness sake!" Alise said.

Callie looked down at Stephen's hand still outstretched in greeting. She put her hand in his and was surprised by its softness. Frowning she shook his hand. She had expected the rough hand of a cowboy. After all, he looked the part in his jeans and button down shirt. She knew he owned a large ranch in Texas. He certainly rode horses, but apparently all that cowboy stuff was just for show. Photo ops for all the business magazines he appeared in regularly.

Stephen Russell wasn't at all what he appeared to be standing in front of her now. Not that Callie was fooled. She knew exactly who he was. He was a filthy rich, white businessman who found sport in preying on the financial needs of others. So, what did he want with them and why is Alise so willing to let him have it? Stephen, seeing Callie's reaction looked beyond her at Alise who shrugged her shoulders.

"I'm pleased to meet you, Callie," Stephen said and flashed that hypnotic smile again.

"Uh huh."

"Trust me," he said as he bent his 6'4 frame to allow his eyes to become level with hers.

"She doesn't even trust me, Steve," Alise said chuckling from behind the bar.

"You won't regret this," he added.

Callie rolled her eyes and sighed. "I already do."

Stephen looked at her and feigned offense at her comment.

"Sorry, but that's the best I can do."

"I guess I'll have to take it then," Stephen said. Then smiling he added, "For now."

CHAPTER 5

Callie drove through the light traffic towards home allowing her mind to drift. A smile came to her lips as she replayed the conversation she had that afternoon. This restaurant could really be something. Stephen had great ideas. It's no wonder he's been so successful. Callie was amazed at how much she liked him and disliked him at the same time. He was charming and brilliant and, of course, one fine specimen of a man. But he was also arrogant and stubborn and she really didn't completely trust his motives. Why would he want to get his hands dirty? He could have hired anyone he wanted to take on every aspect of his new business, but yet he seemed to be representing himself as the lone entrepreneur. Why? Callie had asked him just that question but wasn't at all satisfied with the answer.

"I like to do things myself. I like to be challenged. Take control of my destiny, so to speak. Besides, it gives me an adrenaline rush to know I made things happen with my hard work. Running a company after that is the boring part. The excitement for me is in the newness of it all." His eyes, which had been steady on hers, traveled down just shy of her cleavage and back up, lingering on her lips before meeting her eyes again.

"I like exploring new territory," he said with a tiny smile.

Callie looked quickly at Alise, who had her head buried in the file of papers Stephen had given her, before her eyes returned to stare at him. She fought to control the burning rise of blood to her face. She would not allow herself to react. He must be used to getting away with such juvenile behavior when dealing with women, but this was business and she wasn't just any woman. She had to set him straight.

"Mr. Russell, you -"

"Stephen, no Steve, please call me Steve."

"*Mr. Russell*, this may be a game to you, but -"

"It's not game."

"- *but* I'm in no mood to play games!" Callie continued. Alise's head went up upon hearing the tone of the conversation.

"Callie, this is a good agreement." Alise held up the folder of paperwork, looking apprehensively between Stephen and her sister.

"Don't play with me, is all that I'm saying!" Callie said without taking her eyes off of Stephen. He looked helplessly at Alise and then back at Callie.

"Callie, honestly I am here to do good. I know a good business opportunity when I see one. And this is a great one, believe me. Otherwise, I wouldn't be wasting my time. We can both meet all of our business objectives." Stephen walked up closer to Callie, gazing steadily into her eyes. "Getting together will be good for you and for me."

Again, Callie felt flush and this time retreated. She backed away from Stephen, folding her arms across her chest.

"I'm being sincere. Scouts honor," Stephen said, holding up two fingers and suddenly Callie felt foolish. Here she was making a big deal out of what she now believed was her imagination. She felt a hint of excitement when he made that last comment about getting together, which obvious was an innocent statement on his part. Wasn't it? Could she have imagined the earlier exchange too?

Callie clearly realized she must be losing it. It had been such a long time since she had even thought about a man other than Michael. Had it been so long that she couldn't tell the difference between innocuous conversation and when a man was making a pass at her?

Maybe it was worse than that. Maybe she was deluding herself into thinking something *could* happen between her and Stephen, since he was the first and most *unlikely* suitor to come her way. Clearly any romantic relationship with Stephen would be a total disaster. The disappointment and embarrassment that would follow would only serve to send her back to hiding under her covers where she felt safe. She would be back to thinking of no one else but Michael, which is exactly what she wanted to do anyway. They were so great together; Callie knew any other relationship was doomed to fail. Being with Stephen would certainly prove her theory.

Callie looked at Stephen holding up his two fingers and actually looking like an innocent kid waiting for approval. She smiled. He was extremely good looking, but not her type. Callie liked the tall, educated, strong black man. Stephen was as far from that image as any man could be.

This is absolutely absurd, Callie thought. *I'm acting like he's asking me out, which he isn't, which is good, because I wouldn't go.*

"Ok, ok," Callie said.

"Then we can sign the contract?"

"Right after my lawyer looks at it."

"*I've* looked at it," Alise said. "It's not like it's my first time."

"No, she's right, Alise," Stephen said. "It's always a good practice to let your lawyer look at any contract before signing it."

"That's what we pay them for," Callie and Stephen said simultaneously.

"*Finally* we agree," Stephen said and did a two-step. That brought laughter from Alise and Stephen. Callie managed to smile in spite of herself.

"And on that note," Alise said gathering up the documents, "I'll go call for a courier and send this over right away."

Callie and Stephen watched Alise walk towards the back office. Despite her reservations, Callie thought Stephen Russell might actually work out after all. Now, however, she was feeling a bit guilty. She began to finger the pattern in one of the napkins and became serious as she thought about the whole situation.

56

"Everything ok?" Stephen asked cautiously.

"Yeah, but," Callie paused, "but I need to ask you a favor."

It was amazing how thoughts of Michael still consumed her. Even after everything that's happened she still wanted to protect him. She knew it would hurt him if he knew they had entrusted their business venture to a perfect stranger over him, but Stephen was so much more than that. Even though Michael owned an advertising and marketing company, he had to know she could never work with him. She had just gotten to the point where she could have a conversation with him without her ending up in tears. But that was personal. This was business. The truth is that Stephen Russell was more than some stranger. He was one of the most successful businessmen in the country and he could be the best thing that ever happened to their restaurant.

Even still, Callie felt the guilt. Michael was a brilliant businessman but her struggled everyday because of the color barrier. Many of the big clients seemed to go with the bigger, whiter firms. It was one of Michael's greatest obstacles and one that hit him very hard personally. Too many times she had seen how he would suffer in silent dignity after being down struck, yet again, by obvious racist decisions. The large contracts always went to a white owned company because that was where "big business" felt safer. Although it was true that he got his share of contracts for products that were made for and marketed to the black community, he still struggled to be viewed as one of the *best* in the business rather than one of the *best black* men in the business.

Callie felt a little strange thinking about race at that precise moment. She was feeling extremely guilty and defensive on behalf of Michael. She held on to the fact that everything she was feeling was all related to her business decision and she didn't dare let her mind drift towards the possibility that it could be a lot more personal. She was strangely drawn to Stephen and she felt a little like her attraction to him was some sort of betrayal to Michael. Even if it was, why did she feel guilty? Michael deserved to know what betrayal felt like.

However, none of that mattered anyway because a man, any man –
black, white or purple was of little interest to Callie at this time in her
life. What *was* important was that Stephen Russell would be a
formidable competitor in Michael's very near future and Callie had
positioned herself right in the middle of enemy camp. She knew how
deeply Michael would be hurt to have his own family choose the
competition over him. She would not change her mind, they were
going with Stephen Russell, but she felt obligated to soften the blow of
rejection – at least temporarily.

"Without going through a long drawn out explanation, I would
prefer it if you don't mention that I'm you're client."

"Well, I don't understand. I really have to *mention* the restaurant if
I'm going to *market* the restaurant."

"The restaurant, yes. Me, no."

"Who should I say is the owner? Alise?"

"Alise, nobody, I don't really care. Just don't use my name. I'm a
silent partner and I want to keep my ownership, well… silent."

"Are you hiding something, Callie?"

"I'm not hiding anything!" Callie said defensively.

"Then are you hiding *from* something?" Stephen asked, but quickly
added while shaking his head and waving his hands, "Never mind.
Forget I asked that question. It's none of my business. I don't need to
know."

"Thank you," Callie smiled "It's not anything sinister, it's just -"

"I told you I don't need to know," Stephen said gently and smiled
back.

"Ok," she said softly. She looked down at the napkin she was
holding and back up at Stephen feeling silly. God, the lengths she
would go through to protect Michael. Well, his feelings were no
longer her concern so she should just dismiss them. Michael had
taught her how easily that could be done. Callie began to debate if she
should just withdraw her request when Stephen interrupted her

thoughts with another question.

"Now, it's not the government, is it?"

"What?" Callie said, taken aback by the new line of questioning.

"The government? They're not going to put a lien on the place or anything, right?"

"What? No!" Callie said surprised "It's not-"

"CIA's not involved or anything? Nobody's looking for you, right?"

"Of course not!" Callie said smiling, "I thought you didn't need to know?"

"I don't." Stephen raised his hand in surrender. "Please, I'm sorry. I'm not trying to pry."

"Good," Callie said. They stood in silence looking at each other. His eyes twinkled mischievously and Callie felt her heart flutter just a little before she quickly turned away from him.

"Is it personal? I mean, did you lose a bet and owe some people a lot of money? You don't gamble do, you?"

"No! Stephen what are you talking about?" Callie chuckled as Stephen continued.

"It's just that I watched the entire Sopranos series and, well, those guys can be brutal."

"I thought you didn't want to pry?"

"No, I don't!"

"Good! For the second time, good!" Callie was really laughing now.

"But I don't want to be sitting here and a fire ball hits the place, you know?" Stephen, who had managed to keep a straight face before, was now laughing too. "But I don't want to pry."

"I can tell."

"Let's see, if it's not for the government or for money, then it must be for love."

Callie smiled sadly and then sighed heavily. He watched as she nervously fingered the name of the restaurant embossed on the napkin.

"Well," Stephen said quietly, "I've officially pried. So, a change of subject is in order."

He leaned against the bar and watched Callie. She was pretty, no beautiful, but there was something even more beautiful when seeing her so vulnerable. She had a sadness that tugged at his heart and made him want to protect her.

"Where did the name Callie come from? Alise said there was a story behind it, but I would have to ask you."

"Yeah," Callie said smiling again, "there's a little story behind it alright."

"Care to tell me?" Stephen asked smiling, glad to see her relaxing.

"Well, my father was a musician that traveled and sometimes my mother would meet up with him at the different gigs. Once, he had a big show on the west coast with a lot of famous people and my mother went to meet him and it sort of turned into a little vacation. And after the vacation she brought home a little souvenir." Callie smiled sheepishly as she looked at Stephen.

"What was the souvenir?"

"Me. They were in California."

"Ahhhh," Stephen said laughing, "Callie, I get it. That's good."

"If you say so."

"No, really. They named you to forever be a reminder of what must have been a good time," Stephen said grinning. "That's kind of touching."

"It's actually kind of disturbing. I'm talking about my parents, you know. Not to mention a little embarrassing. Most of the time I keep that bit of history to myself until I get to know a person's sense of humor better."

"So you think I have a good sense of humor, huh?"

"I think you're weird," Callie said, grinning.

"But with a sense of humor."

"Some people might think so."

"I'll take that." Stephen paused and then added, "For now."

"Good, for the third time, good," Callie said laughing as Stephen flashed his gorgeous smile again.

"Ok, well, insults aside, I like your name and as a person *with a sense of humor,* I like the history behind it. You're ok, Callie," Stephen said suddenly becoming serious, "Even if you don't want me to know it."

"Just ok?"

"That's all I got," he said quietly, staring intensely at Callie.

"Well, I'll take that." Callie locked eyes with Stephen, "For now."

Callie felt that now familiar flutter. Was her imagination going into overdrive? The way he looked at her excited her, but was that his intention? Flustered, she walked around him and headed for the back office.

"I have to talk to Alise now," she yelled over her shoulder. "I'll...uh....*we'll* be back in a minute to go over a few other things." She quickened her step. "After that you should probably deal directly with Alise," Callie added before disappearing through the door leading to the back offices.

Callie pulled up in her driveway behind Vanessa's mustang. She had taken to driving home from college in nearby Virginia every weekend no matter what. Vanessa said it made her feel better to come home to her own private room and get away from dorm life, but Callie knew better. Vanessa wanted to check up on her. She was worried about her mother and Callie didn't know how to prove to Vanessa that she really was all right and could take care of herself. The last thing Callie wanted to do was to suck the life out of her own daughter. Vanessa should be enjoying being young instead of taking on the role of caretaker. Callie had to figure out how to put her daughter at ease, because if she didn't, Vanessa would end up as another casualty in this big mess, just like Ashley.

"Vanessa, you've got to get a life," Callie said aloud, turning the ignition off and opening the car door.

Callie was determined to be upbeat and have a great evening with

61

the kids. She walked up the driveway with a little bounce in her steps and realized that she really *did* feel pretty good. She usually worked really hard at pretending, but maybe tonight will be different.

Callie walked through the front door and down the long hallway that led to the kitchen. She stood in the hallway right outside the kitchen door and smiled. Laughter! The high pitch giggle of Maya mixed with the throaty laugh of Vanessa made Callie want to laugh along. But it was the sweet chuckling of Ashley that nearly brought sentimental tears to Callie's eyes. It felt…well.... normal. Like it used to be before the past year happened.

Callie half expected Michael to come around the corner, give her a kiss hello and tell her how much he missed her today before dragging her into the kitchen to join the fun. Callie looked down the hallway towards the front door. No Michael. But somehow her heart didn't break like it had countless times before when she longed for the past. Callie closed her eyes and listened to the laughter again, which made her smile. Grinning she walked into the kitchen.

"What's going on here?"

The girls were sitting at the kitchen table playing some type of board game. They all looked up at her still smiling.

"Monopoly!" Vanessa said.

"Momma come play with us!" Maya added.

"Monopoly! We could be here all night. That's the longest game in the world!" Callie said, walking eagerly towards the three girls.

"Not the way you cheat! You'll have won in no time flat," Vanessa said before taking a sip of her soda.

"I beg your pardon!" Callie said feigning offense. "I do not cheat!"

The room fell silent as the three girls eyed each other.

"Well, I don't!" Callie insisted.

The girls continued to exchange looks before bursting into laughter.

"Ok, ok, ok," Vanessa said. "You don't cheat. You just play

creatively. Pull up a chair and let the "creating" begin."

"What! I don't believe my own flesh and blood has turned on me. Accusing *your own mother* of cheating!"

"Well if the shoe fits," Ashley said, handing Callie the shoe game piece.

"Ha, ha very funny," Callie said taking the game piece.

"And clever," Ashley said, smiling at Callie.

"Alright, prepare to get your beat down!" Callie said rubbing her hands together. "I'll be the banker."

"No!" all three girls yelled at the same time staring at Callie.

Startled by the outburst, Callie widened her eyes as in shock. "Okay, okay. I don't have to be the banker if y'all feel that way about it."

"We do," Vanessa said.

"Absolutely!" Ashley agreed.

"Justice prevails!" Maya yelled raising her fist in the air.

That brought a round of laughter from everyone. Callie looked around at her daughters. They were chatting and smiling and throwing popcorn at each other. It was nice. It felt like family again.

It wasn't until the next morning when Callie was thinking back on the wonderful evening that she realized she had not thought anymore about Michael after entering the kitchen. Blushing, she realized she had, however, thought about cowboy boots.

CHAPTER 6

Callie closed the passenger door of Michael's Range Rover and stood back watching as Ashley put on her seatbelt. She smiled at Ashley who returned her smile and waved as she drove off with Michael. The weekend with all three girls had been great. Callie was beginning to feel like her old self again. Every now and then she would think of Michael and feel a little melancholy. After all, he was the one missing piece to complete the happy family life that she had just experienced with her children.

At some point, she hoped Ashley would be able to completely forgive her for what happened at her party. Callie believed eventually she would be able to find the words to explain her feelings in a way that her daughter could understand. For now, it was enough that she understood her continued separation from Michael had nothing to do with any of the children. Callie didn't know how much Ashley knew of Marlisa's part in the wedge that was now between her and Michael, but she didn't think full disclosure would be appropriate. The important thing was that Ashley knew Callie was sorry for allowing the surrounding circumstances to overwhelm her good judgment.

Maybe she would be able to explain, using her behavior as an example, how easily you can give up control of your life. The hope was for Ashley to learn something positive from this bad experience. Callie believed that she had learned something herself. Besides, she was getting past all that now.

Callie smiled to herself. Who was she kidding? She can tell

Ashley all the right things but she knew that living with the pain of a broken heart was easier said than done.

Callie walked up the stairs and decided to check on Maya who had been put to bed a half hour ago. She tiptoed to the door and quietly opened it. Callie was surprised to see Maya sitting up in bed with her head under the covers. Beneath the covers with her was a flashlight, which cast shadows of two Barbie dolls engaged in an animated conversation about shopping.

Maya, upon hearing the creak of the door, was surprised too. She threw the flashlight and Barbies on the floor and scrambled to get into a believable sleeping position. Callie, unable to suppress a smile, walked over to the bed and kneeled to pick up the flashlight and dolls. Still kneeling, she leaned close to the bed and watched Maya who had her eyes shut tight trying desperately to control her breathing.

"Maya," Callie said softly, watching her daughter squeeze her eyes tighter. "What were you doing?"

"What Mommy?" Maya blinked her eyes rapidly and then rubbed them with her fists. Callie tried to look serious, but couldn't keep a straight face as Maya looked up at her doing her best impression of a sleepy child.

"You are so busted," Callie said chuckling.

"Ok, you got me," Maya said smiling and sitting up.

"I know I did, you faker." Maya giggled as Callie put the dolls and flashlight on a shelf near the bed.

"But here's the deal; no more playing, no more dolls and no more flashlight. Understood?"

"Yeah," she said, lying back in bed. Callie adjusted her covers and sat on the bed, lovingly stroking Maya's hair.

"Mommy."

"Yes," Callie whispered.

"It was nice having Ashley here all weekend, wasn't it?"

"Yes, it was."

"It felt good. I wish Daddy was here too 'cause then it would have

65

been gooder."

"Better. It would have been better."

"That's what I said."

"Yep, that's exactly what you said. Now, I need you to promise to get some sleep. Okay?"

Callie smiled as Maya nodded her head in agreement. Then kissing her on the forehead, Callie got up from the bed.

"Good night, Maya."

"When is Daddy coming home?"

"Go to sleep, Maya," Callie said walking towards the door.

"That's not an answer, Mommy. Why do you always say that when I ask a question?"

"Go to sleep, Maya," Callie said again, just before closing the door.

Callie walked slowly down the hall to the master bedroom. Maya had a good question that Callie couldn't possibly answer. Funny, since she used to have all the answers. She had always been so sure of everything. She thought everything through, analyzing the details extensively before making a move. That was her strength, knowing all the angles before she would commit. She took pride in that. But what do you do when you're taken by surprise? She had done all the right things with Michael and she was sure of his love, even now. So what did it mean that he could love her and still do this to her? She definitely didn't see that coming. No matter how she thought about or analyzed their relationship, she never believed in a million years that he would be unfaithful to her. How can you protect yourself from this sort of thing if don't even see it coming right at you to knock you down? She needed to talk. Callie picked up the phone and called Alise.

"Hello?" a sleepy Alise answered.

Callie giggled. "Is that a question?"

"Yeah, I'm asking you why you're calling at this hour," Alise replied. She sat up in bed.

"It's only nine o'clock. You sure are getting old if you can't stay up past nine."

"Well, first of all, it's rude to call someone's house after nine o'clock unless it's an emergency. And so far this doesn't sound like a 911 call. Second of all, a smart person realizes that they are much more productive if they get enough rest. It refreshes the mind and rejuvenates the body. That's why they call it beauty sleep. Shut up, Callie."

"I didn't say anything!" Callie laughed.

Alise was laughing too. "I heard you thinking of a smart comment about my beauty rest through the phone!"

"But I didn't say it!"

"Well, I heard you anyway. And finally, yes, I admit like every other human being, I'm getting old and going gray. Actually, I was thinking about letting my hair go completely gray. Plus, I'm tired of dying it."

"That's not a bad idea. It will probably look good on you. What about your moustache?"

"Ha, ha, ha. You are *sooo* funny. Is this what you woke me up for? Your comedy routine?" Alise said dryly, but she was smiling.

"No, for an anti-pity party. Ashley just left and Vanessa left earlier to go back to school. Maya's in bed and now it's just me. This is when I miss Michael the most. I don't want to start crying again. I just wonder if I will ever move past this stage."

"I know it's hard. Even with a no good husband like Terrance I thought it would be easier to shift gears, you know? I remember-"

"Whoa, whoa, back it up."

"Back what up?"

"This is *my* party, remember? Why are you trying to take over and make it about you? You do this all the time."

"I do not!"

"Yes you do! Every birthday since we've both been over thirty, you have a pity party and talk about how old you're getting and how you haven't accomplished what you thought you would by now. And

67

then you talk about not finding a man and how you haven't lost weight or maybe how you've gained a few more pounds and how gravity is working against you! And what do I do? I give you my complete attention and support, that's what I do! But what happens on *my* birthday two weeks later? We talk about you again!"

"That's not my fault," Alise said seriously.

"What do you mean it's not your fault?"

"The rule is you have to give the birthday girl at least a month to recover. It's not my fault that your birthday falls in between. Rules are rules. I don't' make them up, I just follow them."

"What rules? You've gotta be kidding me!"

"Am I or am I not, ready to support you two weeks after your birthday?" Alise said while laughing.

"It's not the same and you know it!" Callie was laughing too.

"Alright," Alise said. "I'll try to be more sensitive since you're being such a big baby about this! I was just trying to let you know what was going on with me after I kicked Terrance out. I just-"

"Heard it," Callie said sharply. "Now back to me. Let's focus this time."

Alise giggle. "Ok, ok, back to you. Don't bore me though."

"Is Stephen dating anybody?"

"I thought we were talking about Michael."

"No, we're talking about me and I want to talk about Stephen."

"Are you interested in him?"

"I just don't know when it's ok to think about another man when you're still married and I feel guilty. I go between missing Michael and wanting to be back with him and then thinking about Stephen. There's nothing going on," Callie said quickly. "I just wonder if he's a womanizer."

"Hmmm. Maybe. I really don't know. I never heard him talk about a woman. Any woman. But I'm sure he can have his pick of just about anybody. So womanizing is not out of the question."

"I tried to research it."

"You've been checking up on him?"

"Yeah, for the sake of the restaurant."

"Yeah right, for the sake of the restaurant," Alise said sarcastically. "Anyway what did you find out?"

"I found out he likes to keep his private life private. He's only been linked publicly with a few leggy brunettes but I don't know anything abut the relationships. You know," Callie said thoughtfully, "he probably investigates the women before he's seen in public with them."

"Why do you think he would do that?"

"Because he's so careful! He wouldn't want to fall for a girl just to have her naked pictures show up on the internet. Can you imagine the press he would get? One of the richest and most eligible bachelor's love interest turns out to be a party girl. He's on the cover of Forbes and she's the screen saver for every pervert in the free world. That would be a little embarrassing."

"Well you can't blame him if he's careful. He *is* the ultimate "good catch." I'm sure he has to fight off a lot of gold diggers and "I'll do anything" girls."

"Yeah. Michael's a good catch, too," Callie said pensively.

"What kind of pity party is this? You're crying because you have *two* good-looking, rich men interested in you? For heaven's sake, Callie, back to me! I got issues!"

"I didn't say that Stephen was interested in me!" Callie said defensively.

"Well, you must be interested in him."

"I didn't say that either."

"Then what are you saying, Callie Elizabeth?"

"I'm saying that I don't know what I'm thinking or why I'm thinking what I don't know I'm thinking."

"What the hell are you talking about? That was nothing but gibberish! I am so confused! And for the record I ain't never been confused at a pity party before."

"I'm confused, too. And for the record this was an *anti*-pity party."

"Did it work?"

"Yeah," Callie said smiling. "Surprisingly it did."

"Glad to help. Glad to *support* you."

"Go back to sleep gray bush."

"Gray bush?"

"Think about it"

Alise thought about it for a moment and then smiled. "You are so nasty," she said right before hanging up.

CHAPTER 7

Callie glared at Stephen growing more impatient and angry with every passing second. The glow of their first meeting was completely gone. The honeymoon was officially over. It had been weeks since the first meeting and everything seemed to go downhill from there. They were behind schedule because there had been a delay in just about everything remotely tied to the progress of the restaurant.

As it stood now, the opening had to be pushed back from mid October to late November and nobody, especially Stephen, seemed to be aware of the strain she was under. She was in a perpetual foul mood because of it and he was pretending everything was rosy. Not to mention that Michael had gone from calling her daily to only a few times in a week. Callie wondered how often he was talking with Marlisa and if they were together. She shook the image from her mind. Tonight was about the restaurant, which seemed to be a black hole for her financially and it hadn't even opened up yet.

Callie speculated that perhaps this was step one in Stephen's plan to steal the business that rightfully belonged to her and Alise. Tie things up in order to deplete the owners' finances. Even though she had voiced her concerns to Stephen, she somehow felt his responses were meant to patronize rather than to reassure. They didn't need to be having another meeting over a dinner that would eventually be billed to her. She had told him that the last time, but he had just smiled and winked. It annoyed Callie that he seemed to think his charms and good looks were the answers to everything. And now it pissed her off even more that while sitting just a few feet away from her, he was yet again unmindful of her obvious irritation. Well, hell hath no fury.

"Am I being billed for this?" Callie asked as she looked over the above average menu prices

"Well it *is* a business dinner," Stephen replied. Tapping the menu he added, "This sounds delicious. I think I'll have the 16 oz steak."

"And I think we're going to McDonald's if you expect me to pay for your beef eating habits."

"What's wrong with beef?"

"Nothing if it's ground up, wrapped in paper and comes with fries. Stephen, I don't mean to sound cheap but-"

"Yet, somehow you do," he said with a grin. "That's a joke," he added when Callie didn't return the smile.

"These dinners are an unnecessary expense for me and I told you that already! This is the fifth night in a row we've gone out on a business dinner and frankly, we could have been just as productive over the phone.

Listen, I'm not crying poor, but this restaurant business is a *drain* on my finances and I told you that, too -remember? I thought I knew what to expect with this type of investment but I may have under estimated things….well…..just a little.

The bottom line is that it's going to take awhile for us to really be in the black and I need to be careful. I need to payback loans and recoup my own investment before I can see a dime of profit! The studio is doing great, but I have to remember I only have my income to depend on right now."

"I thought you were married."

Callie grew silent momentarily. "I am married," she said tensely.

"Your husband doesn't contribute to the household finances?"

Callie bristled. "My husband and what he does or does not do, is off limits. I'm talking about you and me and your bills to me, *which I have yet to see!* So I would appreciate an *itemized* up to date invoice. I don't want to get smacked with one giant, whopping bill with a lot of little ambiguous expenses- like this dinner. So, if you plan on billing me for this "business dinner" we might as well go right now!"

"Ready to order?"

The waitress had just walked up and stood smiling, poised to take their order. Callie and Stephen just stared at each other for what must have seemed like an eternity to the waitress who, feeling began to fidget. She was excusing herself to give them more time to decide when Stephen began his order. He spoke to the waitress, but did not take his eyes off of Callie.

"I'll have the 16oz steak, medium, no make that a 20oz steak, medium with the large salad, ranch dressing, mashed potatoes and gravy, a side of home fries because they're my favorite. I'll also have an apple pie a la mode, because I'm feeling really hungry. Oh, a big bottle of your best and most *expensive* wine because I'm beginning to believe I'll need to be drunk to get through this dinner! And for my guest here," Stephen gestured towards Callie, looking up briefly at the waitress before making eye contact with Callie again, "give her anything she wants*, my treat.* I like to think of this as a charity dinner.

"Oh yeah, I'll need the receipt for the expense report I'll be submitting to *my* marketing company. I can afford it."

"You bastard!" Callie pulled the napkin from her lap and threw it on the table and then stood up. "You son of a bitch! You arrogant son of a bitch ...you... you.... jackass, son of a bitch bastard!"

"Ooh, do you kiss with that dirty mouth?" Stephen said smiling, showing his sparkling white teeth.

The splash of cold ice water on Stephen's face was not completely unexpected. After all, he knew Callie wasn't a shy one and this would not be the first time he would "wear" his drink. The second glass of water took him by surprise, just a little. However, it was the third and fourth glass of water borrowed from the table next to theirs that proved to be a complete shock to his system. Callie rolled the last empty

73

water glass across the table where it landed heavily in Stephen's lap, before she stormed off towards the exit.

Stephen, unmindful of the murmurs and awkward stares, quickly wiped his face with the napkin the waitress offered and then gave her a twenty. Then, as if on second thought, he peeled off two more twenties and gave it to her before chasing after Callie.

Callie found herself standing in the middle of the lamp lit parking lot as if she had just dropped out of the sky.

"This is ridiculous!" she muttered.

Her anger had ruined her concentration and she had completely lost track of her car. After clicking the unlock button from her key ring Callie listened for the familiar beep and watched for the flash of lights from her Lexus. Upon spotting her car, she marched up to it, grabbed the door handle and pulled hard, fully expecting the door to fling open wide by the force of her motion. The door, however, was slammed shut even before it opened completely.

"We're not done yet," Stephen said in her ear.

He stood behind her with his arm stretched over her shoulder, his hand still resting on the car door where he had slammed it shut. She could feel his warm breath on her earlobe as well as the rise and fall of his chest as he labored to breathe. He was winded from running to catch up with her.

Without turning around, Callie said as viciously as she could, "You'd better move or I will tear your head off your shoulders."

"Oh, so you have a foul mouth, no table manners and a tendency for physical violence. What else should I know about you?"

"What? You didn't read the Black Women's Handbook?"

"Y'all got a handbook?" Stephen asked innocently.

Callie smiled in spite of herself. No! He wasn't getting off that easy. Callie quickly replaced the smile on her face with a scowl. Stephen let go of the car door and backed away.

"Too late, you smiled. I saw your reflection in the window. "

"So?" Called said as she turned around. She folded her arms and

74

leaned up against the car. "I'm still pissed off."

"Ok, I get it," Stephen said with an apologetic smile, "I kinda deserved what I got. Maybe I got carried away. Just a little."

Stephen held up his thumb and index finger drawing them close to demonstrate. "Maybe just a little bit."

"Maybe? You acted like an ass in there!"

"I said I was sorry! What else can I say?"

"Actually, you didn't say you were sorry. What you said was-"

"Ok, ok, ok," Stephen said quickly. "I'm saying I'm sorry now. Really. I sincerely apologize." He shrugged his shoulders and put his hands in his pockets.

"I almost think you mean it."

"I do," Stephen gave a small smile. "Do you want me to say Scout's honor to prove it?"

"Don't get cute with me, Stephen. I don't do cute."

"I'm not trying to do anything but apologize for my bad behavior!"

Callie stared at him narrowing her eyes and tightening her lips.

"*I mean it.* If you don't believe me maybe it's because I'm a little nervous right now."

Stephen eyes widened and he whispered aloud, "The truth is you're scaring me"

"Oh, I'm scaring you now."

"Yeah. Here we are alone, in a dark parking lot and you've already assaulted me *four times*. Who in my shoes would not be terrified?"

Callie rolled her eyes and sighed loudly, willing herself not to smile.

"Ok, alright, I'm sorry. I'm being serious now. I am very sorry for saying those things. I intentionally meant to rile you up, but Callie you practically accused me of trying to run a scam on you. I just can't believe you don't trust me."

"I don't *know* you!"

"How can you say that? We've been together almost every single

75

day for weeks now! And when we're not together we might as well be because we're talking on the phone!"

"That doesn't mean I really *know you* or know what your motives are!"

"Success is my motive! It's my motivation for everything I do. The grand opening is next weekend and there's not a reservation available for the entire opening weekend! It's standing room only!

"And at the risk of sounding like that arrogant, son of a bitch, jackass, bastard you called me, you have to admit I had a lot to do with that! Don't you get it? *Your* success is *my* success. I told you that when I first met you and I meant it."

He walked up to her and placed a hand on each shoulder. "Just trust me. That's all I really want from you. I haven't asked for one thing more."

"Yeah, but why me?"

"Because I like you."

"That's not an answer, Stephen, because you didn't even know me when you signed on. Sure, you like me *now* after you've gotten to know me."

Stephen looked down at his wet shirt and back up at Callie. "You're pretty sure of yourself, aren't you?"

Embarrassed, Callie covered her face with her hands momentarily. "They'll probably never let me into that restaurant again. I am so, so sorry. I acted like a wild woman in there."

"That's ok," Stephen leaned up against the car next to Callie. "I had planned on washing this shirt tonight anyway. I just didn't plan on being in it at the time."

"You are so corny," Callie said chuckling. "That's why the jury is still out on that sense of humor of yours." They smiled at each other and fell into a comfortable silence.

After awhile Stephen said, "Don't you trust anyone, Callie?"

"I trusted my husband. And I trusted my sister. And I trusted them when they were together." Callie paused. "That was the biggest mistake of my life."

"You mean…," Stephen said, unable to finish the sentence.

"Yeah, I mean…"

"I…um…. don't know what to say."

"Neither did I."

They fell silent again. The wind rustled the trees nearby and the stars seemed to twinkle brighter to Callie for some reason. Looking at the moon, she was beginning to feel the tension ebb from her body when Stephen's voice broke the silence.

"Callie."

"Yes"

"I'll tell you."

"Tell me what?"

"You wanted to know 'why you', right?"

Callie nodded and turned towards Stephen curious now, but he stared beyond the trees and out into the distance.

"First, a little background. My life has the classic beginning of a sad story"

"You were the son of a sharecropper?"

"No."

"Raised by wolves?"

"No."

"Abducted by aliens?"

"No!" Stephen smiled. "You know, you're a little corny, too."

They both laughed and Callie was suddenly feeling completely relaxed.

"It's like this," Stephen continued, "I had a maid…"

"You had a *maid*? That's the beginning of your sad story? You had a maid? Oh, please, somebody get me a tissue, I can tell this is gonna be a real tear jerker. What's the matter, you only had one measly maid? Wait a minute," Callie had a sudden thought, "Do I remind you of your maid or something?"

"No, she was a nice, sweetheart of a lady."

"Very funny," Callie said dryly. "Just tell your sad story, poor little rich boy."

"Well, I was an only child of rich parents. And to make a long story short, I was really more like an orphan. I hardly ever saw either parent. There was always a gallery opening, business meeting, fundraiser or some social or business gathering that was more important than me. I got everything I wanted for my birthday, Christmas or just because I wanted it. Everything, that is except for my parents."

Callie had been prepared to make another joke when she looked at Stephen's eyes and realized he seemed to be lost in thought. He had drifted back deep into his past and she could see the hurt and pain on his face. She tried to imagine how it would feel to be so alone. As misguided and clumsy as her parents had been with their emotions, she had never been made to feel abandoned. She also had siblings and while she wished them away quite often, being alone was never *really* an option. She felt a pang of sadness for what he must have gone through. She couldn't imagine how lonely he must have been.

"I can't remember any happy times as a family. I honestly don't remember both parents being there at the same time without one of them getting ready to rush out the door. When I think back to my childhood, the most important people in my life were the two people my parents paid to be with me, Ella and Inga." Stephen said Inga with a Swedish accent. He looked at Callie.

"Inga was my nanny. She was very good at what she did, but she was completely without emotion. She used to say her job description read *efficient* not *affection*. So, she just did her job. I'm not even sure if she liked me. But Ella was a different story.

Ella was the one who tucked me in at night and held my hand because I was afraid of the dark. She would hug me whenever I was sick, or lonely or just unhappy and tell me everything would be all right. Ella was my family. She was also the one to introduce me to the blues."

78

"The blues?" Callie asked incredulously.

"Yeah, the blues. Jazz and blues." Stephen looked at Callie's face, which showed her obvious confusion.

"You know, *the blues*? Um…. music?"

"I have a hard time envisioning you enjoying any music not sung by somebody named Willie or Hank."

"Well, no self respecting cowboy would ever admit it, but I *was* just a kid." Stephen paused and smiled at Callie whose eyes had softened and showed no signs of anger anymore.

"She had quite a record collection, too," he continued. "All the greats, you know, but there was one song in particular that she played all the time. She used to hum it around the house all the time, too."

"What song was that?" Callie asked intrigued.

"*God Bless the Child*". Billie Holiday. I hadn't heard that song in years. Not until I walked into the well-run establishment where I met the enthusiastic, breath of fresh air, assistant manager."

"Let me guess, Alise"

"Yep, Alise. I have to admit she impressed me. After nosing around a bit, I found out while she was just getting assistant manger pay, she was running everything. The manager's position had never been filled and probably wouldn't be. Why pay a manager's salary if your assistant manager doesn't need help? The owners were never around, either. It was just Alise."

"They've been using her like that for years," Callie said clearly annoyed. "Don't get me started!"

Stephen chuckled. "Don't worry, I don't want to get you riled up again," he said, patting his damp shirt.

"You only get one apology a night, so stop trying to make me feel bad."

"Ok," Stephen said and chuckled again "Back to my story."

"Your long story."

"Cutting to the chase," he added quickly. "Anyway, after talking with Alise I asked her if she had ever thought about opening her own

79

place."

"Hmm, I know you got an earful."

"But she made me a believer. She was so *passionate* about it. You've got to have passion, you know?"

Stephen looked into Callie's eyes just long enough to make her uncomfortable. Embarrassed, Callie looked away and down at her feet. Since Stephen has been around she has come to know that particular view very well.

Nice shoes Callie, but you've got to stop turning away. Try as she might, she could not look back into his eyes. She could only get as far as his neck before he continued with his story.

"I was toying with the idea of partnering up with Alise. She was so….oh, I don't know….confident. But then she told me she had an investor who was also going to be, at least initially, her headliner. Her semi-star of a sister Callie.

Then she put on her sister's debut CD track number six. She said to me right before the music started that she thought the song would speak right to my heart. And it did. I knew what I had to do."

Stephen looked at Callie who was frowning trying to remember the song on track six. Her eyes stretched wide as the realization dawned on her and she pointed her finger at him

"*God Bless the Child.* Track number six."

"I took it as a sign."

"Oh, my God!" Callie said as her hand flew up to her heart and her voice quivered. "That's got to be the most beautiful, wonderful," her voice went flat as she thrust her hand firmly on her hip, "and the most *unbelievable story I have ever heard.*"

Stephen raised his eyebrows and stood looking at Callie who returned the stare. It wasn't long before Callie saw the corners of his lips turn upwards.

"Ok, what the hell, it was worth a try," he said smiling mischievously.

"Oh, you are so unbelievable!" said an exasperated Callie.

80

"You made that perfectly clear."

"No, I mean you-"

"I know what you mean," Stephen said grinning. "But for your information a lot of that story was true, but because you were so rude I won't tell you which parts. You'll just have to wonder"

"Oh, so you're trying to tell me all of this was because of a song?"

"I'm not saying a word, not even if you begged me. After all, rudeness shouldn't be rewarded."

Stephen turned his face away from Callie as if terribly hurt by her words. Callie was trying hard not to laugh.

"Well, I just don't believe you made a business decision based on a song and childhood memories. I don't even know if I believe that song was even part of your childhood memories. As a matter of fact, I don't even know if I believe you were ever a child. The only thing I know that's true is that you somehow met Alise."

"Yeah, well knowing you, I honestly didn't expect you to believe everything I said, but I didn't think you would be so vicious," Stephen said, amused by Callie's comments.

"Well, you deserve it. You are some piece of work, Stephen Russell."

"You got me there, Callie Armstrong. But for the record, everything I said was true except the part about Alise playing me the song. I listened to your CD on my own and I just liked it and I liked Alise and I thought working with you two was a good idea."

Stephen was smiling but suddenly he turned serious as he looked at Callie.

"I told you all that to buy time. I was trying to figure out if I should tell you everything. I keep telling you to trust me, but there is something that I'm keeping from you. This next part is a lot harder to say."

"What part?" Callie placed her hands on her hips and narrowed her eyes while looking at Stephen.

"The financial part. I fronted Alise her portion of the money to be paid back when the restaurant begins to make a profit." Callie's jaw dropped open in surprise as Stephen continued, "For my generosity, I have the option to buy in by forgiving half of Alise's debt and claiming one half of her ownership. And I think it's only fair to tell you," Stephen, very serious now, met Callie's eyes, "I plan on exercising that option because the restaurant will be successful. I'm sure of it."

"How can you be so sure?" Callie snapped.

"It's my business to be sure. That's why I'm not billing. I'm not being sneaky, but it's kind of silly to send out bills…well to myself. I just want to turn a profit on this thing as soon as possible. I don't want to drain you financially or do you any harm at all, Callie. Trust me. I'm not up to anything. It's just business."

"Trust you! There you go again, throwing that word around. How do you really think I'm supposed to react after you and Alise been keeping secrets and scheming behind my back?"

"Now, wait a minute. It was Alise's idea to keep you temporarily in the dark. She thought you would be a little concerned about our arrangement."

"Well, she was right about that one! At least I know what Alise's motivation is in getting this restaurant off the ground. She needs this. It's her dream. But you?"

"Callie, listen to me." He grabbed her by the shoulders and turned her towards him. "I just need you to understand where I'm coming from. You're right; I do have an additional motive. There is something in it for me as long as you're successful."

"What happens if we're not successful?"

"We just part ways. I won't try to collect from Alise, but I won't have to collect because it'll be a success! I pride myself on my business instincts and I can make this happen! Plus I have a lot of connections.

You don't have to look over your shoulder at me because I'm not out to get you. I really, really wish you the best."

Callie shrugged her shoulders and took a step back and out of his grasp.

"I wish me the best too because I'm the only one who's taking a risk here! Alise has no money invested and you're rich enough not to miss this drop in the bucket if things don't work out!"

"It *will* work out, Callie. That's what I keep trying to tell you. Alise is a good businesswoman. If you don't trust me, than you can at least trust her, right?"

Callie laughed a deep throaty laugh and shook her head slowly from left to right.

"What am I missing, here? You don't think she can handle this? She *is* a good businesswoman."

"Oh, Stephen, you have no idea," Callie said to a puzzled Stephen.

"The numbers break down like this;" She continued matter-of-factly. "I put up one hundred percent before I knew anything about your involvement. Alise paid back half. For some reason I thought she took a second on her home but now I know where she got the money."

"Ok. That's all in the open now."

"I'm not done yet. Oh, and by the way, that reimbursement is the money that I'm putting out again because of all of these delays."

"But you'll recoup that."

"Well, I hope so. But this is our businesswoman in action. When she gave me the money for her share, she asked if I would agree to allow her to buy into half of *my* share. Being that she is my sister and this is her dream, I had no problem with that at all. So the bottom line is if the restaurant is profitable, we'll do an ownership shuffle. You buy into her share and she buys into mine. She'll still own half the restaurant, with controlling interest and-"

"Without initially putting up a dime."

"Not one red cent."

"And if it's not successful, she walks away," Stephens said.

"Uh-huh," Callie mumbled pensively.

83

"She's good," Stephen said quietly. They both stood silently lost in thought for a moment.

"Why am I even talking with you about this? When we first met, you said you weren't interested in investing in the restaurant business. Now come to find out, you're a secret investor."

"Alise didn't think you would go along with it any other way. She wanted you to be a part of this. And for the record, I *wasn't* interested in another restaurant, but I wanted to help Alise. And I never would have done it if I didn't think it was a good business move or if I thought Alise couldn't handle it."

Stephen rubbed his chin and smile. "That little story has given me more confidence in my decision than you could have ever imagined."

"It all comes back to "just business" with you doesn't it? Never mind you just flat out lied to me!" Callie yelled. She was getting angry again.

"Jeez, you can go from zero to a hundred on the "angry-o-meter" pretty quickly, can't you?" he said to a scowling Callie. "All I can say is that I'm telling you the truth now, Callie. I don't want to give you any real reason not to trust me."

"Stephen, you make a living out of stealing people's businesses right out from under them. I think that's reason enough to be suspicious of your Good Samaritan routine."

"I also help people. Hey, wait a minute," Stephen pointed his finger at Callie "I don't steal!"

"Well, you lie. And my mother always said if you lie, you steal. But hey, since you're being so honest now, what about that "start up" marketing company? Was it just a cover to explain why you would be around, digging your nose in our business?"

"Well, I had always-"

"Truth, remember? No more secrets and no more lies."

"Ok," Stephen sighed. "The truth is, it's not really a start up company. It's more like an expansion. I just opened an office here expecting that I could concentrate on the restaurant. It was a bit of a cover but…." Stephen grinned nervously. "I just got another big client."

"I'm going to beat Alise up," Callie stated flatly.

"No! You can't tell her you know!"

"What? What ever happened to no more secrets? Honesty, remember?"

"Yeah, honesty right after opening week. Listen, Callie," Stephen reasoned, "Alise is about to jump out of her skin as it is. She's nervous and scared and I think anything unexpected will send her right over the edge. If you're stressed and strained because of the constant delays, think about how Alise feels. This is her dream remember? Right now she's the glue. And I think she would just die if she lost your support in this."

Callie thought about it and knew he had a point. She really wanted everything to go off without a hitch. She could let Alise have it later.

"We're all in this together and it just wouldn't be good for business to have her lose focus." Stephen continued. "I promise you this will work out. If not, expect an anonymous donor to pay off your restaurant debts. *After* opening week we can both tell her and become one big, happy…uh, partnership. Ok? "

Callie fumed in silence as she considered his offer. If he was true to his word and would become her financial safety net, then things weren't that messed up. And they *were* in it all together. But Callie still wasn't convinced Stephen could be trusted. Callie made a mental note to get tonight's declaration in writing.

Everything boiled down to a business arrangement with him. He could be setting her and Alise up to be financially dependent on him. She had already invested so much, she couldn't back out now even if she wanted to. Callie was sure it would not be the first time a business owner stood in her shoes. But what choice did she have?

Callie had done a little research on Stephen, so she knew he had a track record for reaching out and helping people as well as ruining their livelihood. He helped the little guy. He crushed the little guy.

85

Which man was she talking to tonight? Callie looked away still contemplating when Stephen grabbed her hand and fell to one knee.

"Please, Callie," he said before kissing her hand and then flashing that smile

"Ok, ok, just get up," Callie said, knowing that it was becoming easier for her to let him manipulate the situation.

She really did like him, but he certainly hadn't earned her trust. Why was she letting him get to her like this? Because he could make her laugh? Because he could do something as ridiculous as fall on his knees in a parking lot and not care how it looked? Not having a man around seemed to be lowering her defenses against these kinds of pathetic moves, as long as they came with a pretty face. And his face was gorgeous, but there was something else about him, something that fascinated her. Callie felt a stirring inside just thinking about it

"You know, you don't strike me as some big powerful business tycoon. You're too...," Callie hesitated as she searched for the word.

"Handsome?" Stephen suggested while brushing the dirt off the knee of his pant leg

Callie laughed and shook her head.

"That's not what I was going to say."

"Charming?"

"I wasn't going to say that either, cowboy. Although, you are quite the charmer," Callie admitted and smiled.

"Finally, a compliment."

"But sometimes you lay it on a little too thick."

"Oooh, through the heart!" Stephen held his heart as if he had been stabbed. "While I'm dying here, I have one more confession."

"There's more? You've got to be kidding me." Callie rolled her eyes.

"No, I'm not kidding, so here goes. This is personal, but I feel like I owe it to you. You're right. I have hurt some people in the past and in the name of business. It was never my intention, but I felt like I had something to prove to my father. He didn't have a whole lot of faith that I was worthy of the Russell name, and I couldn't help but think that he might be right. So, I went through this thing when I was in my twenties, you know trying to find myself. Or run from myself is more like it. I wanted nothing to do with anything that would tie me to the Russell family, so I left.

"I kicked around a few places as a ranch hand, but then one day I realized I liked sitting behind a desk more than sitting on top of a horse. So, back to the office I went to prove myself to Daddy and eventually fill his extremely large shoes. But to do that I couldn't let myself see the faces behind the profit, just the numbers. The only face I wanted to see was my father's. I needed to know that I made him proud."

"And did you?"

"I don't know. He died before I could ever find out. I'd like to think so." Stephen rubbed his hands together nervously.

"I'm sure you did."

Callie reached out and grabbed one of his hands, clasping it in hers. She smiled at him and then said, "You have the softest hands. You can't be much of a cowboy with such delicate hands."

Laughing, Stephen squeezed Callie's hand and replied, "Yeah, well, I'm a cowboy at heart. I have a ranch and I still like to ride but it's more of a hobby. Besides, when someone wants to do a story on me they want a down to earth cowboy, not a business suit."

"I guessed that," Callie said. "Although, you still kind of act the part."

"That's because I like the cool part of being a cowboy." Stephen stuck out his chest and winked at Callie. "The chicks dig it."

Callie laughed. "Oh, Lord! Alright, are we done with true confession for tonight, at least?

Stephen nodded his head and spread his arms wide. "I'm done. No more secrets. My life's an open book. I want us to be friends, but to get there you have to believe in me. I just wanted you to get to see the real me. I'm not exactly proud of some of the things I've done, but

I've tried to make up for it."

"Fair enough," Callie said, eyeing him suspiciously. "Hmm…. I just don't know what to expect from you."

Stephen reached down and opened the door to her Lexus and then politely gestured with one hand towards the driver's seat. Callie took her seat and Stephen stood next to her in the open door.

"You should expect the unexpected. It always happens when you least expect it," he said and leaned in to kiss her on the cheek. "Have a safe trip home, Callie," he whispered in her ear.

She felt his warm breath on her earlobe as he lingered near her ear. She half expected him to nuzzle her neck and the very thought made her shudder, probably just as he had planned. Before he could move away, Callie gently guided his lips to hers and softly kissed them.

"You drive safely, too," she whispered barely pulling away from his lips in order to speak. Then she stroked his chin lightly before reaching for the door handle.

Stephen moved out of the way and Callie closed the door. She could see the look of surprise on his face. After pulling out of the parking spot, she rolled down the window and added, "Oh yeah, I *do* kiss with this dirty mouth."

Callie smiled and waved at him as she pulled off.

"Betcha wasn't expecting that, cowboy," she said softly, smiling to herself as she drove out of the parking lot.

Callie pulled into the garage still replaying the events of the night. The kiss was nice. Very nice and as much as she hated to admit it, it had left her wanting more. But as nice as the kiss was, the look on his face was the best. Callie chuckled to herself. It had thrown him off balance and *that* was nice. He wasn't used to giving up control and now Callie knew without a doubt that all of those meaningful looks and sexually charged comments weren't her imagination. He was flirting with her. Seducing her! He had good looks and charm and a gorgeous smile that he used as weapons.

88

Callie wanted to believe in Stephen and trust him, but she wondered about his motives for keeping Alise in the dark. He had a good enough reason, though. Alise *was* just one big bundle of nerves and the conversation Callie was planning on having with her *would* be a distraction. Callie really didn't want to take a chance on upsetting her at this point. This was her dream come true and Callie wanted everything to be perfect.

However, suppose Stephen was just running interference because he didn't want the two of them to compare notes? Callie wasn't sure she could ever untangle the confusion she felt when she thought about Stephen. He did have a history of helping people with no strings attached, so maybe he really was just trying to help. He was so sincere, but she couldn't let go of her doubt just yet. She didn't want to allow herself to trust him or anyone else for that matter.

Callie was still contemplating whether her trust issues had more to do with Michael than with Stephen as she made her way from the garage to the kitchen. She had armed the alarm, grabbed a bottle of water from the fridge and was on her way upstairs when she saw the message light flashing on her phone in the living room. Making her way back down the stairs, she kicked off her shoes and walked quickly across the plush carpet. Normally all the calls came on her cell phone. At least the important ones did. Maybe it was just a few telemarketers insisting on ignoring her wishes to be left alone. Callie pushed the button on the machine and heard what she least expected.

"Callie, it's me, Marlisa. You know I wouldn't be calling if it wasn't important. We need to meet ASAP. Come to the office tomorrow morning so we can get this over with."

The line went dead. Callie stared at the machine. What could they possibly have to talk about?

CHAPTER 8

Callie got up earlier than planned. She didn't sleep well. No matter how much she told herself she wouldn't let Marlisa's phone call bother her, she had to admit it unnerved her a bit. What could Marlisa be up to?

Callie showered and dressed and contemplated breakfast. She wasn't hungry so she decided she would just have coffee. She was just finishing her second cup when the phone rang. It was Alise.

"Hey," Alise said cheerfully, "I wanted to call you last night, but it was pretty late when I got in. Did you get your invitation?"

"From Marlisa?"

"Yeah, she left a message on my machine at home. She has my cell phone number, so if she really wanted to talk to me she would have called that instead."

"Well, apparently she didn't want to talk to either one of us. She left me a message on my home phone, too," Callie said stirring her coffee.

"Oh, I don't blame her for not wanting to talk to you. She was probably scared you'd discovered a way to punch her in the eye over the phone."

"Well, if I do discover a way to do it, she'd better be prepared to get three or four calls a day from me."

"Three or four a day? Is that all? You know she'd be on your auto redial so you could just push and punch, push and punch!"

Callie and Alise both laughed, happy for the distraction.

"What do you think she wants?" Alise asked.

"I don't know, but I don't have the patience to deal with her. She had better not be starting something."

"Well, I'll meet you there, but *don't go in without me*. I know Marlisa loves to push *your* buttons and if I do say so myself, them buttons getting easier to push!"

"I know, I know," Callie admitted.

"I just have to drop Jackson and Anthony off at their father's place this morning. Finally he planned to see them. Now, a real father would have come and gotten his boys himself, but as usual he had some excuse – his car is in the shop or something like that." Alise made a clicking sound with her tongue. "Dumbass. Anyway, that's a different family drama. The boys agreed to see him and I didn't want to be accused of standing between them so I'm taking them to him."

"Alright. I was about to leave, but I'll wait and have another cup of coffee before leaving."

"Another cup! How many have you had?"

"I'm on my third."

"Three cups of coffee! You know how you get when you drink coffee! Oh Lord, let me hurry and drop my kids off 'cause you gonna be wound up like a fighting machine by the time I get there."

Callie smiled. "I think you're exaggerating, just a little. I can remain civil."

"Callie, don't forget I saw you launch yourself like a rocket across a dining room table. I ain't saying she don't deserve whatever she gets, but I'm just trying to keep you out of jail. Besides, you're a local celebrity and it'll make the papers and that'll be bad for our restaurant."

Our restaurant. Callie bit down on her lip to stop herself from commenting based on her conversation with Stephen last night. Not a word until after the opening. Besides, she didn't know what drama Marlisa was setting in motion. The questions she had about Stephen and the restaurant could wait.

91

"Alright, alright. I'll meet you over there."

"And you will not go in without me."

"And I will not go in without you."

"Good. See you in a bit." Alise hung up and Callie slowly set the phone down. What could Marlisa be planning so that she not only invited her but Alise too? It certainly couldn't be about the production company they owned jointly, since Alise was not a part of that.

"What are you up to, Marlisa?" Callie asked aloud.

She poured herself another cup of coffee, added cream and sugar and then took a sip. It was good. Then she took another sip before pouring it down the drain. Alise was right about coffee getting her wound up. She rinsed her cup out and put it into the dishwasher before grabbing her purse and car keys. It was time to face Marlisa.

Callie got out of her car that she had parked in her reserved space in the parking garage. The building, which housed her successful production company, belonged to Callie and Marlisa along with the adjacent parking garage. Several businesses were paying rent and the parking garage itself had a fee.

There were a few metered parking spaces on the street, but good luck finding one. Being near a hospital insured that the garage would always be full since the parking on the street would be hard to come by. They had to section off an area for the business owners; otherwise they would never get a space.

Callie and Marlisa had gotten a good deal on this piece of downtown real estate and it had quickly paid for itself over and over again. Callie walked briskly towards the elevator and pushed the button, turning when she heard someone call her name. It was Alise.

"I thought I told you to wait for me!" she said a little out of breath from her brief jog to reach Callie.

"I was...uh going to wait for you upstairs."

"Uh huh," Alise said, not believing that for a second.

92

"Well I'm here now, so let's go," she said stepping into the waiting elevator. They rode in silence to the top floor where the business offices for the company were located. They were both lost in their own thoughts and barely heard Marlisa's secretary greeting them and informing them to go right in, as they were expected. Angie, the secretary, had no idea she couldn't have stopped them even if she wanted to.

Callie threw open the door to Marlisa's office with such force that it startled Marlisa, who was sitting behind her big oval shaped desk, as well as the mystery guest who, sitting in the winged back chair across from Marlisa, had spilled a little coffee from her cup. Callie couldn't see who it was since the chair was completely blocking her face, but she recognized the voice instantly.

"My goodness! You still like to make an entrance, don't you Callie?"

Callie and Alise looked at each other puzzled before turning their gaze back to the mystery guest who stood up from the chair and turned to face them. It was Paula. They hadn't seen or heard from their oldest sister in years.

"What's going on?" Alise asked.

"I have some news that will affect everyone in this room," Paula said so dramatically that Callie half expected to hear the cliffhanger scene soap opera music swell in the background. However, the tension in the room did rise up a notch.

Callie scanned the faces of everyone in the room. She first looked at Alise, who could barely mask the look of disgust on her face as she stared at Paula. Then Callie looked at Paula, who seemed to be relishing in the theatrics of it all and finally her eyes rested on Marlisa who looked uncomfortably down at her desk.

If the truth were told, Marlisa still had trouble looking Callie in eyes.

Good, Callie thought. *She should feel uncomfortable.*

They used to be close friends as well as sisters, but that was before

93

Marlisa torpedoed their relationship. It was all her fault and Callie never wanted her to forget it.

There were a lot of hard feelings in the room right now. Callie looked around at her three sisters and wished for a magic wand, which she would promptly use to make Marlisa and Paula disappear. She didn't need them anyway, only Alise. If she didn't know it before, she knew it for sure right now. She had too many sisters - two more than she could stand to look at right now. Callie turned to leave but hearing Paula's voice stopped her.

"Callie this is important. You need to hear this. It could change everything."

CHAPTER 9

"First of all, you all know that I was administrator of Daddy's will."

The four of them sat around the table in the conference room. Callie had insisted the surprise, mandatory meeting be moved to neutral territory.

"Yes, we know," Alise said rudely.

"No matter what anyone says, he was my Daddy. My *only* Daddy," Paula said as she continued looking around the table.

This was it, Alise thought balling up her fist. Paula was going to get that well deserved pop in the mouth. Each time she said "my daddy" the words burned through Alise's will power. She had a mountain of flashbacks whenever she looked at Paula. Painful reminders came again and again, triggered just by Paula's presence. Alise didn't want to relive those times when the sisters were left to fend for themselves, but that was when she discovered the real Paula.

The four sisters grew up in a three level row house in northwest Washington DC. Their father, who was an established musician, practically lived on the road. He performed, toured and recorded with a lot of famous names. However, he had one problem that deeply affected his family. He gambled. Even though the money he earned should have been sufficient to take care of his family, much of the time the money never made it home.

Their mother didn't work outside of the home because she never wanted anyone to watch her children. While both of her parents worked, her caretaker had abused her and her siblings. Because of this personal suffering, she couldn't bear leaving her own children with anyone. She had promised herself that no one would ever abuse her own children, so she kept her girls close.

Although they could have used a second income, she believed they would just have to make do with what they had, but sometimes it was harder than she imagined. She struggled to take care of everyone, but sometimes she couldn't help anyone – not even herself.

No one talked about depression as a disease in those days, but looking back it was clear that their mother suffered from severe episodes of depression and needed help. Eventually, she would fight her way through the dark fog that enveloped her, but not until after she had taken to her bed for days at a time.

In today's time, she could have received a diagnosis and treatment, but back then no one knew what was wrong with her. The girls just called them her sad days, but the neighbors thought she was crazy. With their father on the road and their mother in a darkened room until God knows when, the girls turned to Paula.

Paula was a product of their mother's first marriage and much older than her sisters. Her real father took off and left her and their mother when she was little. But he didn't just disappear and leave the city- he simply left the family. Everyone knew he lived just three blocks away, but he never acted like a father to Paula. After a while he didn't even acknowledge her and his abandonment left her with serious "Daddy issues". She spent the better part of her life trying to force a man to love her.

Loving Paula however, was not an easy job. She was selfish, self-absorbed, insensitive and overbearing. It was her way or no way. Bend to her will and bow at her feet. Alise had seen enough of it growing up - the world according to Paula.

While running after a man, she would lavish gifts on him and his family. His brothers and sisters, nieces and nephews would get brand new shoes, school clothes, toys and gadgets, while her own younger sisters of the same ages would go without.

Paula knew how tough they had it sometimes. During their mother's episodes it was like they were orphans and it was obvious that they needed someone. But Paula's philosophy was every man, woman and child for themselves unless, of course, it was her that was in need of something. You could count on Paula to be there to take her share as a family member when times were good. She liked the benefits she received from being the oldest, like ruling over them with their mother's approval. But when her little sisters really needed her, she had no problem turning her back on them.

Alise knew she could take care of herself, but Callie and Marlisa were just too young. Making sure they ate or got off to school or got bathed was not convenient for Paula, so Alise, who was six years her junior, took on the role that she had tossed aside so easily.

What really bothered Alise was that when their mother was feeling "normal", she placed Paula on an extremely high pedestal. She was the smart one; the pretty, light skinned one with the sensitive heart. Paula could do no wrong and no one believed that more than Paula.

Yet, all the praise in the world couldn't raise her self esteem and stop her from being a doormat for one man after another. She was desperate for the love of a man, a father figure, but when she found it, she couldn't handle the relationship. She struck out with anger and obnoxious behavior stemming from her own self-hatred.

Man after man bounced her to the curb, but only after taking advantage of her desperation. However, once she reached a certain level for crazed behavior and the stalking began, they were sorry they ever laid eyes on her. Thank you for the booty calls and the gifts but goodbye - too many "daddy issues". No man wanted to put up with her destructive, self-serving behavior and neither did the sisters.

Paula always made it clear she cared more for her current man than her own family. She even told Alise as much. Alise had always wondered if that were true why didn't she just move on? She had

97

reached adulthood long before her sisters. She was working. Why didn't she just stay away? Alise, Callie and Marlisa had talked about it often as adults and tried to figure out her motives. If her family wasn't important, she should have said her good-byes and "broke camp."

Alise always believed she stayed because she felt powerful in the household. She had the power to control their happiness. Only a miserable, unhappy person would be driven by this idea. Marlisa and Callie had made peace with much of the harm Paula had caused them, but Alise had been older and understood more of what was going on when they were growing up.

Alise did not have to give much weight to the mean, bossy things she did to them like making them beg for food or not allowing them to sit on the furniture whenever the mood hit her. Those weren't the really cruel and destructive things Paula was capable of doing. Things happened that were unforgivable in Alise's eyes. Some of her behavior Callie and Marlisa did not know about and even both parents went to their grave not being fully aware of what Paula had done.

What was worse is that Alise could remember when she actually had put Paula on that pedestal that their mother had built for her. She *was* pretty and she *was* smart and Alise was so proud of her. But that was her big sister seen through the eyes of a little kid. Now, she could barely stand to look at her. The flashbacks came fast and furiously.

Flashback to Paula slapping Alise across the face calling her a whore for trying to entice Paula's twenty five year old boyfriend. At the time Alise had just turned twelve and had fought off one of Paula's boyfriend's advances after he had detoured into her room from his trip to the bathroom.

She was relieved to see Paula storming into the room, believing Paula would protect her, only to find the opposite reaction. As Alise stood holding her torn halter-top in place, Paula berated her for causing the entire episode because of the slutty way she was beginning to dress. Then she lovingly took Richard's hand and walked with him out of the room. Alise could still feel the sting of humiliation she had felt when she heard Paula apologize to him for the "problem" Alise had caused. It would be years before Alise accepted that she was not to blame.

Flashback to the Christmas Eve when she was thirteen years old. Marlisa was five, Callie was six and Paula was nineteen. Paula had just gotten a raise at the telephone company and was making "good money" as she used to say. Alise knew no presents would be coming from their parents. Their father couldn't make it home for the holidays and their mother had been in bed for a week.

She didn't much care for herself, but the girls would be heartbroken. They were so excited about Christmas and Alise became frantic trying to find a way to salvage it. Alise had searched her mother's drawers and found some money. It wasn't that much, but she could use it to buy a trinket or two at the five and dime store. She also had her favorite Barbie dolls that both girls admired. She had decided to give them to the girls. After all, she was getting a little old for dolls anyway.

Alise had gone to her room for her coat to make the trip to the store but stopped at Paula's door. Paula had been spending a lot of time over at her new boyfriend Robert's house, so Alise was surprised to see the light under the door. She knocked softly and when she didn't get an answer, she slowly opened the door.

Presents! There were four large shopping bags overflowing with gifts! Alise was so excited. Paula had come home on Christmas Eve to give them their gifts. She didn't want to be selfish, but she couldn't help snooping to see which gifts were hers. But present after present had unfamiliar names. Alise had emptied all 4 bags and had not found one present addressed to anyone in the house. She was sitting in the middle of all the packages strewn around the room when Paula walked in.

"What are you doing!" she screamed viciously at Alise.

Incredulously, Alise looked at her and said, "None of these belong to us"

"Of course not. They belong to my other family. Robert's family, which is more like my real family anyway."

"What about us?" Alise asked, with tears in her eyes. "We won't have any presents at all."

Alise remembers what happened next with particular clarity. Paula had leaned down close to Alise's face and whispered, "At least *I'll* have a Merry Christmas", before snatching the gift Alise was holding from her hands. Strutting over to door, she turned back to Alise.

"You better clean up the mess you made by the time I come out of the bathroom." And with that she was gone down the hall humming *Santa Clause is Coming to Town*.

Alise was devastated and hurt beyond belief. But she was also outraged! This was the incident that Alise believed to be a turning point for her. It was the first time she would strike back. While Paula took a shower and pampered herself in the bathroom getting ready for her big night as Santa, Alise was carefully removing the contents of each present and replacing them with an array of items from Paula's room – old, beat up books, broken toys and dirty clothes. Robert's mother was receiving dirty panties and bras rather than the expensive cashmere sweater. Alise knew that Paula would attack her like a rabid moose when she found out, but it would be worth it.

After finishing she walked up to the closed bathroom door where Paula was still busy primping and whispered, "Now, I'll have a Merry Christmas, too."

Flashback to Alise graduating from high school. Paula did not attend the ceremony, but when Alise got back to the house Paula couldn't wait to give her a very special "present". She asked Alise to her room for privacy.

At twenty-four years of age, Paula had still not moved out of the house completely. She first came back after flunking out of college and then after each live-in boyfriend kicked her out. This one occasion had been the only time she had asked any one of her sisters

100

into her room. Even after everything that had happened, Alise looked at Paula hopeful that she was reaching out to her as a sister. That's when Paula began with the teasing comments leading up to the big bombshell.

"Don't you wish your daddy was there to see you graduate today?"

Alise looked at her puzzled.

"He was there today."

"No, no, no, not your stepfather, your *real* father. Philip Elliot, the man you have called Daddy for your entire life, is your *step*father. Your *real* father is Thomas Alexander."

Alise, in shock, stood staring at Paula.

That's right," Paula continued. "We have the same father. He knew about you and he left you, too."

Alise could feel the tears coming but she fought them back. She would not cry in front of Paula.

"How do you even know?" Alise managed to say without her voice giving away her anguish.

"I found out when you were four years old. Daddy had just found out and he and Mama were fighting. Mama made me promise not to tell you. She said you were too young. She said you never needed to know. She said this was supposed to be something that only adults could talk about and that we were still sisters and blah, blah, blah.

"Anyway, I was just a kid myself then, but now we're both adults. You've graduated from high school, you're eighteen and I thought you needed to know."

"You're lying!" Alise yelled.

"Need proof?"

Paula pulled out worn documents and shoved them in Alise's face. Alise snatched the papers from Paula and quickly scanned them, becoming more confused by its implications.

"What... what is this?" Alise asked puzzled.

"Custody papers. Our father tried to exercise his parental rights for visitation. Now, don't get your hopes up, it wasn't even his idea.

101

Apparently, our grandmother put him up to it. She wanted to be a part of our lives and the only way she could get to us was through her son.

"So, between drunken binges he managed to get the legal stuff started, but when he went back to jail that kind of put an end to *that* drama. But it opened up a new drama about you." Paula smiled. "You know what they say 'Mama's baby, Papa's maybe.' When the truth came out, it hit the fan!"

Alise balled the papers up while eyeing Paula intently. Then she dropped the wadded paper at her feet, turned and left the room. She forced herself not to retreat to her own bedroom and went downstairs as if nothing was wrong.

Later on, she carefully cut the heads off of all the stuffed animals in Paula's prized collection, but instead of removing them, she kept them propped up in place. It wasn't until days later as Paula adjusted them that all the heads began to fall off. Paula threw a fit, but before she could confront Alise, she discovered some of the pages of her diary had been removed. They were the pages that held the most personal and explicit details of her love life. She had no idea what Alise might do with them, but that was when she realized how dangerous Alise could be. Alise hadn't cried or ran to her parents like Paula expected. She was no longer a little kid, and it was then that Paula knew she would have to be smarter when dealing with Alise.

Even though Alise had never repeated the conversation to anyone, she was devastated to find out a lot of people knew anyway. And when Thomas Alexander died, Alise was named as a beneficiary in the life insurance policy his mother had taken out on him. The funeral program also listed her as one of his surviving children.

Alise never thought of her parentage except when Paula was around. She always made "Daddy" comments as if Alise should feel hurt or ashamed or like an outsider, the way Paula herself must have felt. But Alise only felt anger, not at her mother or either father. She only directed her anger towards Paula.

Paula worked hard all her life to create strife and unhappiness in

102

the family. It was worse now because supposedly she had found religion. Now she backed all of her cruel and selfish behavior with the Bible. She could isolate verses in the Bible and twist them to fit into the context of whatever was going on in her life. With her version of scripture, she could prove she was morally right to do anything she wanted, including judging everyone else. She would give personal insults veiled as messages from God because according to Paula, she was just a vessel sanctioned by the Word of God.

Of course, God never told her anything *she* needed to do. The only way finding the Lord changed Paula was to make her feel more powerful in her plans of destruction and that made her more dangerous. She had already been kicked out of a few churches, but according to Paula, they were intimidated by her relationship with God. She considered herself a spiritual giant and she realized she was too big for those other churches, so she became a self-proclaimed pastor. Alise shuddered at the damage she could do if she ever gathered a following. But now she was here, out of the blue, talking about daddies

"Well, I guess I should just get to the point," Paula said. "The will was written so that almost all of the money from our daddy's estate would go to his biological children. Alise and I did get a *small* settlement. A *very small* settlement compared to his two other daughters."

"Paula, you know why the will was written that way. We got money from our biological father, so it was only fair that Daddy gave to his own blood."

"Well, that's your opinion, Alise. I felt that I was his daughter just as much as anyone else in this room. I was treated as his real daughter right up until I read the will, then I became a stepdaughter.

"Besides, all of the money from *our* mother's insurance was given to Daddy, who basically passed it on to his "real" daughters. He didn't set aside anything from her policy for me, did he? I didn't think *that* was fair, but that's not the point right now.

103

"I'm here to carry out the stipulation made in the will to the best of my abilities and something has come up that needs to be addressed. I would be derelict in my duties if I did not pursue this issue."

Paula tried to remain calm and business-like but Alise could see behind her eyes. She was about to drop a bombshell and she was almost jumping out of her skin with glee.

"What is it, Paula? You win; you got us on the edge of our seats. We get it; you're in control, alright? Now what is it?" Alise said. She had been in the room with Paula too long and her patience was running out.

"I'm getting to it," Paula said before slowly reaching into her briefcase to take out a single piece of paper. "As we all know, the will stipulated just about everything was to go to Daddy's biological children, Callie and Marlisa. The only problem is that one of them is not his daughter."

The room became completely still. Everyone was silent and then suddenly, they all began to speaking at once.

"How could you say that?" Callie said.

"What are you talking about?" Marlisa asked.

"What's on that piece of paper?" Alise demanded.

"If everybody would be quiet, I'll answer all the questions. First, this is a letter found amongst Daddy's things. I had it the whole time, but I never read it until recently. This letter is from Mama and she wrote it to Daddy just before she died. Look at the date. Mama had a way of writing everything down when she started getting into one of her moods."

"If this is true, it implies she was some sort of serial adulterer. I don't believe that," Callie said, folding her arms across her chest.

"Let's face it. She was not well. And Daddy *was* gone nine months out of the year."

Alise looked away. She had heard Paula say that before, more than once, as a matter of fact. That was her response each time she asked about a couple of their mother's "friends" who made her feel

104

uncomfortable. She didn't like Mr. Leroy, who came around to fix the furnace even in the summertime or Mr. Tom, who was a little too nice and delivered free steaks to them at home. And she couldn't stand Mr. Al, a neighbor that did handyman jobs for her even at night. After a while, Alise stopped asking. She thought she knew the answer and she wouldn't allow herself to care.

She could remember how her mother would suddenly snap out of her depression and start singing to herself and getting all dressed up to go out. Wearing sweet smelling perfume that her father sent her from far away places, she would squeeze into her tightest skirt and high heel pumps.

She was a pretty woman with a voluptuous shape and could get more than her share of attention from men. The extra twisting she did when walking never failed to draw all eyes to her *and she liked it.* Alise remembered most of all how much she liked it. Soon, their father stopped traveling so much and none of it mattered, except now it did.

This admission may be an astonishing revelation to Callie and Marlisa, but Alise understood the possibilities. So did Paula.

Paula now looked meaningfully at Alise. Callie and Marlisa looked on as Paula and Alise eyed each other, curious about the exchange, but anxious to continue the meeting.

"Anyway," Paula continued, "what you see here is only a copy. As a matter of fact, I made copies for everyone." She retrieved copies from her briefcase and passed them around the table.

"The original is safe with the lawyer," she added with a smile.

Callie snatched her letter and read in horror. It was a confession of infidelity resulting in the birth of a daughter that he thought was his own. It was a very personal letter of apology and remorse. She was asking for forgiveness.

Callie re-read the letter trying to absorb it all. She couldn't rely on anyone. Not Michael or Alise or Marlisa, not even her own mother and father. All the people that were supposed to make her happy had let her down. Had kept secrets from her. This was too much to take.

"I take my duties very seriously and the settlement of the will was mismanaged. One of you ladies," Paula looked from Callie to Marlisa, before continuing, "is the *illegal* recipient of a monetary settlement from Daddy's will. Now, I have made arrangements for both of you to take a DNA test to prove paternity and the results will then provide us with the rightful owner of this business property."

Marlisa's mouth dropped open. "We both own this studio!"

"It was purchased with money from the settlement. Remember, I saw the checks? You two practically got it all. The money from the sale of the house and the money he had squirreled away from his royalties for all the songs he wrote. Not to mention, the insurance money. But one of you has to give it all back because you're not a biological child. One of you will lose everything."

"You're enjoying this, aren't you?" Alise asked.

"My joy has nothing to do with this! The Holy Spirit would not let me be if I didn't clear this up. I prayed on this situation because I knew people would get hurt, but it's the truth that we're after. God is not the author of confusion and you have to admit this is just a big mess!"

"That you created!" Alise was yelling now.

"I could not be still on this!" Paula stood up. "I told you the Holy Spirit had me convicted! But God did speak to me and tell me a way that this could work out and bring us together as a family."

"Y'all better duck 'cause we have a better chance of locust flying through that window than family harmony!" Alise yelled pointing at the big glass window in the conference room for emphasis.

"Oh, habbada shalab manaca ba drrrool." Paula had her eyes closed and hands reaching up to the ceiling.

"Oh, she supposed to be speaking in tongues." Alise laughed and pointed at Paula. "You going straight to hell!"

Paula stopped suddenly and sat back down. "The devil is not gonna stop me from my mission!" she said forcefully, looking pointedly at Alise. Then she turned her attention to Callie and

106

Marlisa.

"You could both take the DNA test and one of you will lose everything. And you both worked hard to build this business. Both of you! *Or* the two of you could agree to share the business."

Feeling relieved, Callie and Marlisa looked at each other. They were already sharing the business.

"With all the sisters," Paula added.

"What?" Alise said in amazement.

"I'm trying not to destroy one of their lives, while still upholding my obligation to the settlement of the will. If the owner —one of the two of them – agrees to share with her siblings equally, then it doesn't matter who the real owner is."

"Uh uh. Leave me out of this diabolical scheme of yours!" Alise said and stormed out the door.

"Then that just leaves the three of us and one unsettled will. Here is the date and time for your DNA test." Paula handed each of them an appointment card. "It's up to you if you want to keep your appointment."

Paula pulled out more paperwork from her briefcase. "Now, if you decide to share the settlement, I have some paperwork that you might want to look over. It's -"

"This meeting's over," Callie said standing up and then walking out of the room.

CHAPTER 10

The lure of the wine bottle was calling again. Callie resisted. She didn't need to drink; she needed to think with a clear head. So instead of drinking, she paced. Around and around she went in her office. Her sanctuary. This entire situation was almost too much for her to bear. Her whole life was turning into some kind of test. How much can Callie take before she breaks completely? Her relationships were in shambles. In her mind, everything took on the feeling of comparing before and after pictures.

Before, she was completely and totally in love with the man of her dreams. Now, she had no choice but to divorce him as he betrayed her in the worst possible way.

Before, she had a younger sister that she loved and trusted with her life. Growing up with only a year between them, everyone thought they were twins. Now, they couldn't be further apart and their relationship could never be mended.

Before, all three daughters lived under one roof. Now, Ashley is only a visitor in her own home.

Before, she knew exactly who her father was. Now …Callie couldn't bear to think of what the after picture could look like.

She looked at the appointment card in her hand. Her scheduled time was three days away. Did she want to know? If Marlisa was the real daughter, Callie could lose everything. Marlisa would have no problem setting her belongings on the doorstep. If she would sleep with her husband and the father of her children, then kicking her out of the business would be a piece of cake.

Callie wanted to think of herself as a better person, but she wasn't going to fool herself. After a pang of guilt, she would happily send Marlisa packing. With their strained relationship it would be a relief to remove her from the office, the only place where their paths were forced to cross.

Then there was the other part of this horrible mess. Which one of them just lost a father? If Philip Elliot was not her father, than who was? With their mother gone it would be next to impossible to find out, even if she wanted to. How could her mother do this to their family again? Maybe, she was the daughter of Thomas Alexander, like Alise.

Callie ran downstairs into the den and opened the bottom drawer of the built in wall unit. The den had been decorated with all warm colors, exactly as Michael had desired. It had been his favorite room in the house. Next to her own office, it was also her favorite room in the house, with its large windows and soft leather furniture. There was always a beautiful view out of the windows and a real coziness in this room. Callie used to sit for hours curled up in the large brown easy chair reading or just talking with Michael while the fireplace crackled. Nowadays, Callie shied away from the den. It reminded her too much of Michael and how happy she was with him. Sometimes she thought she could still feel his presence.

She sank down now in that brown leather chair and curled her legs beneath her, holding onto the photo albums she had pulled from the hutch. Closing her eyes she took a deep breath. The room still smelt like Michael or maybe it was just her imagination. Callie opened her eyes and softly touched the cover of the first photo album. She didn't know what she was looking for, but maybe, if she looked closely enough at the pictures, she could figure out if she belonged. At the very least she hoped the memories would give her a connected feeling again.

Callie flipped to the first picture taken of her and Marlisa. There she sat holding the new baby that had just come home from the hospital. Just a baby herself, Callie was grinning at the camera while her mother sat next to her and supported baby Marlisa. Her mother was also smiling at the camera. Smiling at her father. How could she be so happy if Marlisa wasn't his?

Callie flipped through the album, stopping on any picture of either her or Marlisa, until she came to one where she was eight and Marlisa was seven. No wonder people thought they were twins. Same hazel eyes, same smile, same hair. Callie slammed the album closed. All traits they both could have gotten from their mother.

What about their personalities? Callie was a lover of music like her father and grandmother. That was always their bond. When he was home from the road they would sit for hours "performing". Callie would sing while her father played his trumpet. Most of the songs Callie wrote herself, but her father could follow along. Sometimes, the whole family would get in on the act. Callie smiled at the memory. The poor neighbors.

But other than the music, they were nowhere near alike. Callie was neat and organized and planned every move, while her father was spontaneous. He had a zest for life and always lived totally in the moment…like Marlisa.

Callie also stood apart from her father and Marlisa when it came to making friends. Callie was always careful not to let anyone too close and it would take awhile for her to warm up and get to know people. When she let people in and showed her vulnerability, it was because she trusted they would be a part of her life for the long haul.

Her father and Marlisa both embraced everyone – the more the merrier. They laughed easily and never took anything too personally. Friends? Easy come easy go. Their mother always said Marlisa was her wild child, carefree and irresponsible, just like her father.

Just like her father.

Callie covered her face with her hands determined not to allow herself to cry and lose control. Think Callie! What are you going to do? Take the chance and lose everything? Then go through the rest of your life wondering who your real father is? Or take the easy way out. Sign over part of the business to Paula and just pretend none of this ugliness and uncertainty ever existed. If she's never tested, then no one will know for certain one way or the other if she is an Elliot. Even if Marlisa takes the test and it comes back that she is his daughter, that won't prove that Callie *isn't* his daughter, too. Callie thought back to the letter her mother wrote. Her mother could have been wrong.

"She was wrong. I'm sure of it," Callie said aloud.

"Who was wrong?"

Callie uncovered her eyes to see Michael standing in the doorway.

"Hi," she said in a small voice.

Michael walked slowly into the room studying Callie, a look of concern on his face. He knelt down next to the chair leveling his face with hers.

"What's wrong?"

Callie smiled wryly. "You got to be kidding me right? That can't be a serious question coming from *you*."

Michael stood up and took a step backwards without loosing eye contact. He continued to stare at Callie before saying, "It's not about me this time."

His eyes went to the photo albums containing her childhood pictures.

"What's wrong?"

"Nothing."

Callie sat looking down at her hands. How could he tell just by looking at her?

Michael walked over to the sofa and sat down. Callie smiled seeing him sitting there. Just like old times.

"I just dropped Ashley off and I have nothing planned for tonight besides having a lonely macaroni and cheese microwave dinner. Sitting here listening to you trying to convince me nothing's wrong for the next couple of hours would definitely be an evening upgrade.

"So, I'll ask again, *what's wrong*? But before you answer this time, I have to warn you, I'm not giving up easily. I can ask you ten thousand more times before I will even *think* about the possibility that I won't eventually get a straight answer from you."

Callie smiled at him. Her defenses were already broken down. She needed someone to talk to and, in a way, the financial ramifications would affect him, too. She reached in her back pocket and handed him her copy of the letter and then began to pace. She explained the emergency meeting and the sudden appearance of Paula, as well as Paula's idea of a solution. She finished by handing him the appointment card.

"This doesn't sound right. I'm not sure if they can do this, especially after all this time." Michael looked at her skeptically holding up the letter. "Have this been authenticated? We could fight all of this if you want to. I'm sure of it. We should have a lawyer look into this."

He was saying 'we' and that touched Callie more deeply than she could have imagined. He was letting her know she didn't have to go it alone. But he didn't quite understand what Callie herself just realized. It wasn't about contesting wills or finances, even if she had the strength to fight. It was about living a lie her entire life. It was about knowing who she is. Belonging. And it was about losing her father all over again, something that would be utterly devastating. Callie stopped pacing and turned to Michael. Tears were beginning to form in her eyes.

"Michael, I loved my father more than anything. And if I…if I find out that I was a product of my mother's betrayal…every time he looked at me he must have felt…he must have…"

Callie choked back the tears. She couldn't bring herself to say the word 'hate'. Her father must have hated the visual reminder of her mother's infidelity and deceit. He must have hated calling her name, too. It held no special meaning except to remind him that he had been deceived. Callie almost laughed at the irony. It was all too much to

112

think about, especially when everything else in her life was uncertain. Not knowing if her whole existence was just a lie was too much to bear.

Silently, Michael looked at her, feeling her pain. He saw the relationship she had with her father and how difficult it was for her when he died. When Callie loved, she loved hard and she loved completely. She also felt a loss equally as hard. He knew that better than anyone. He knew she was more emotionally fragile because of his own betrayal. Michael stood up from the couch and opened his arms. He had to make things right again. He had to make Callie happy again.

Callie walked into his embrace and then all the tears she had held inside poured out. Her body went limp as she cried, feeling safe and protected in his arms. She stood there crying and holding on to Michael wishing things were back to the before picture with them, but knowing in her heart they never could be that couple again.

Michael held Callie and caressed her back, desperately trying to soothe her. He kissed her forehead and promised himself that he would make everything all right between them again or die trying.

CHAPTER 11

Marlisa stood before the tall, glass, living room window of her condominium contemplating her options. She held a glass of wine in one hand and her copy of the letter she had gotten from Paula in the other. Paula sat behind her on the sectional sofa stirring her scotch and water with her finger. When she finished stirring, she sucked her finger and then took a long swig. This was her second drink and she chided herself that she should slow down a bit on the liquor.

She was Marlisa's houseguest and seemingly only minutes away from being her partner. She didn't want Marlisa to think she wasn't focused. Some people didn't believe that a pastor could drink and still be an effective vessel of God. Paula wasn't one of them, but she didn't want Marlisa to feel uncomfortable. No need to alarm her or have her lose faith that everything she was just told was the truth. Marlisa turned to Paula and shook the paper that she held in her hand.

"How do I know this letter is real, or even true for that matter?"

"You don't. But believe me it is. It's both real and true. It's dated two months before Mama died. The day after she came back from her last check up with the doctor. She knew she was dying, Marlisa."

Paula put her drink down on the table in front of her and leaned back comfortably on the cushions of the sofa. Then she continued in her most sympathetic voice.

"She had a lot of time to think about dying. She wanted to come clean before God and everyone. If she didn't know her heart could give out at any moment, then maybe she would have thought about things differently. I think she believed it was the right thing to do."

"It just seems wrong. What you're doing to us is wrong," Marlisa said sitting down opposite of Paula.

"What *I'm* doing to *you* is wrong! What about me!" Paula snapped suddenly, lounging forward with eyes glaring. Just as quickly, she regained her composer and settled back on the sofa. "I'm sorry for getting upset, but I put a lot of thought into this and it's been a strain on me deciding what to do. This is the only way to honor the will and keep both of my sisters from getting hurt. Otherwise, one of you will lose everything that you worked so hard to build and I don't want to stand by and let that happen."

"Well, I don't know...I have to think about it and get my lawyer involved before signing these papers to share our business." Marlisa fingered the stack of papers Paula had set on the coffee table in front of her. "One thing Callie did teach her gullible younger sister was never to sign paperwork without reading everything first and having a lawyer do the once over. Lord only knows where the company would be if she hadn't drilled that into my head."

"That's a good policy," Paula agreed. "Have a lawyer look over everything, but maybe I should warn you...oh never mind."

"'Never mind', what?"

"Oh God, I prayed on this, but I'm still not sure if I should tell you."

"Tell me what?"

"I think ethically it's wrong...but....well...," Paula sighed deeply and looked at Marlisa who was practically on the edge of her seat. "Callie is Philip Elliot's real daughter."

Marlisa gasped and leaned back in her chair. Her mouth was open and she was staring wide eyed at Paula.

"That means....," she trailed off.

"That means you should just sign the papers and forgo the DNA test."

Paula slid the papers in front of Marlisa.

"If Callie knows that you will not make this a big legal battle and just agree to share the company, she may do the same thing. Remember, she doesn't know she's the biological daughter and may not want to gamble her company away."

"But how do you -"

"How do I know? There was another paragraph to that letter." Paula pointed to the letter still clutched in Marlisa's hand. "I covered it before making copies."

"Oh my God," Marlisa said studying her copy. She looked closely and thought she could see where it had been doctored to cover another paragraph. Paula took a pen from her purse and laid it next to the written agreement.

"Just sign the papers and no one will ever have to know," she said before picking up her drink and walking out of the room, down the hall and into the guest bedroom. Closing the door to the room, Paula rested her face against it and closed her eyes.

"God forgive me, but I'm in too deep to turn back now."

CHAPTER 12

Michael hugged Callie once more before stepping out the front door. It had been a great evening. No, better than great, it had been a dream! Michael walked to his car, unsure if his feet ever hit the ground. As he drove away from the house, he pushed play to start the first CD on the player. The soft twinkling on the piano echoed in the speakers before Callie's voice began to sing as if only for Michael. He grinned thinking about Callie and how they had connected tonight.

They had talked, really talked and enjoyed each other's company. He felt closer to her than he had in months. Marlisa and his infidelity had not been interjected throughout the conversation as a wedge keeping them at arms length. For once they talked about it honestly and listened to each other - something they had never done before because emotions were always too raw. He could never make up for what he did, but he tried to explain as best he could where his head was at the time.

Their relationship had been perfect for so many years that he assumed everything would always stay the same. But Callie changed when she went into business for herself and Michael wasn't sure how to deal with it. It boiled down to insecurities - his. He knew she loved him, but she didn't seem to *need* him any more. She never asked what his thoughts were on important subjects or even seemed to care, not like she had in the past and not since she had her own business to run.

Ironically, it was Michael who had encouraged her to chase after her dreams and find her own rainbow. But when she found it in the success of the production company, it had given her a new confidence

Michael had never seen before. Even without a college education she was able to slay the dragon of fear, which was a very worthy opponent and consistently lay in wait for her. She was afraid that she couldn't measure up in the business world. She had always been smarter than most people Michael knew, but his graduate degree had opened doors for him. It had put him on a higher level. A level that Callie never dreamed she could reach on her own to stand next to him. So she supported Michael and loved him and had his babies.

Michael had to admit that he liked her being his cheerleader, his adoring fan and even his shrink. He talked over everything with her, good or bad, and she always made him believe everything would be all right. She believed in him and he needed her to believe in him.

However, once she achieved CEO status of a company whose bottom line rivaled that of his own company, she didn't seem to have time to talk as often or as long about what was on *his* mind. She now made decisions around the house without consulting him. Even though she had made the same type of decisions without consulting him in the past, he still took offense. She never asked his opinion on issues dealing with *her* company, she didn't have time to discuss his opinions as it related to *his* company and it seemed as if his opinion didn't matter even within his own household.

Somehow, his "better half" at home, was his equal half in the business world and Michael had felt angry and neglected, and even a bit jealous. For the first time everything in her world didn't completely overlap into his world and, although it was hard to admit, he didn't like it.

Then along came Marlisa, feeling more like an employee than a partner in her own business. Callie had shut her out because of a few costly mistakes she had made. She complained to Michael about how his wife treated her as if her opinions didn't count and he immediately understood. His own chauvinistic insecurities led him into Marlisa's bed. He felt even more guilt because he knew Marlisa was in love with him. She had professed her love the very same night he had

118

proposed to Callie.

For Michael it was just a coincidence that Alise was his favorite waitress in the restaurant he frequented while in college. He always left her a big tip, even when he would only order a cup of coffee. She kept him laughing and he always had a kind word for her. Alise thought he was too great of a guy to be single and she couldn't stand any of the women that surrounded him. So, she decided to play matchmaker. She finally told him she thought he should meet her younger sister who was coming home after traveling in a musical for the last year and a half.

Michael didn't think much of it until he met Callie in the restaurant while she was visiting Alise. He fell in love instantly. She was performing in a band locally and Michael made an effort to see every performance. He often sat with Marlisa at Callie's shows. The two sisters seemed so close and the three of them got along so well, it felt natural when they began to hang out together as friends on a regular basis.

But while he was very fond of Marlisa, it was Callie that held his heart. Even though they had not officially dated, they talked on the phone a lot and he met her after rehearsals and every performance. Every free moment he had he would seek her out, and when he wasn't with her, he was thinking about being with her. That's when he knew for sure he was head over heels.

He wanted to let her know how he felt. His heart was on the line, but he had decided to propose. It was two days before Christmas and Callie had called him as he was on his way to the club to see her. She wanted to be sure he would be there because she had planned to perform a song she had written for him.

Michael was happy and scared at the same time. He was crazy about Callie and wasn't sure how she would react to a marriage proposal. They had started out as friends, but the spark had always been there between them. He couldn't see any other woman but her. At first he thought he had lost his mind to be proposing, but the heart wants what the heart wants. He was *really* in love.

Michael, dressed in a suit, grabbed the single red rose from his kitchen table and walked towards his door. A letter had been slipped under the door and lay on the foyer floor. It was from Marlisa. In it, she declared her love and requested that they meet at her place that night, before the show. Michael looked at his watch. He wanted to explain his feelings for Callie to Marlisa in person, but he just didn't have time. He had to see Callie. If it all went well, she was his future. He would have to talk to Marlisa later.

He grabbed the ring, a single 24K gold band. It was all he could afford without involving his parents, but he promised himself somewhere down the line he would give her the biggest diamond ever imagined. But on their 15th anniversary when he tried to replace the simple gold band, she had turned him down flat. She told him the ring she wore, a simple gold band, was priceless and could not be replaced.

Michael now drove listening to Callie's CD and smiling at the sweet memories of young love. He remembered standing in the back of the club and watching Callie sing that night. She had never looked so beautiful. She had on a sexy red dress. Red to match the rose he would soon give to her. Michael had smiled and looked down at the rose he held. In the middle of the petals lay the ring.

When she announced the special song written for a special friend and began singing it, he watched her mesmerized. He was drawn to her and started walking towards the stage, just as she was ending "SoulMate" They stood face to face, with just the rose and the microphone between them. The applause had died down and as he looked into her eyes, he whispered 'Marry me'. Callie reached for the rose and with trembling fingers removed the ring. She was speechless. She could only nod her head.

The audience, which had grown completely silent when they heard Michael's whispered words across Callie's microphone, erupted in

120

applause. Michael slipped the ring on Callie's finger and to the chants of 'Kiss her! Kiss her!' he then kissed Callie gently on the lips. He turned to the audience and in the mist of smiling faces he saw one that was shocked and hurt. Marlisa. She turned and ran towards the exit.

Michael shook his head as if it would shake off the guilt he still felt. He never spoke with Marlisa about the letter and he never told Callie either. All these many years, he felt as if he were lying to Callie by not revealing Marlisa's confession. Michael had told himself it was just a harmless crush, but he suspected there was more to her feelings. He felt acknowledging her feelings would give them life and hope, rather than letting them die. So, through the years he had ignored her knowing looks and insisted any love she felt was that of friendship only.

He had managed to keep her at arms length until things changed between him and Callie. The day he took her to bed, she confessed her love to him again. After all this time, she was still in love with him. Michael wasn't sure what to do with that information, but he was sure Callie would never understand why he kept it from her.

Signaling, he turned onto his street and then into his driveway. Callie was still singing and Michael turned off the car's motor, but kept the CD player on. He picked up the CD cover and looked at the face on it. She was beautiful and she meant everything to him. After tonight he felt hopeful that she would be willing to give him another chance. He closed his eyes listening to her soothing voice and pretended she was singing only to him. The ringing of his cell phone interrupted his reverie. He quickly answered it, hoping it was Callie needing him again, but it was Marlisa.

"Michael! Oh thank God!" She was sobbing loudly.

"Marlisa, what'is going on?"

"Something happened today. Something that is just unbelievable!" she said choking back tears.

"Is this about the DNA test?"

"You know?"

121

"Callie told me. I was just with her."

"You were with Callie?" Marlisa asked, curiosity overpowering her hysteria.

"She told me everything."

"Not everything," Marlisa said, tearful again, remembering her conversation with Paula.

"Well, what did she miss?"

"I don't want to go through it over the phone. Can you please come over? "Marlisa was sobbing loudly again.

"Look, it's late…"

"Please Michael! I have to tell somebody the *whole* story, but I have so much to lose! I don't know if I can do this alone!"

Michael hesitated before answering. Marlisa was on the verge of total panic. She sounded scared and hurt and he did feel sorry for her, but Callie was his priority. Going over to Marlisa's house late at night is not something that Callie would understand. For the sake of his relationship with Callie, he would have to keep Marlisa at arms length, something he had always done until that one time. He wouldn't make that mistake again. She would just have to get another shoulder to cry on.

"I'm sorry, Marlisa. You might want to call one of your friends to help you through this."

"One of my friends? Are you saying you're not one of my friends?" She asked, voice trembling.

"I'm saying I'm your brother in law."

"But not for long…..right?" she asked in a quiet voice.

"Good night, Marlisa."

"Are you and Callie getting back together?" She began to cry again.

"Good night, Marlisa"

Michael hung up the phone. He looked at Callie's face on the CD cover again.

Arms length, he thought to himself. *Arms length*.

122

CHAPTER 13

Paula stood in the hallway outside of Marlisa's bedroom listening to her side of the conversation with Michael. She had heard enough to realize she had to make a move tonight. If Marlisa had told Michael of their conversation it would have upset the whole plan. She had counted on Marlisa's shame and her self-preservation to keep her quite. She never thought that Marlisa's guilt for keeping what she believed was not hers would urge her to confess that Callie was the deserving daughter. It was vital that Marlisa didn't walk away and hand Callie everything. After all, where would that leave her?

Paula started dialing on her cell phone and then thought better of it. She would make her visit in person. She grabbed the keys to her rented sedan and practically ran down the hall to the elevator. Impatiently, she tapped her foot waiting for the elevator doors to open and she began to imagine how the scene should play out.

Callie would be more difficult to handle. She was honest and straightforward and always plagued by doing the right thing. Paula knew her only advantage was the fact that she was on bad terms with Marlisa. The wedge between them would probably never be removed – not that Paula blamed her. Marlisa had always been disgustingly needy, but going after her sister's husband was the lowest of the low. Paula chuckled. She knew something about low as she herself had been with other women's husbands. They were many, but never related.

Maybe this "will" situation is good for Marlisa. She won't have Callie or Alise to lean on as usual. Lean on? Actually, sucking the emotional life out of them is a better description of her capabilities. Marlisa will have to finally grow up and stand on her own. That or go nuts. Either way, Paula didn't really care. Marlisa had already worked herself into a frenzy before her call to Michael, but whatever he said during the call really set her off. Paula could still hear her crying when she walked past her bedroom on the way out. And not just crying but whaling loudly like a sea otter. Pathetic. Paula tightened her grip on her briefcase that held the documents signed by Marlisa. Pathetic and simple.

The elevator doors opened and a handsome, middle-aged gentleman stepped backwards to give her ample space to enter.

Not bad, Paula thought as she quickly surveyed the man while smiling warmly. Paula glanced down at the wedding band on his finger.

Good, just the right type.

She smiled at him sweetly and as the doors closed, she was sharpening her mental claws, thinking of which opening line to use. He would be the perfect distraction while staying with Marlisa. She hoped he would be a challenge. The ones she worked hardest to get were always the best in bed. Maybe it was the guilt mixed with the excitement of the forbidden fruit that made them more passionate.

Yes, he'll do nicely.

Paula walked off the elevator and swished her hips with just the right amount of sex appeal. She knew he was watching her walk towards her car in the parking garage. Although she wanted to run to the car and speed over to Callie's, she didn't want to blow the ground work she had already laid with her soon to be conquest, Winston Taylor. Their brief chat in the elevator told her exactly what she needed to know first – he was very interested. She also found out he

124

was married and a lawyer which was a double bonanza. In light of the current legal matters she had set in motion, information from him could definitely come in handy. So let him watch and enjoy.

Once Paula reached her car she turned towards Winston and waved. As she suspected he had stood and watched her walk the entire way to her car. Paula smiled feeling powerful. It was about time she used men instead of getting used by men.

Once inside the car, Paula focused more on the difficult mission at hand – Callie. She would have to be careful, but when the dust settled, Paula was sure she would have all that she set out to get – maybe more.

The knock on the door startled Callie. She was still sitting in the den looking out the darkened window at the distant lights twinkling beyond the trees. It was a beautiful night and Callie had sat there thinking mostly about Michael. She secretly wished he had stayed longer, maybe even overnight. She knew it was too soon, but she wondered what she would have said if he had asked. She missed him so much. And one thing she knew for sure was that she would always love him. After tonight, it didn't seem so impossible that they could get back together. If she could just compromise a little more, she could begin to concentrate on their future together.

Callie was beginning to believe they could be happy again. She smiled as she walked to answer the door. Maybe he felt how right everything was again tonight, too. Maybe he came back and was waiting right outside the door. Callie's smile disappeared when she saw Paula's face as she stood on her doorstep.

"Can I come in, Callie? It's really important."

"I thought you already gave all of your important news."

"Well, there's one more piece of information that I wasn't going to share, but my spirit won't let me rest."

"What is it?"

"Callie, can I come in? I drove all the way here because I needed to see you face to face. I could have done it over the phone, but I thought I owed you more than that."

Callie saw the look of concern on Paula's face. Stepping backwards, she allowed Paula to step inside before closing the door.

"Is there someplace we could talk?"

Callie rolled her eyes and walked towards the den. No, not the den. It was too private, too personal. She doubled back and led the way into the formal living room. Callie waved her hand towards the sofa inviting Paula to sit, then she plopped herself down in the chair across from her.

"What on earth do you want to talk about now?"

Paula opened her briefcase on the coffee table and took out the letter.

"I have one of those, remember?"

"Well, there's something that you need to see." Paula pointed to the blank space and explained how she had covered up part of the letter. Callie looked at it closely and could see what she had so easily overlooked earlier. But so what? The part that she could read was clear enough. Puzzled, she looked at Paula and shrugged her shoulder.

"So?"

"So, do you want to know what I covered?"

"Not really."

"Well, I'll tell you anyway, Callie, because it's the moral thing to do. I thought I was protecting everybody and being fair to everybody. I thought no one would get hurt."

Paula paused for dramatic effect but Callie wasn't biting. She was just looking at Paula with a look Paula couldn't quite read, but she saw there was no curiosity, no concern and no interest. She imagined that if she had just announced what she had eaten for dinner she would have gotten the same reaction. Paula had to keep the conversation going, but with Callie she had to be careful of what she said and how she said it

126

"Well, I know you loved Daddy a lot and that's why I'm here. He loved you, maybe, most of all. You two had a bond with your music that none of us could even compete with. He would have been so proud of you and what you've done with your talent. Your CD is a hit and I'm sure this new venture with Alise will be just as successful! I know that his love for you-"

"POINT, Paula! Get to the point!" Callie was now clearly agitated.

Good, Paula thought.

"The point is something I didn't want everyone to know. If you just sign the papers and we all share the company, no one will have to ever know. Daddy loved you so much! I don't think he wanted you to be hurt, so I covered it up! I thought God wanted me to hide it, but now I know I have to tell you the whole truth!"

"What truth!" Callie shouted.

Paula used the dramatic pause again, but this time she was satisfied. She saw it all now on Callie's face - the pain, the curiosity, the anger and the fear.

"Marlisa is Philip Elliot's biological daughter."

Callie looked at Paula, eyes filling with pain.

"I covered the paragraph of the letter which told who it was," Paula added. "I thought if we all shared everything as one family, then this," Paula pointed to the letter lying on the coffee table next to her briefcase, "wouldn't matter."

"Well, just because Marlisa is his daughter doesn't mean that I'm not," Callie said indignantly. "This could be wrong," she said, now pointing at the letter herself.

"Well, then keep your appointment for the DNA test. You can find out once and for all. But then so will Marlisa. It will be a part of the will and the settlement. Marlisa would get it all."

"Well, then so be it. I have to do the honest thing. That's *my* moral thing to do."

"Oh, Callie," Paula sighed before taking the documents Marlisa signed from her briefcase and laying them on table. "Marlisa already signed the paperwork I drew up. She wants to share and just get on with her life as is. She knows she can't handle the business alone. She would have probably lost it a long time ago if it wasn't for you, and she knows that. What she doesn't know is that she is the biological daughter and rightful owner of the company. She doesn't know, but she doesn't care."

"But I do. That's the difference between Marlisa and me. She never takes anything too seriously."

"And you take everything too seriously."

"Too seriously?" Callie asked in amazement. "You think finding my true parentage and accepting an inheritance that may not be mine shouldn't be taken seriously?" Callie jumped up and stood over Paula with her hands on her hips.

"You know what, Paula? I think it's time for you to go."

"Ok, ok." Paula grabbed the letter and the signed documents and put them back in the briefcase. She then pulled out the papers with Callie's name on them and placed them on the table.

"I'll just leave these here for you to look at and -"

"No, don't leave anything. I want you to take everything you came in here with!"

"Fine," Paula said calmly as she closed her briefcase but kept the unsigned documents in her hand. Holding them out towards Callie, she added, "But remember, if you sign these then you shouldn't take the test."

Callie responded by crossing her arms in front of her body and glaring at Paula.

"Callie, you might not believe this, but I really care about all of my sisters," Paula said gently.

"Oh, thank you so much for your concern," Callie said with the same feigned sincerity.

Walking towards the door Paula looked over her shoulder and said, "Call me before making a final decision. Oh, I don't know if I told you that I'm staying with Marlisa."

Then as if an afterthought she added, "I'm not comfortable being there alone yet. I hope she's back from meeting Michael."

"Meeting Michael?"

"Yeah," Paula turned to face Callie, her face displaying a practiced innocence. " She called him right before I left. I guess she was really upset about what happened today – who could blame her? She needed someone to talk to and apparently she's using Michael's shoulder to cry on." Paula looked at Callie with the right amount of concern in her eyes. "That's ok, isn't it? I mean you and Michael aren't together, right?"

"Right," Callie said, barely able to contain her emotions.

She couldn't believe he would go to Marlisa to comfort her. Not tonight. Not after leaving her own doorstep. Not after they finally connected again.

"But I know she signed everything because she wanted to and not because he told her to. She wanted to do the right thing for the whole family."

Paula continued walking towards the front door again. This time she waited until she had her hand on the doorknob before delivering the final blow.

"I guess she's lucky to have someone to give her business advice like he's been doing."

"What are you talking about?' Callie asked.

This time when Paula turned she began to walk back towards Callie, just as she had in the scenario that had played out in her head earlier. "He helped her during the time you had your little break down."

"I didn't have a break down," Callie snapped.

"Well, whatever you want to call it, Callie, and ....um... I'm sorry for being insensitive," Paula said softly. "But the fact is, Marlisa had to make a lot of decisions because you ....well you...weren't making them. She told me she leaned heavily on Michael and that he was

129

really there for her."

There for her! There for *her*! Callie felt the rage and pain bubbling to the surface. It was making her dizzy. She sat back down in the chair and closed her eyes.

"Are you alright, Callie? Can I get you some water or something?"

"No, I'm fine. I just want you to go."

"I'm sorry, Callie, really. I thought it would make you feel better to know that the company won't go under even with Marlisa at the helm because she's smart enough to lean on Michael. He'll be able to help her." Paula back away from Callie. "You look like you need some rest. I'm going to go now."

"Yes, please."

Callie opened her eyes and stared at a picture of her three girls that sat on the end table next to her chair. She had to put her girls first. Their welfare was the only thing that mattered at this point. She was sure of what she felt when it came to her girls. However, she couldn't trust her own instincts when it came to her relationship with Michael. Tonight had felt right! But apparently, it wasn't quite right or else he would have never gone to Marlisa. She had to look out for the best interest of her children with or without Michael! And the truth was she couldn't afford to lose her main source of stable income. Paula was at the door with her hand on the knob again when she heard Callie's voice.

"Leave the papers on the table in the foyer."

Paula smiled. Then she happily laid the documents down as instructed. They still weren't signed, but Paula was confident they would be within the next two days. There was no way Paula would let Callie keep her appointment for the DNA test. She could not let either sister be tested to find out what she already knew. They were both the biological daughters of Philip Elliot.

Paula reminded herself that she told both sisters the truth when announcing that the *other* sister was the biological daughter. The letter written by their mother was a very convincing touch, albeit deceptive. Paula had found it in their father's old chest that she had taken when he died hoping to find some things of value. The letter proved to be very valuable, indeed.

Paula grinned as she walked to her car sitting in Callie's driveway, and then quickly chided herself for getting cocky. Documents still needed to be signed and she only had two days, the weekend, to work on Callie. Come Monday, the day of the appointment, it would be too late. At least she knew which pressure points Callie responded to now. She had to get her signature and file papers before anyone realized they had been manipulated. Paula realized she could use some lawyerly advice. She drove off smiling because she knew just where to get it.

CHAPTER 14

Alise studied her copy of the letter. She was wrapped in a blanket and lounging cozily on the window seat in her family room. She had a glass of wine in one had and took a sip before reading the letter yet again.

She couldn't understand her mother's motives, or anyone else's motives for that matter, when it came to being unfaithful. She knew her mother had been lonely and depressed much of the time during the marriage, but hell, who wasn't? Her marriage to Terrance had not been, by any stretch of the imagination, a wonderful experience, but she had never, ever cheated on him. Not even when he had cheated on her, which he had more times than she could count.

Alise had thought she was doing something noble by staying with him. She had three young boys who needed their father, so she did what she had to do in order to keep the family together. A lot of good her sacrifices did because he managed to hurt her boys worst of all.

He was sadistic at times, offering them his love and his attention only to pull it away again and again. They couldn't depend on him even when he lived in the same house. She couldn't depend on him, either. And even though he deserved it, she couldn't bring herself to break her marriage vows. They were sacred to her and she was devastated each time Terrace broke his, until the last time. Something in *her* broke and she finally saw that Terrance was stealing her youth, stealing her compassion, stealing her love and stealing her peace of mind. But the real revelation came when she realized that *he* wasn't stealing *anything*. She was *giving* it all away. And she was making her boys give away parts of themselves, as well. There was nothing noble in giving Terrance a family that he didn't deserve and often didn't even want.

Alise had told herself that she kept taking him back because of the children, but deep down she also did it for her own reasons. She didn't want to chance starting over with someone new who could end up being worse than Terrance. She also didn't want to give Terrance the boot just to see him learn his lesson and be a great husband to some other woman. She didn't think she could handle it if, after wasting her time and effort pruning, watering, sunning and fertilizing that raggedy, black piece of driftwood, he would then go and blossom in another woman's backyard. That was just beyond comprehension. But Alise finally got to the point where it was beyond comprehension to make excuses to *stay* with him and soon she was able to walk away without a backwards glance. When, how, if, and with whom he may or may not blossom for, was no longer a concern of hers.

The hard cold fact was that she had to choose between Terrance and the possibility of living the rest of her life alone. Terrance seemed like a better choice for a long time. However, the day she filed for divorce was the most liberating day of her life. Although, she had to admit, when the final papers came, she felt a little melancholy, but there were no regrets.

That's why she wondered what had happened in her parent's marriage. If they had such problems, why did they stay together? Was her mother's depression her reason for doing what she did to her husband and family?

Alise knew she would never understand her mother's motives. She could only understand the subject of infidelity from the one side. She certainly understood Callie's pain and she found it difficult to forgive Michael and nearly impossible to forgive Marlisa, the other woman. But at least Michael loved Callie. He *really loved her* and that was something that had been missing from her marriage to Terrance.

133

Maybe it was it missing from her parent's marriage, too.

Alise read the letter again and sighed deeply. She looked out of the window and saw a moth fluttering up against the pane, attracted by the soft light from her reading lamp. Alise watched it flutter tirelessly and realized that that was the feeling she had been having all day. There was something fluttering around in her mind that she couldn't quite grab on to. Paula had said a lot that was hard to absorb.

Alise turned off the lamp and slowly folded the letter before putting it back in her purse. She looked back at the window to see if the moth had flown away but it was still there, stubborn little thing. Just like the moth in her mind – scratching persistently against the window, but still not quite able to get through.

CHAPTER 15

Callie woke up on the couch in her office and looked at the clock. It was 7:30 in the morning. She had dozed off and surprisingly, she had managed to sleep for several hours. Her head throbbed and her mouth was extraordinarily dry. If she knew she was going to wake up feeling like she had a hangover, she would have at least given herself the pleasure of actually drinking. But Callie certainly knew how horrible a person could feel the morning after a night of crying. Alcohol would have only made it worse.

She felt stupid and betrayed by Michael, yet again. After Paula left, she had gone to her office to view Michael's cell phone records on the Internet. She still had the password to his account and wanted to verify Paula's story. Had Michael talked with Marlisa after he left her home last night? Or did Paula just make that up to get to her?

Although Paula's motives were still in question, there was no doubt that she was telling the truth about the phone call. Callie saw that Michael received an incoming call from Marlisa's cell phone. A three minutes call. Callie had stared at the record of the call and realized it didn't necessarily mean anything. She had called him, but they didn't talk long. However, if what Paula said was true, three minutes was ample enough time to plan a quick meeting – if that's what the call was about. Callie was ready to table the incident in anticipation of speaking directly with Michael until she began scrolling through his call log and discovered a steady pattern of calls – from and *to Marlisa*.

135

Ten minutes. Twenty minutes. Forty-five minutes! There were calls to and from Marlisa's home, her office, and her cell phone at all times of the day, evening and night. Callie realized over the past several months he had talked to Marlisa, perhaps more than he had talked to her. She knew Michael had not cut ties with Marlisa, but he had always said it was because of Ashley. Looking at the call log of his personal cell phone, Callie knew it was more to it than what he had told her. It was not just to help Ashley stay connected with an aunt she cared deeply for, hoping that connection would help her work through family issues. Michael also cared about Marlisa.

She believed Paula when she said Michael had helped Marlisa with matters dealing with their company. Maybe Marlisa needed the help or maybe she just needed Michael -but so did Callie.

Everything that was wrong with their relationship was because of Michael's action. Callie conceded that she could understand him feeling isolated after she became so busy, but he should have talked to her. Instead he went running into Marlisa's waiting arms.

She knew he wanted her forgiveness because he made a mistake. However, it was not just any mistake. It would take time and effort to heal the hurt that stood between them. Callie had let him know that Marlisa also stood between them. That's why she didn't understand why he continued his relationship with Marlisa, as evidenced by the lengthy phone calls. Why can't he just walk away from her?

Callie wanted to get mad at Michael again but she couldn't muster up the strength. The only thing she felt since discovering the phone log was hurt. Michael had been there for Marlisa, helping her with business or whatever she needed, but Callie also knew Marlisa had been there for Michael during the break up of their marriage. They had leaned on each other. They had supported each other through the crisis that the two of them had created while Callie stood alone.

Callie looked at the three-minute phone log and realized that apparently they still supported each other. So the guilty would stick together. If there was a victim in this triangle, Callie thought it should be her. Yet somehow, she felt like the villain because she couldn't forgive and forget. Even her own daughter pushed her away.

Callie thought back to when the three of them had been inseparable. It was a long time ago, but even after she and Michael had gotten married, Marlisa was still never far away. Michael cared for Marlisa, but what Callie needed to know was how deeply? Did he care so much for Marlisa that he would never be willing to sever ties to their relationship, even if it was to save the one he held with her?

Callie would never force him to choose between her and her sister for one simple reason: it should be no contest. The fact that Michael would even have to make a choice would mean that he allowed his relationship with Marlisa to be in direct competition with his relationship with his wife. As far as Callie was concerned, he had already made his choice the moment he decided to keep his friendship with Marlisa while his marriage was falling apart. After all, it had fallen apart *because* of their "friendship". They deserved each other and Callie decided she was better off without either of them.

She wiped away her fresh tears and headed to the bathroom where she washed her face and brushed her teeth.

"It's a new day," Callie said as she looked into the mirror. "Don't waste it on people who don't deserve it."

She moved close to the mirror and examined her teeth and then satisfied, leaned back in order to check the bags under her eyes. Yep, still there like two old friends.

"Well, old friends," she said dabbing a special cosmetic cream under her eyes, "we managed to lose a husband, a father for the second time, a daughter, a company and a sister - good riddance to her. The important thing is guys, we managed to do it all in just one year."

"Do you talk to your eye bags all the time, or am I witnessing a really special conversation?" It was Vanessa who walked into the bathroom and sat on the counter next to where Callie stood.

"You just wait a few years and you'll be talking to your body parts, too."

137

"I can't wait," Vanessa said dryly, but then snapped her fingers and stretched her eyes in remembrance. "Actually, I don't have to wait because I've been talking to my boobs since I've been thirteen. I've been asking what it will take to have them grow into big *mugombos* like my mother's."

"You're going to look back on those conversations with great fondness once the talk turns ugly. Just wait until you're arguing with you butt to get into a pair of jeans, wondering what it would take to have it *stop* growing like your mothers!"

"Oh please, you look good and you know it."

Vanessa and Callie looked at each other in the mirror. Callie had not only applied the eye cream, but an exfoliant also covered half of her face. An outrageous case of "bed head" completed her unfortunate appearance.

"Care to take back that last comment?" Callie asked.

"Absolutely! I apparently spoke out of turn."

They laughed and then Callie continued applying the facial treatment. Vanessa turned sober and put her hand on Callie's.

"Mom, I heard what you said about losing so much in one year. I just want you to know that things are going to get better. You're due for the good stuff now."

Callie smiled and squeezed her daughter's hand.

"Now, before we get mushy and you try to hug me and exfoliate me to death, I just came to say we're headed to Aunt Alise's house."

"All three of you? Why so early?"

"Yeah, well, we're kinda having a cousins' weekend with videos and music and stuff like that. Today there's some sort of fair or something going on by Aunt Alise. I have a friend that'll get us in free with free rides coupons if we get there before nine o'clock."

"Oh, ok," Callie said.

She was glad her children were so close with their cousins. They used to be together all the time when they were little. Now that they were all getting older and busier, it was hard to get them all in the same room sometimes. This weekend, both Vanessa and Jamal were home from college and another cousin, Shauna, was in town early for Thanksgiving. So, it seemed like the perfect opportunity for such a gathering.

"You're going to be ok by yourself here, aren't you? Did you have something planned for us?"

"Me? No. I have no plans. You guys have fun and tell Alise I said 'good luck'."

Callie splashed water on her face to wipe off the cleanser. With eyes closed, water dripping from her face and reaching for her face towel, she had a sudden thought.

"Oh wait," she exclaimed, "I want to make sure Maya packs everything she'll need."

"I'll take care of it," Vanessa said handing her mother a towel. "You need to take care of yourself and stopping scaring your daughter and other little children."

"What are you talking about?" Callie asked turning towards Vanessa as she wiped her face.

Vanessa grabbed Callie's shoulders, quickly turned her to face the mirror and then pointed at her reflection.

"Oh," was all Callie could say.

"Yikes is more like it!"

She had missed wiping quite a bit of the cleanser from her face, the smeared remnants of yesterday's mascara now gave her raccoon eyes and her hair had somehow gotten worse.

"Anyway, we'll be back tomorrow night," Vanessa informed her before slipping out the bathroom door.

Right after the kids left for Alise's house, the phone rang. It was Stephen. Even though Callie had talked to him just a few days ago, he seemed to be part of another lifetime. She had all but forgotten about the restaurant, the opening and yes, she had forgotten about Stephen, too.

"Hi," he said and Callie imagined him flashing that gorgeous smile.

"Hi, yourself."

"I've been thinking about you."

"Really?" Callie replied, knowing she could not say the same. "And just what have you been thinking?"

"About how we got started on the wrong foot. I want to make it right. I mean, I'm not a bad guy, but I understand how you could view me as a, let's see…how did you put it? Ah, yes… *a jackass*." Callie chuckled as a grinning Stephen continued, "So…. I was thinking that maybe we could do something together which doesn't involve money or companies or business of any kind. What do you say? Are you up for something fun?"

"Well, I don't know…"

"Before you say no, just hear me out. I have to go to Florida on business and…"

"I thought you said no business of any kind?"

"I did say no business -"

"But I just clearly heard you say Florida and business."

"I did just say Florida and business, but-"

"Then which is it, business or no business?"

"It's business, but it's *my* business."

"Then what are you telling me for?"

Stephen sighed loudly "You're doing this on purpose, aren't you?"

Callie was grinning "Yeah, I am."

"May I ask why?"

"Because it's funny!" Callie was laughing now.

"It's not funny," Stephen said, but he was laughing too.

"It's a little funny."

"No, it's not."

"Yes, it is"

"No, it's …Ok, you're doing it again, aren't you?"

They both laughed.

"Ok, here's the plan," Stephen said still smiling. "Why don't you

140

come with me for a little R & R? I have a house in Florida that I like to show off. It's a beautiful rambler on a bunch of acres with horses and everything. It'll be a peaceful getaway. It's beautiful there. I love it because it's a place to go to step away from your life. It's sort of like being someone else for a little while, no worries, no cares. Sometimes we need that, if you know what I mean."

"Yeah," Callie said seriously "I know what you mean."

"Is that a yes?"

Callie thought about the mess she called her life. She could use a recess from it. If she said no she would be alone all weekend to do nothing but think and analyze and talk to herself about all the "what ifs". She'd already had many similar weekends over the past year and wasn't eager to experience another one. A little getaway sounded perfect.

"No business talk, right?"

"Right."

"I just get to free my mind?"

"Promise."

"Ok, let's go."

CHAPTER 16

The plane touched down on a private airstrip near Orlando. Stephen leaned forward to look out of the window of his private jet, and then he turned to Callie, who had dozed off while reading a magazine. He had never seen her looking so peaceful. She was always so guarded and tense. Her eyes were usually wary, even afraid as her mind quickly absorbed everything she was observing and analyzing. She worked hard at hiding her vulnerability by being tougher than she needed to be. But Stephen could see past all of that because he saw her pain. He looked beyond the hurt and he liked what he saw. She was tough and smart and funny and at the same time delicate. Stephen reached up to gently move a lock of hair from her face. Callie stirred and Stephen's hand instantly retreated. It was time to go. The car was waiting.

"Wake up, Callie," Stephen said, gently nudging her arm.

Callie cracked her eyes open and looked at Stephen. She was beautiful. Stephen realized that he had forgotten to include beauty in her list of assets.

"All right, sleeping beauty," he said unbuckling his seat belt and gathering his briefcase and other personal items that lay on the table in front of his seat. "If you don't wake up and come with me to the car now, you'll be bedding down on the plane tonight."

Callie closed her eyes tightly and pretending to sleep, made snoring sounds.

"All right, have it your way," Stephen said walking towards the

142

front of the plane.

"You'd really leave me here?" Callie asked, sitting up in her seat. Stephen stopped at the front entrance to the plane and looked at Callie.

"Yes, I would. But then I would feel guilty and I would eventually come back for you."

"Gee wiz, you're such a swell fella," Callie said imitating his southern drawl.

"That's the same thing my mama used to say. Now, come on woman. I don't have all day."

"Jackass," Callie said, suppressing a smile.

Stephen tipped an imaginary hat and said in a deep southern drawl, "I do believe we have established that, ma'am."

Then he winked at her before stepping through the door of the plane.

He was right about his house, it was beautiful. Callie was surprised to learn Stephen designed it and had had a hand in decorating it as well. She never imagined he had such artistic vision. But as she stood in the foyer looking around, there was no denying his good taste and she was pleased with what she saw.

Callie showered and changed into a short-sleeved white tee shirt and jeans. She exchanged her boots, perfect for the late November day they had left up north, for sandals. Walking out of the dinning room's large French doors and onto a spacious patio, Callie felt the warm sun on her face. She stopped and lifted her face towards the sky. Smiling, she spread her arms out wide and wiggled her exposed toes. Florida in the winter was something she could definitely get used to.

"Great, huh?"

Startled, she turned around to see Stephan dressed like her, in a white tee shirt and jeans. Her eyes quickly registered how wide and tone his chest was and how his muscles pulled the sleeves on his shirt taunt. He was gorgeous. Callie turned away embarrassed as if he could

143

read her thoughts.

"Yep, it great all right," she said.

"Wanna tour of the place?"

"Sure, but I thought you had a meeting?"

"I do, this evening. It'll be over dinner. I have to shake a few hands and pat a few backs. You'll be ok having dinner alone?"

"Of course, I do it all the time. It's pathetic, but even leaving the state couldn't get me a dinner date. Oh, I mean, not that you're a date or anything."

"I know what you mean. I have the same problem."

"*You?*"

"Yeah, guys get lonely, too."

"Wait a minute. You are a rich, eligible, good-looking bachelor. There's no way I'm going to believe that you have a hard time finding a woman."

Stephan stared at Callie and then slowly smiled.

"You said I was good looking. You think I'm good looking! I knew you wanted me!"

Callie laughed, embarrassed by his teasing. "What are you talking about – 'I want you?'"

"Don't deny it now. Let's explore this a little more."

"Stephen."

"Yes, Callie?" Stephen replied raising his eyebrows.

"Show me around and then feed me."

"Ooh, I like bossy women. But I'm way ahead of you. Carmen is fixing us lunch right now. I thought we could do a quick tour of the house, and then lunch and then we can do a tour of the grounds- on horseback."

"On horseback? I've never even been on a horse before."

"I figured that city girl, but I'll help you."

Callie frowned and Stephan could see the anxiety on her face.

"It'll be ok, I promise," he said gently and then held his hand out to her. Callie slipped her hand into his and made a weak attempt to smile. Stephan squeezed her hand reassuringly.

"Come on," he said "let's go see the house."

Callie was impressed with the entire house. It was a combination of elegance, warmth and comfort. The color schemes changed to give every room a separate feel, yet the design of each room flowed effortlessly into the other. The hard wood floors in every room of the house, including the kitchen were beautifully crafted. The rooms were all spacious and sunny and had spectacular views.

Callie thought there was one room in the house that stood apart from the rest and it was immediately her favorite. It was not as large as the other rooms, nor was it as open and bright, but it felt the most lived in. All four walls were rich wood paneling. However, three out of the four walls actually served as shelves and were covered floor to ceiling with books. A large fireplace overpowered the final wall. Two giant leather easy chairs were sitting in front of the hearth on a soft rug. A small table sat between the chairs making the perfect conversation area. In the middle of the room sat a beautiful, large mahogany desk with exquisite detailed carvings. Callie could tell even from a distance that it was extremely expensive, and if the look on Stephen's face as he admired it was any indication, it was well worth every penny.

"This is my favorite room," he said walking towards his desk. "It's like...my refuge. I don't know if that makes sense to you or not, but that's the only way I know to explain it."

Callie smiled "Believe me, I get it. But what I don't get is this." Callie pointed to the fireplace. "Who uses a fireplace in the sunshine state?"

"Ahh, spoken like a true Yankee. It gets a little cold sometimes in the south - even in Florida."

"Hmmm. Learn something new everyday."

"Glad to teach ya."

"I'm sure you are," Callie said dryly.

"Hey, don't get rude with me. Not when I'm about to feed you."

145

Callie perked up.

"Thank goodness. I'm starving."

"Well, let's go. We're gonna eat by the pool."

Callie sat back in her chair with a sigh.

"That was delicious!"

"Yeah, Carmen's great in the kitchen. She makes it look easy too," Stephen said.

Callie looked at the water shimmering in the pool and feeling the warmth of the sun, she reminded herself again that it was November.

"Like I said before, I could get used to this."

Stephen leaned forward in his chair and rubbed his hands together.

"You ready for the next part?" he asked.

"Ready as I'll ever be," Callie said nervously.

They rode in a golf cart from the pool area to the stables and where Oscar, the stable hand, met them. He had already saddled and prepared two horses for riding. He stood between the horses holding a rein in each hand.

"Hello, Mizter Russell!" he said cheerfully with his Hispanic accent. "I have Butter, your favorite, all ready for you!"

Callie looked at Stephen. "Butter? Please tell me you didn't name that poor animal Butter?"

Stephen became rigid in his seat and looking straight ahead said, "I hope you know this fine animal was named after my very first horse that I received when I was just three years old. The horse, just a pony really, had an accident and died less than one year later. As a tribute, I've had at least one horse in my stable named after Butter all of my life. Butter is a good name."

Stephen looked serious and wounded at the same time. Callie realized that she must have really hurt his feelings until she saw how he was struggling to suppress a smile.

"You are *lying* your behind off! Again!"

Stephen turned suddenly towards Callie. "I beg your pardon?"

146

"You're sitting there trying to get sympathy *and* make me feel bad on a lie!"

"What part am I lying about?" Stephen asked, unable to maintain his serious composure. He was smiling broadly now.

"I did get my first pony when I was three!"

"Named Butter?"

"Named Stallion but-"

"Figures. Did Stallion die a year later?"

"Could have, I don't exactly know what happened to him after my Dad took him back. Because he was bred from racing stock, my Dad changed his mind about gifting him to me. He got a trainer for him and took him to the track. Tried to give me another horse, but I was pretty mad about him stealing my first one, so I refused. Ended up getting a puppy."

"Let me guess. You named *him* Butter?"

"No, Champ."

"Did you ever have *any* animal named Butter?"

"You're looking at him." Stephen pointed to the horse and after getting out of the cart, he walked with Callie to stand beside him.

"Oscar's little daughter Rosita named him." Stephen patted the stable worker's back and Oscar grinned looking from Stephen to Callie.

"My Rosita give names to all the horses," he said with pride.

"What were you saying about the name Butter, Callie?" Stephen asked putting his arm around a smiling Oscar as they both stood facing Callie.

"I....uh.... was saying it was a beautiful name," Callie answered smiling as Oscar, again, swelled with pride.

She looked up at Stephen who, towering above Oscar's head, was mouthing the word "liar". Chuckling, she grabbed Ocsar's hand and shook it.

"Hi, I'm Callie."

Oscar, who was now laughing too, said, "I'm Oscar. Nice to meet

147

you, Miz Callie."

"Oscar, can you help me get on this other horse. Uh, what's this one name?"

"Whip Cream!"

Callie grinned broadly at Oscar, but did not dare to look at Stephen for fear she would lose her composure. Stephen kept looking at Callie hoping for eye contact as he mounted his horse.

"Okay. Um….Help me get on….Whip Cream, please."

"I bet you that's not the first time you said that," Stephen yelled from behind her. Callie grinned broadly but still ignored him.

"Oscar, please."

"No problem, Miz Callie."

Oscar held onto the saddle with one hand and with the other, he grabbed Callie's hand, all the while giving instructions. Callie attempted to hoist herself onto the horse, but was unable to swing her back leg across the saddle. Finally, in desperation, Oscar let go of the horse and with both hands planted firmly on Callie's buttocks, he pushed her above the saddle, letting out a loud grunt. Callie squealed, which was all it took to make the normally calm Whip Cream a bit nervous and she began to move away from Callie. The more Oscar pushed, the more Callie squealed and the more Whip Cream moved away.

Stephen watched amused as they went around and around in a circle before getting off Butter to come to their rescue. He steadied Whip Cream and calmed her by stroking her and gently speaking to her. Oscar then gave one final push and up Callie went plopping down soundly in the saddle. Oscar was sweating and trying hard to catch his breath.

"*Aye, Dios Mio*. That was not so gude!"

Stephen handed the reigns to Callie and walked back to Butter. However, before he had a chance to mount him again he heard Oscar yelling.

"No! No, Miz Callie! You must control! Stop her! Pull the reigns!"

Stephen turned just in time to see Callie trotting by.

"How do you stop her!" she yelled.

"Pull back on the reigns."

Callie gently pulled but could not bring herself to pull hard enough. She kept seeing the scene in the *Lone Ranger* when the horse would rear back on his hind legs, front hooves swinging. She was deathly afraid the horse would react badly if she pulled harder. Besides, she was sure Whip Cream didn't like her because of the way she kept looking back at her. Callie couldn't help but see how her giant eyes were staring unappreciatively at her unwelcome passenger.

She began to scream for the horse to stop, but Whip Cream picked up the pace. Callie's cries for help were instantly translated to 'go faster' as far as Whip Cream was concerned. The horse was galloping now and Callie was completely frozen with fear. The force of the wind in her face made her feel as if she couldn't breathe and she felt the panic rising in her throat. Callie closed her eyes and leaned forward willing herself to calm down when suddenly the horse slowed down. Callie was grabbed around the waist and swung onto another horse. She opened her eyes and saw that she was sitting on Butter facing Stephen. She closed her eyes and hugged him tightly.

"And that, my dear, concludes the tour."

"Thank you," Callie whispered.

She continued to hug Stephen while trying to catch her breath and waiting for her heartbeat to return to normal. Stephen gently stroked her back having the same effect on her as he did on Whip Cream earlier. After what seemed like an eternity, Callie regained her poise and released the vice grip she help on Stephen.

"Let's head back now," Stephen said when he was sure she was all right.

"No, I'm too embarrassed."

Callie peeked around Stephen and saw not only Oscar leading Whip Cream back towards the stable, but a host of other stable hands, Carmen and several children, one of whom must have been Rosita.

"Can we just go somewhere so that I can find my pride?"

Stephen smiled. "Sure. You'll have to turn around. Here, I'll help you."

Stephen stopped Butter and held her waist firmly as she maneuvered her position on the saddle. After Callie was situated, Stephen put his arms around her in order to grab the reigns. She immediately stiffened.

"Relax, I don't bite."

"Word of advice - if it has teeth, it bites."

Stephen smiled. "You always have a comment for everything."

"Not everything," Callie said, allowing herself to relax as she leaned back against Stephen.

They rode in silence until they came to a clearing where a stream was running through a rock bed. The grass was lush and green and the sun was shinning through the tops of the tall trees that surrounded them. It was so beautiful that it took Callie's breath away. Stephen stopped Butter and climbed off the horse. Then he carefully helped Callie from the horse.

"My thinking spot," he said once her feet were on the ground.

"It's beautiful. It's like something out of a fairy tale."

"Fairy tale, huh?" Stephen said and then pointing to the stream he added teasingly, "Maybe you should find a frog to kiss and see if it turns into a prince."

"Maybe I should kiss you and see if you turn back into a toad."

Stephen shrugged his shoulder.

"Ok," he said and then held out his arms, closed his eyes and puckered his lips. Callie laughed and shook her head.

"What, no kiss?"

"No, I'd rather see you suffer as a human toad."

Callie looked around and finding what looked to be a comfortable spot, plopped down in the grass.

"I see why you come here – to think. Your house and your property it's all just so ....oh, I don't know...peaceful. Perfect."

150

Stephen sat in the grass beside her.

"I agree."

"Unlike my life."

"Nobody's life is perfect."

"Yours is."

"From the outside looking in, maybe."

"What's so wrong with your life? Too much money? Too many fast cars? Beautiful women? Private jets?"

"No," Stephen sighed. "Too many birthdays and holidays spent alone. Not enough people to trust."

Callie looked at Stephen waiting for that tell-tell sign to let her know he was kidding, a wink of the eye or a curve of his lips, but none came.

"See, you have three beautiful kids that adore you."

"Two."

"Huh? Two what?"

"Two beautiful kids that adore me. One beautiful kid who's on the fence."

"Well you have two sisters that -"

"Three." Callie held up three fingers.

"Three?"

"Yeah, I have three sisters."

"Ok, you have three sisters who love you, I'm sure."

"One sister who loves me. The other two couldn't possibly love me and I couldn't care less what they feel," Callie said before falling backwards in the grass and looking up beyond the treetops towards the rays of sunlight peeking through. Stephen lay down beside her.

"Well, ok. The point is you have people in your life that care if you live or die. They care if you come home at night. They'll wonder what happened to you, not because you miss a couple of board meetings, but because they miss you in their life. You also have, whether you want to hear this or not, a man."

"I don't want to hear this."

151

"A man that loves you a whole lot. Now don't tell me I got that one wrong."

Callie closed her eyes and was silent.

"I don't think I can ever forgive him. I want to. I want things to go back to the way they were, but I don't think love is enough to get us there."

"You love him a lot, don't you?" Stephen asked.

"Yeah, but the thing is…I hate him just as much. Crazy huh?" Callie turned and propped herself up on her elbow to look at Stephen.

"Naw."Stephen grinned and looked over at Callie. "Now, don't get all eager thinking I can give you any advice about this 'cause I can't. If you need info on a corporate takeover, I can handle that with no problem. Relationship questions? I draw a blank. I got nothin'."

Callie rolled onto her back and looked at the clouds.

"What good are you then?"

"I do depart of this piece of wisdom," Stephen said in a fake British accent. "If you find true love, then it's worth fighting for."

Callie stared at the clouds a moment longer before closing her eyes and sighing deeply.

"That was the worst fake accent I've ever heard," she said eyes still closed.

"Really? I thought it was quite good."

"You would," Callie replied opening her eyes and smiling. She then grew serious in the silence that ensued.

"Stephen, I'm just so scared."

"Of what?"

"Of everything."

Callie then explained about the paternity test and how she could lose her identity and about Michael and his ongoing friendship with Marlisa. She began to tear up again talking about Michael and how she felt betrayed again so soon after reconnecting with him.

"Half of me is scared that I'll spend the rest of my life loving a man that I don't trust. Never letting my guard down because I have to be ready to protect my heart. I'm so afraid to have that kind of tainted love in my life. But the other half of me is scared that I'll *stop* loving him all together and he'll stop loving me. Then what will I have when the love is all gone? I'll just be alone and I ...I don't think I could take that."

"You still have me beat."

"How's that?"

"Because you've experienced true love."

"Are you saying it's better to have loved and lost etcetera, etcetera?"

"Yeah, I guess I am."

"You sound sincere."

"I guess I am."

"Well," Callie said closing her eyes again, "How profound."

"One of us has to be," Stephen said reaching out to grab Callie's hand. And for once, Callie let him have the last word. Together they lay in the grass in a comfortable silence, each lost in their own thoughts, until the sun began to go down. Then they got back on Butter and rode back to the stables.

Callie and Stephen spent Sunday lounging around the pool laughing and joking until it was time to go. They stayed away from any topic that had the potential of becoming serious. Callie did feel better after spending the weekend in Florida with Stephen, where their motto was 'don't worry, be happy'. But now she was on her way back to the real world. Back to her life and the chaos and fear and loneliness. As the plane touched down Callie realized just how much she would miss Florida.

CHAPTER 17

Paula watched Terrence pace around the small apartment.

"So you got nothing?" he asked.

"No, not a thing," Paula answered. "I followed them all week before they even knew I was in town. But they just did regular kid stuff."

"Did you see them with Marlo? I know he's a pothead. He smokes all the time."

"Yeah, but he didn't smoke with them. I'm telling you, Terrence, this is a good thing. You should be proud. Most parents would look at this as *good* news."

Terrence pulled out a chair and sat with Paula at the dinning room table. He drummed his fingers on the table before slouching forward and resting his head between his hands. This was his last resort. He just knew he would get the evidence he needed to threaten Alise with custody. If he could show the judge the juvenile delinquent behavior he had witnessed with his own eyes on a regular basis, then he would have leverage to use against Alise.

Of course, he would never show any judge the tapes he had hoped Paula would provide him. He would only *threaten* to show them and *threaten* Alise with removing the boys from her care. He didn't really want them. No, the plan was not to actually get custody, but just to bully Alise into selling the house so that he could get his share of the equity. He didn't care if they smoked and stole until their little hearts were content. They could and *should* be locked up in juvenile detention – that might be good for them. His goal was to get Alise out of the house. After all, it was *his* house and *his* father had paid the down payment on it as a gift to *him*. But for now, Alise had full and exclusive use of the house and there was nothing he could do about it. He wasn't even allowed to come in, for Christ sake!

It was that stupid divorce lawyer's fault! He should have made the terms clearer in the divorce agreement and stipulated *when* Alise had to sell. As it stands now she has to *agree* to sell and he could grow old and senile waiting on her. She had promised to sell in three years, but then changed her mind claiming it was better for the children if they didn't move.

Of course, Terrence knew better than that. The children had nothing to do with it. Alise just wanted to make him miserable and holding his one hundred thousand dollars over his head was payback for cheating on her. He was a fool to have ever trusted her! He deserved his money and finally a little happiness. After all, he went through more than twenty years of hell in the marriage too, but all he has to show for it was this tiny apartment. Even his own children had been turned against him. It wasn't fair and he was tired of waiting!

His calls to her about selling the house were useless since she never bothered to pick up the phone or respond to his messages. It wasn't as if he would be putting his starving ex-wife and children on the street. They would have her share from the sell of the house to live on and he knew Alise would get a roof over their heads. She could take care of the kids and she could take care of herself, but there was no one to look after what he needed.

Here he was with nothing and she was about to have a successful restaurant and make money, more money than he had ever made, and she could still live in *his* house! Terrence had no idea how she even got the money for her new business venture. He figured Callie was involved somehow, but regardless, she proved that she didn't need him and she had managed on her own.

Well, he was ready to start a few things of his own too, but he couldn't as long as he was tied to her. And he didn't have a rich sister to bail him out if he needed it. He wanted his money and this was his last ditch effort to get it! He was sure that he had found a way to force Alise to do things his way.

Getting Paula to spy with the video camera was easy. She could hardly stand Alise and was angrier about being made an outsider than he was. But he couldn't believe she found *nothing!* Terrence looked up at Paula.

"Are you sure there's nothing?"

"I'm sure," Paula said, shaking her head in mock sympathy. "I got nothing. You know I would gladly hand over everything to you if it meant you taking away her boys. But I don't have anything to offer you. My cover's blown since they know I'm in town. They'll see me a mile away now."

Terrence got up and started to pace again.

"Think, Terrence, think!" he said aloud.

Paula looked at Terrence trying not to roll her eyes. Alise was right. He *was* a dumbass. Paula couldn't imagine putting up with him for all the years Alise did. He could care less about what happened to his own children just as long as he got the money from the house and made Alise miserable.

Paula put her hand in her pocket and fingered the mini videocassettes. They contained plenty of footage of her nephews doing plenty of illegal things, as well as being unsupervised late at night.

Alise had the woes of a single parent working hard for a living. She couldn't be everywhere at once and now, since her youngest was almost fourteen, she thought she could trust them to do as they were told. Paula assumed doing what they were told *did not* include what she had witnessed -the selling and using of drugs, not to mention stealing bikes, car radios, shoplifting and even an assault and robbery. Paula hid a smile from Terrence. He had given her the idea of how to protect her own interest against Alise. Why waste a perfectly good blackmail scheme on greedy Terrence? All he wanted was a house.

156

Paula wanted a future and her fair share.

On the off chance that someone would figure out the misleading letter and the DNA request, Paula knew it would be Alise. Marlisa just didn't have a clue and Callie was too wrapped up in her love drama with Michael. No, Alise was the only one she was concerned with and she had to be able to fight back. Now she had ammunition with the help of poor, misguided Terrence. If Alise threatened to expose her, she would counter with a threat to take her boys away. They could go to Terrence or jail, either way Paula really didn't care, just as long as Alise believed she would lose them. Paula watched Terrence circle the floor one more time. Enough was enough.

"Terrence, I'm sorry but I have to go. If I get anything, I'll let you know."

And with that she was out the door of his shabby little apartment. She shook in disgust and reminded herself to take a shower as soon as she stepped foot back into Marlisa's beautiful condo. Hopefully, if everything worked out, she would never have to speak to that man again for the rest of her life.

CHAPTER 18

Callie drove to Alise's house humming. Stephen had sent her home in his limo, but once the driver pulled off Callie felt very alone. She called over to Alise's house and heard a hub of activity, laughter and music. The kids were still there having a great time and Callie had the sudden urge to be surrounded by family. After quickly freshening up, she grabbed the keys to the car and was soon on her way happily anticipating seeing Alise and the kids. Callie didn't get a chance to knock because as soon as she reached the door, Alise opened it up and gave her a great, big hug.

"I could use reinforcements!" she shouted over the music and the chatter of the children.

Callie walked through the downstairs and realized there were several children in every room. At least four animated children inhabited each the living room, kitchen, family room, dinning room and basement.

"It's not just the cousins. I have a couple of kids from the neighborhood and two of Jackson's buddies over. If you can find your kids, you can take 'em. And if you don't find them, then just take a few of somebody else's. Believe me, I won't mind!"

Alise laughed and headed towards the den. Callie followed stopping to say hello to each of her own children. Maya was in the mist of an animated game of Cranium with her twelve year old cousin and two of the kids from the neighborhood. She grinned and waved at her mother before quickly turning her attention back to the game.

Callie shouted 'hello' from the top of the basement stairs to Ashley, whom she could hear playfully arguing with another cousin about a score obtained from a Playstation game. It was not until she reached the den a few steps behind Alise, did she find her eldest daughter Vanessa sitting on the floor watching a movie and eating a bowl of ice cream.

"Hey, Mom," she said, acknowledging Callie's entrance, but not taking her eyes off of the television.

"We were just watching a movie," Alise said taking her place back on the couch.

The den was by far the quietest room in the house, but not for long. Callie knew that with both her and Alise in the same room, they would soon be talking over the television. It would irritate Vanessa, who would probably leave to go to an upstairs bedroom to watch the show in peace. At least, Callie hoped she would leave on her own. She wanted to talk to Alise alone, but didn't want to alert the kids. If they knew she wanted a private audience with her sister, they would figure it was something good and juicy. Both her and Alise's children's had an unusual talent for becoming a fly on the wall when it came to getting the low down. They didn't know anything about the mess Paula brought to town with her and Callie wanted to keep it that way.

Callie sat down in the armchair next to where Vanessa sat on the floor and rubbed the top of her daughter's head. Then she pressed "Info" on the remote control to display the description of the movie they were watching.

"This is a Christmas movie and it's not even Thanksgiving yet!" Callie exclaimed.

"I know. It starts earlier and earlier every year," Alise said. "What they should do is just move Thanksgiving to December 23rd so we just have to see all our relatives one time a year."

Callie laughed along with Alise before adding, "No, what they should do is move it to December 25th so we only have to gather to *eat* with them once a year, too. I would hate to have to watch Aunt

159

Evelyn chew with her mouth open for two family dinners with only a day to separate *that* phenomenon!"

Callie and Alise laughed loudly and Vanessa sighed and eyed them both.

"Come on, y'all! Shhhh!"

Callie and Alise both covered their mouths trying to stifle the sounds of their giggling. Then Alise's eyes stretched wide as she stared at the television screen watching the young male actor seducing Susan Sarandon.

"Ohhh, now that's a man!" Alise exclaimed.

Callie quickly looked at the TV screen.

"Wow! What is he? Black? Puerto Rican?"

"Does it matter?"

All three of them watched as he kissed Susan Sarandan, who was clearly uncomfortable with his advances and nervously pushed him away.

"Oh, no she didn't! They should have gotten me to play her part!" Alise said, eyes still glued to the screen.

"If that was me," Callie said matter-of-factly, "my leg would be around his neck right now."

"Eeeow!" Vanessa said in disgust as she slapped her hands to her ears, dropping her spoon. It clanged loudly as it fell into the nearly empty ice cream bowl. "*I did not* just hear my mother say that! I think I've gone deaf now!"

"Say what? Who's deaf?" Jamal, Alise's son, had just walked into the den holding a basketball under his arm. Alise and Callie laughed and continued the conversation ignoring Vanessa and Jamal.

"If that was me," Alise said, sitting up in her seat on the sofa, "I would have his shirt off by now and *rubbing all over that chest!"*

Alise thrust her hands forward to demonstrate by caressing the air. Then, for emphasis, she stuck out her tongue and used it in an imaginary lick.

"Uuuuhhh!" Jamal yelled dropping the ball to clamp his hands

160

down over his ears. Then using his fingers, he also covered his eyes as he exclaimed, "I'm deaf *and* blind!"

Alise and Callie laughed while Vanessa and Jamal continued to voice their disgust in an effort to drown their mothers' voices out.

"Look, if that was me," Callie added "the director would be saying 'Cut! Cut! Can someone please get her off of his back? And *where in the world* did she get the blindfold and the handcuffs?' "

"That's it, I'm leaving!" Vanessa said

"Me too! This is messed up!" Jamal added.

Vanessa got up and headed towards the door while Jamal retrieved his ball.

"What's goin' on in here?" Maya asked, puzzled. She had heard all the noise and laughter and had come to investigate.

"Don't worry about it, just run! Run as fast as you can!" Vanessa said pushing Maya out the door. But Maya, not satisfied with that answer, pushed Vanessa aside to look back into the den.

Alise and Callie were still laughing and exchanging scenarios when suddenly Callie jumped out of her chair and began to shake her hips.

"I'd say 'Come here and show me what you're working with!' "

"I know what you mean!" Alise said, joining Callie in the floor to gyrate her hips.

Maya stood frozen in the doorway with eyes stretched wide and mouth open watching her mother and aunt wiggle and jump around in the floor. Vanessa grabbed Maya by the collar and pulled her away from the door.

"Come on, before even years of therapy won't be able to erase these disturbing images from your mind!"

This time Maya went without protest and Callie, seeing their retreat, walked to the door and looked out to make sure the kids had indeed gone. After securing the door, she went back to her chair and plopped down.

"Now we can talk," she said.

Alise also fell back on the sofa. "How much time we got?"

"Oh, they're gonna be disgusted for at least thirty-five, forty-five minutes."

"That little jail pose you did…that was pure genius," Alise said, still a little winded from all the jumping around she had just done.

"Now don't sell yourself short 'cause when you did that tongue lick, I was disgusted myself. *I* almost left. Even though I've done it, many, many times."

Callie and Alise both burst out laughing.

"I never knew teasing the kids could be so much fun," Alise said still chuckling "But let the record reflect, I meant everything I said about that hunk of a man. The teasing was just an extra added bonus."

"Girl, who you telling? I just put that man on my Christmas list."

"Speaking of a man for the Christmas list, how was your weekend in Florida?"

Callie smiled shyly a little embarrassed by the phrasing of the question.

"My weekend was fine. Actually, just what I needed."

"Just what you *needed*? Care to explain?"

Callie looked at Alise clearly surprised by her implications.

"What are you trying to ask?"

"I'm just saying, that's a good looking white man. Don't tell me that you never noticed?"

"I…I'm still married."

"Not for long."

"So you agree with the divorce?"

"I agree with you being happy. Maybe Michael can't make you happy anymore. I mean, doing what he did…it's…well, it'll be hard for anybody to bounce back from that. Things can never be the same. They can be better or worse or just different, but never the same. I think both of you are kidding yourselves if you think you can go on and not deal with what happened."

"I am dealing with what happened. I'm getting a divorce."

162

"No, that's not what I'm talking about. That's more of a reaction, anyway. I mean, it's like the elephant in the room. You know it's there in the way, you know it's causing problems because you argue about it all the time, but you're not doing anything to *move it*. You don't deal with it emotionally. That's what I mean.

"Sometimes people pretend that it's not even there after awhile. They pretend like they're healed, but they're not. Then they just go on like nothing ever happened."

"I could never go on like nothing happened," Callie said looking down at the carpet she was just gleefully dancing around on only moments before.

"Maybe *you* couldn't but *he* could and that's one of the biggest obstacles ya'll facing. Neither one of you have any idea what you want or need your new relationship to be. And you need to figure something out because you have kids and you still care about each other. The problem is Michael wants to pretend his behavior with Marlisa *never* happened in the marriage and you want to pretend that that was the *only* thing that happened in the marriage."

"Oh, so I'm the villain in your eyes too, Alise?"

Callie could feel the sting of tears in her eyes. She willed herself not to get all wound up over the subject. She didn't want to get into this with her sister anyway. She wanted to talk about the test and everything that had happened during their meeting with Paula.

"No, you're not the villain at all," Alise said gently, sensing Callie's fragileness. "I'm just saying that you need to commit to forgiving Michael and working to keep your marriage or commit to forgiving him but walking away. But you have to forgive him. Not for his sake but for yours, otherwise you'll just keep yourself in limbo.

"It just seems like you're dragging your feet on the divorce like you want to stay married, but yet you won't work on your marriage 'cause you always talking about divorce. If you can figure out how to let go of all that hurt and pain, you can at least see your marriage clearly. You can decide if it's worth another try. If you still love him."

163

"Alise, I love him more than you could ever know," Callie said hoping Alise could understand her confusion. "I'm tired of trying to figure things out."

"Well, I'll tell you what *I've* figured out. If you're blessed enough to find true love like what you and Michael have, then it's worth fighting for."

"I never heard that before," Callie said wryly, thinking of her conversation with Stephen just the day before. "Hey, weren't you *for* the divorce a few minutes ago?"

Alise ignored her and continued excitedly. "Listen, if you're not ready to go back to Michael, Stephen can be a wonderful diversion. It'll be new and exciting and different because he's an extremely rich playboy. *And I mean rich!* Girl, he's the kind of rich that will fly you to Paris for dinner if you say you have a taste for French food."

"I can fly myself to Paris for French food."

"Yeah, you can charter a private plane, probably one of his since he's got about *ten* of them."

"True."

"And when you get there, you'll book a beautiful hotel suite, probably in one of *his hotels* while he stays in the owner's penthouse."

"Yeah, that's true too."

"And then -"

"Ok, Alise, I get your point!"

"Good. Now where was I? Let's see, he's good looking and has a darnn good body – all turn ons. But on the other hand, everybody can see he can be a little full of himself, you know, a little *too* charming and that can be a *big* turn off.

"Hmmm, who knows how this diversion will work out? Honey, he might just send you screaming back to Michael or well….," Alise smile mischievously, "maybe just *screaming.*"

"Girl, your mind sure is in the gutter tonight! Maybe *you* need to find *yourself* a diversion."

"Who says I haven't?"

164

"If you had, I would know every detail by now."

"Yeah, well I'm just a prude at heart. Anyway, after Terrance I'm afraid that I'll have an uncontrollable urge to take the pillow and smother any man that I'm with. I'll see a flash of Terrance in my mind's eye and before I know it, I would have killed an innocent man. You know," Alise added in a matter-of-fact tone, "Terrance almost died twice by way of pillow. Woke up coughing."

Callie knew her sister was kidding and they both burst out laughing, lightening the mood again. However, once the laughter died down, Callie was sober again.

"Are you nervous?" Alise asked, watching Callie carefully.

Callie nodded her head.

"What if he's not my father? What am I gonna to do?"

"I don't know," Alise said.

Callie and Alise sat in silence while the television droned on showing a commercial for a teeth whitener. It promised a smile three times brighter in only seven days.

"You know," Alise said finally, "there's something not quite right about this whole situation."

"What part?"

"Everything Paula said from beginning to end. Something's bothering me."

"Well, I tell you what's bothering me," Callie said. "I was so upset about what she was saying that I never asked how this DNA test is even possible. I mean, you can take my blood all you want to but whose blood are you going to compare it against? Daddy's dead and we ain't digging up no grave for this."

"Being the vampire that she is, she probably carries a vial of Daddy's blood around her neck."

"No, I'm serious, "Callie said, furrowing her brow. "How can we do a paternity test without Daddy's DNA? And if she has a sample of his blood, when did she get it and why have she kept it so long after his death? It's like testing to find his biological daughter is something

165

that she was always going do. Part of some plan to find his 'deserving biological daughter'."

Alise sat up straight, thinking hard. Something Callie said was digging into a deep memory.

'Testing to find out who his deserving *biological daughter is'.*

Alise finally remember what had escaped her before and what had always bothered her about Paula's story. But before she acted on her theory, she had to find out if she was right. She would go directly to the source and confront Paula first. Even if Paula didn't admit it, Alise was certain she would be able to tell by Paula's reaction if she was right.

"Do me a favor, Callie. Take the test tomorrow but whatever you do, don't sign those papers she drew up."

"Why? What do you know?"

"I don't know anything for sure, except that you can't trust Paula. Promise me that you won't sign over your business to her until you talk to me first, okay?"

"Okay," Callie said, puzzled by Alise's response.

Alise leaned back onto the sofa and smiled. Stubborn little moth. Finally, finally it had scratched its way through the glass window.

CHAPTER 19

Marlisa sat at her desk and stared at the phone. Today was the test and she felt as if she would fall apart. She had no one to lean on except Michael. She had to get in touch with him. She had to speak with him and try to convince him to go to the appointment with her. She had already left Michael at least four messages –two on his cell and two at his office. Usually he called her back in a timely manner, but this time something was different. Was he avoiding her? If he had written her off, she didn't understand why or rather, why now.

She expected to be ostracized after Callie caught them together, but Michael insisted that it was all his fault. He felt that it was his marriage and he was responsible for what happened in his marriage. He even felt a little sorry for her and tried to shield her when the whole family on both sides turned against her. Even his mother had taken a few shots at her. Ursula didn't like Callie, but she respected who Callie was to her son and she adored her grandchildren. Now, she downright hated the sight of Marlisa.

Marlisa knew it was the guilt that kept her and Michael on friendly terms. He felt guilty that everybody had turned on her because of him and he was determined not to join the masses. It seemed as if Michael felt so bad for what happened that any punishment would be wasted if it weren't directed at him. So why turn his back on her now? Maybe something had happened to him. Should she be worried?

Marlisa's appointment for the test was scheduled for 10 am and Callie's was set for sometime in the afternoon. Paula set their times far apart to eliminate any possibility that they would run into each other. Marlisa was nervous, especially since Paula insisted on her keeping the appointment. She had thought that once she signed the papers she could just ignore the truth. Callie was the daughter that deserved everything and she was the daughter that would lose everything. Why get hard cold facts to prove how undeserving she really was? And why was Paula so eager to get her hands on the proof? Maybe she struck some type of deal with Callie to make sure the illegitimate sister was left with nothing. Marlisa knew Callie hated her that much, but did Paula?

Marlisa looked at her watch. It was 9:30. She only had a half hour to get there. She needed to get going. The only reason she came into the office was to avoid Paula at home because she certainly knew she wouldn't get any work done. She would try Michael one more time.

"Armstrong Advertising. How may I help you?"

It was Mrs. Taylor, Michael's secretary.

"Hi, Harriet, this is Marlisa again. Has Michael come in yet?"

Harriet Taylor stiffened at the sound of Marlisa's voice. She had some nerve still chasing after her sister's husband so openly. Harriet always felt a pang of guilt for not warning Callie, but one thing she learned living these fifty-five years was when to mind her own business. She didn't want to get involved with family matters, even though she had worked for Michael for so many years that she was close enough to be part of the family. She suspected Marlisa's motives a long, long time ago and she knew Callie didn't see it because she was her sister. But Harriet Taylor could tell a fast-tail hussy from a mile away and now that she had shown her stripes, the gloves were off.

"Michael has come and gone already. I don't expect him back today."

"Did you give him my messages?"

"Well, Marlisa …," Harriet licked her lips and paused just long enough to sense that Marlisa's anticipation had her on the edge of her seat.

"He decided to spend the day with his *wife*, Callie. As he has told me countless times before, no one will *ever* be as important to him as his wife. He loves her so much. It's touching really. I wouldn't be surprised if they were back together before the end of the year."

"Why do you say that?" Marlisa asked, trying to conceal the panic in her voice.

"Well, you know it's the holidays and he'll be spending them with Callie and the kids. And you know this time of year is especially romantic for them since he proposed around Christmas and all!"

"I know, I know. I was there!" Marlisa said, close to tears.

Good, Harriet thought, *she was really hurting now. Time to put the cherry on top.*

"I thought I heard talk about them renewing their vows on the anniversary of his proposal. Wouldn't that be great? It's like they're promising to start over new in the New Year! Callie is so blessed to have a man that loves her the way Michael does."

"I gotta go Harriet."

"Oh, should I tell him you called again, dear?"

"No...um...I'll find him."

Harriet hung up the phone and did a quick prayer of forgiveness. Everything she just said was not quite the gospel, but it needed to be said in order to get that Jezebel to back off.

She genuinely liked Callie and Michael, and she liked them being together. They had both bent over backwards to help her get custody of her grandson, who was living in a drug infested, dangerous environment. Both Callie and Michael always let it be known that they considered her more than just an employee. Harriet Taylor was certain that the two of them belonged together. However, the renewing of their vows was more wishful thinking on her part than anything else.

"Who was on the phone?"

It was Michael, standing in the doorway of his office. He was holding his coat over one arm and in his opposite hand he held his briefcase.

"Oh, that was no one important." Harriet waved her hand in the air dismissing the call. "Nothing for you to worry about. Are you gone for the day?"

"Yeah. You know how to reach me in case of an emergency?"

"Sure do. You'll be at Callie's all day then, right?"

"Yeah, this is going to be a tough day for her and I can't let her go through this alone. But use my cell and not the home line if something comes up."

"Oh, don't worry. I can't imagine anything or anyone being important enough to disturb you."

Harriet waved to Michael and watched him pass through the glass double doors out to the elevator. She thought about Marlisa and made a mental note to have all incoming calls from her number go directly to voice mail. Jezebel.

CHAPTER 20

Marlisa walked off the elevator and onto the second floor of the medical clinic, slowly approaching the door that displayed the suite number from her appointment card. She opened the door to enter and was met by Paula.

"Where have you been? You're late."

"I drove around for a few minutes," she said, remembering her detour past Callie's house looking for Michael's car. "What are you doing here? I can do this by myself, you know."

"I know, but I wanted to make sure everything was ready."

"What's there to be ready? You poke a needle in me and out comes blood."

"*Your blood.* But I had to make sure Dad's sample was here in order to get things started right away."

"What's the rush, Paula?"

Marlisa rolled her eyes at Paula. She was just a little too gleeful this morning. For Marlisa, it had been an awful morning so far, especially now since the avoidance of Paula at home had been for nothing. Paula had come to town and turned everything upside down, and yet she seemed fairly pleased with herself, particularly today.

"Listen, I'm tired of being the bad guy. I just want to do the right thing before God," Paula said, attempting to be solemn.

"This is not about God and you know it."

171

Just then the nurse opened the door leading to the exam rooms and called Marlisa's name. She followed the nurse through the door but turned, and scowling at Paula said, "By the way, you *are* the bad guy."

Paula would have laughed if she hadn't been so shocked. The spoiled little brat finally found her tongue. Well, who cares? Nothing could get Paula out of the clouds today. Callie's little weekend disappearing act before signing the papers had made Paula amend her original plan. It was actually *better* if they *did* take the test, as long as she controlled the results.

"Ms. Alexander," the young receptionist called to Paula, bringing her out of her deep thoughts.

"Yes?" Paula answered as she stepped over to the desk.

"The blood work you brought in earlier from Marlisa Elliot and Callie Armstrong is in the process of being run against the main sample now, but...... it says here we are doing Marlisa and Callie again?"

"Yes, there was a mix up with the earlier samples, so I thought it was best for them to come into the office in person to avoid further confusion."

"So, there will be two sets of results? I can cancel the first set of test, if you like. No need to pay for tests you can't use."

"No, no, no. Let's just leave everything as is before my head explodes," Paula said and smiled warmly. "With the state I'm in today, I'm afraid anything I do will just foul things up more. Let's just leave things the way they are and I'll sort through it later." Paula smiled at the receptionist. "But thank you so much for your thoughtfulness."

"You're welcome," the receptionist said, pleased with her customer service skills.

"Can we double check the address the results are being sent to? I want to make sure I gave you the correct information."

"Sure."

After verifying the address Paula left the office and went to the elevator thinking of how she would spend the day. She was in such a good mood that she decided she would visit Winston, her lawyer friend. They would do it right in his office. He was due for a little excitement that according to him, only Paula could give him. He had complained that his wife was so dull and boring in bed and he would love it if she could spice things up for him. As soon as she got in the car, she would call him with a preview of coming attractions. However, the ringing of her cell phone interrupted her thoughts of Winston and what she planned to do with him. Paula picked up immediately still thinking of her eager lawyer friend.

"Hello, this is Paula," she said in her sexiest voice.

"Oh, please spare me. What did you think, Playboy was calling looking for you?"

"Why do you make everything so sordid, Alise?"

"Because that's the kind of woman you are. You know it and I know it. You could never fool me, Paula. Never. *Not... about... anything.*"

Paula tensed up a bit.

"Do you have something to say Alise? Just say it and stop wasting my time."

"I will, but I want to do it face to face. Why don't you meet me at Callie and Marlisa's office?"

"Ok, I'm not far from there. I'll meet you at *our* office in about fifteen minutes."

Paula hung up before Alise could respond. Change of plans.

Sorry Winston, looks like there's going to be a different kind of excitement today.

Paula got on the elevator smiling to herself. She couldn't wait.

CHAPTER 21

Michael knocked on the door and waited patiently for Callie to answer. Even after all this time, he still felt a little strange knocking on the door of his own house. He still looked at things based on the way they used to be and the way he was sure they would be again. This house was still his home and Callie was still his wife. To his surprise, Vanessa opened the door.

"Dad!" she exclaimed and gave him a hug. "What are you doing here?" she asked smiling broadly, stepping aside to let Michael enter.

"Oh, I can ask you the same question. Is school out or something?"

"More like or somethin'. This is Thanksgiving week, so we're out early anyway. I just decided not to go back until next week."

"Next week? Don't you have mid-terms or something?"

"More like or somethin'. Now Dad, don't lecture me," she held up her hand to stop the next question on the tip of her father's tongue. "I have it all under control. Don't worry about me and school.

"I'm here to help Mom. She's in the den now. I don't know exactly what's going on, but I know it's something big. Something so big she won't tell me, so I'm here just in case she needs me. And now that I see *you* here today, I know it's something so major that it could blow the roof off. Care to tell me what's up or do I have to snoop around to find out?"

"Well ...," Michael hesitated and sighed.

"What?" Vanessa said impatiently. "I'll find out one way or the other and you know I will," she said smiling slyly at her father. "So, you might as well just tell me. What are ya'll trying to do, hone my skills as a master super sleuth or something?"

"More like 'or somethin'," Michael said grinning and then added as he walked towards the den, "Didn't know I could talk that fancy college talk like you, did you?"

Michael quietly entered the den and set his briefcase down near the sofa. Callie was sitting in the big armchair staring out of the window. She was still in her bathrobe and sat with her feet tucked beneath her, her slippers lay in front of the chair. She glanced briefly at Michael and her mouth went up into a tiny smile before she turned her gaze back to the window.

"Hi," she said still watching the clouds that seemly had formed into a large sailboat.

"You don't seem surprised to see me," Michael said, sitting on the sofa.

"I'm not. I think I willed you here."

"You did?"

"Yeah, I did," Callie said turning to look at Michael. "And here you are. I needed you and you came."

Callie began to tear up and then feeling embarrassed she rolled her eyes and shook her head.

"This is stupid. What is, is. And there's absolutely nothing I can do about it. It doesn't change who I am, right?"

"Right," Michael said gently. "You know, I love the hair."

Callie laughed and reached up to feel her hair, still uncombed from a restless, sleepless night.

"Oh, thank you. And you know the best part of this style is that the up keep is *so* easy."

They both laughed and Michael could see Callie relax a bit.

"Have you eaten?"

"Naw, I'm not hungry."

175

"Well," Michael said standing, "you know how I feel about that, so I'm going to the kitchen to get you some juice and a little something to eat."

"Michael, no, really," Callie said pleading. "I'm fine."

"Oh yeah, fine is *exactly* what you are," he said, eying Callie mischievously "But we're talking about food now."

Callie grinned and put her head down suddenly feeling shy. Michael could do that to her, make her feel like she was a teenager with a crush. She missed that – the way he could make her feel desired. She missed being taken care of. She missed him.

"I'll be back in a minute."

"Wait, wait," Callie said standing. "I'll meet you in the kitchen. I have to take a shower."

"Yeah, that would be a good idea," Michael said, wrinkling his nose.

Callie laughed "Oh, shut up."

"And while we're on the subject, brush those teeth, too! You ever heard of morning breath?"

Callie stood with one hand on her hip in front of Michael.

"You know I don't even leave the bedroom without brushing my teeth!" she said indignantly. "As a matter of fact, we couldn't even have morning scx until the breath thing was taken care of."

Squinting her eyes, Callie continued, "And I do believe, Mr. Armstrong, that was because *I* could not take *your* breath, not the other way around."

Michael laughed and looked down at Callie standing before him. "I remember," he said becoming serious. He bent down and kissed her gently on the lips, touching her face softly.

"Mmm, minty," he said while gently running his thumb across her bottom lip.

Callie took a step back and tried to steady herself. She felt weak in the knees just like she always did when Michael kissed her. Even his touch electrified her. As usual, her heart was saying yes and her mind

176

was saying no. She couldn't give him the power to hurt her again. She stood looking at him remembering the cell phone calls.

"Michael, I have to ask you something," Callie said, listening to her heart. What both Stephen and Alise said had finally sunk in. The love she had with Michael was worth fighting for and that's what she had to do. She was sure there was a reason for the cell phone calls and she needed him to tell her. Once that was cleared up, she could put her mind at rest. She had to try to believe in them as a couple again.

"The night you came over and we talked, I mean we finally really talked…that was what, a couple of nights ago?"

Michael nodded his head in agreement.

"I felt as if we had turned a corner somehow," Callie said, turning her head away from Michael before willing herself to look him in the eyes. "I felt close to you again."

"Me, too," Michael said moving closer to Callie. "I felt the same way."

"But," Callie said placing her hand on Michael's chest to stop his advancement. "Things happened after you left and the bottom line is that Marlisa entered the picture again."

Michael took a step backwards and eyed Callie.

"What are you talking about? Marlisa entered what picture?"

"Didn't you talk to her on your cell phone after you left here?"

"Is that what you're talking about?" Michael asked in amazement. *Oh goodness*, he thought as he realized she must have reviewed his call log. Well let her, he had nothing to hide, nothing that he was ashamed of.

"Yeah, she called me hysterical and wanting a shoulder to cry on. I assumed it was about this new situation that came up. After all, it was a bombshell for her, too."

Callie stiffened. He couldn't possibly be feeling sorry for her.

"But I didn't bother to find out," Michael added quickly, looking Callie in the eyes. "I told her I couldn't help her anymore. The only reason I dealt with her before was because I felt guilty. I used her to

177

hurt you and in the process ruined your relationship as sisters. And I know what you're going to say," Michael quickly raised his hand to quell her protest, "she's responsible for her own actions, but so am I. And the fact is Callie, I broke *my* vows. Me. Marlisa was not responsible for that, but she's the one that became the viper of the entire family. I just didn't want to abandon her, too. And that's the truth."

Michael stood looking at Callie knowing his next words would hurt her deeply.

"I wanted to help her get through the bad situation. She was always so much weaker than you and she needed me and it seemed like you didn't."

He could see the tears forming in Callie's eyes and he wanted to cry too for hurting her by the choices he made.

"But I was wrong. You did need me. I just couldn't see it. But Callie…through it all there was always you. I was always thinking of you."

Michael turned his head and smiled sheepishly. "You know I bought your CD when it first came out and listened to it every night thinking of you," he said. Then he shook his head embarrassed by his confession and added, "I still listen to it every night. I just need to hear your voice." Michael grinned at her and said, "I got it bad."

He moved towards her and stood closely, lifting her chin to keep her eyes on him. She had to see him, really see him. He needed her to look past his eyes and into his heart.

"It's always been you, Callie. Only you. Now and forever. I love you and I need you to love me. And if you only love me half as much as I love you, I'll be happy because I know that's more than I deserve. Without you I'm ….I'm …just broken inside. Don't you see Callie? You make my life make sense. You make me feel complete."

Callie kissed Michael deeply and then melted into his arms. She felt exactly the same way. Feeling his arms around her, she nuzzled into his chest and suddenly everything made sense again. Everything

178

would finally be right again, she was sure of it.

Vanessa stood just out of sight, smiling and watching through the French doors of the den as her parents embraced. She couldn't get close enough to hear the conversation without giving herself away, but actions were speaking louder than words.

She tiptoed backwards and wandered towards the living room lost in happy thoughts of reconciliation for them and the entire family. However, her happy thoughts were quickly replaced with those of anger as she looked through the living room window. Sitting in the driveway behind her father's car was Marlisa's car. Then Vanessa saw Marlisa step onto the porch headed right for the front door.

Vanessa raced to the front door. She couldn't let Marlisa knock or ring the bell and interrupt her parents. Hurriedly, she swung open the door and stepped outside, pushing Marlisa back. Then she quietly closed the door before turning her glare on Marlisa.

"What the hell are you doing here?" Vanessa snapped.

"Is that any way to greet your aunt?" Marlisa asked amused.

"Oh, you're nothing to me." Vanessa's eyes narrowed as she spoke. "You gave up your rights as an aunt when you tried to be my stepmother!"

"Oh, so you know. Look 'Nessa I'm sorry for everything that -"

"Save it 'cause you don't have to apologize to me, I always knew you were a little nasty," Vanessa said bluntly.

Marlisa's mouth dropped opened. She had never been shown such disrespect from any of her nieces or nephews and frankly, it surprised her.

"I can't believe you just said that," Marlisa said, astonished. Then pointing a finger at Vanessa, she continued in a manner meant to reprimand. "No matter what happened between adults, I'm sure your parents would be surprised to hear how you're talking to me. Vanessa, I know you were raised better than that!"

Vanessa eyes flashed in anger. "You better get that finger out of my face!" she said in quiet fury. She still spoke quietly because she did not want to alert her parents of Marlisa's presence. "Who do you think you talking to like a child! You don't know anything about me! Lord only knows it's taking every fiber of my being to restrain myself from finishing that choking job my mother started on you the last time your were at this house!

"You know what," Vanessa grabbed Marlisa's arm and pushed her off the porch and into the walkway, "I don't have time to deal with this. You have issues. And since you're not welcome here, you need to take your issues and get to steppin'!"

"I came here to talk to Michael, not you!" Marlisa attempted to approach the front door again, but Vanessa blocked her way.

"I said get to steppin'," Vanessa said in a tone that unnerved Marlisa so much she backed away.

"You are violent just like your crazy mother! I'm not going to do this with you today, but I'll be back. I need to talk to Michael and I'll do it one way or the other."

Marlisa turned angrily and walked away. It wouldn't do her cause any good to be found in a physical confrontation with Michael's daughter on their front lawn.

Marlisa got in her car and drove away with tears stinging her eyes. They'll be another time. She wouldn't rest until she spoke with Michael. She had to know why he was avoiding her when she needed him the most. Why was he just throwing her away? Didn't he know how much she still needed him? How much she still loved him?

She couldn't loose Michael now, not when they were so close to being together. She had stood by and loved him from a distance for twenty years. She couldn't, no she *wouldn't*, go back to that again.

"I won't lose you to her this time," Marlisa said, wiping a single tear that slide down her face. It never occurred to her that he was never hers to lose.

CHAPTER 22

Paula sat in the conference room chair at the head of the table. Everything had been set up perfectly for Alise.

"Come said the spider to the fly," she said smiling, as she tapped the projector that was aimed at the large whiteboard. Usually the projector was used for business presentations, displaying well-designed PowerPoint slides. However, today she had a private show for Alise, although company business *was* on the agenda. Alise just didn't know it yet

Paula looked at her watch and got up to pace. She hated waiting and Alise knew that. She was already twenty minutes late and it was probably on purpose. She knew how to push her buttons. It was part of the game they played with each other. Tit for tat. Alise was definitely a worthy opponent and like any worthy opponent she knew any little advantage was important. She was furious with herself for being furious about Alise being late. Paula slammed her hand on the table and uttered a curse word under her breath.

"Careful Pastor, I think you could go to hell for that one."

Alise stood at the door looking at Paula who was trying to regain her composure.

"Been waiting long, dear sister? Not too long, I hope. I know how impatient you are."

Alise walked into the room and closed the door behind her.

"You know," Paula said, folding her arms across her body, "at this point, I'm not even interested in sparring with you for a couple of rounds like we usually do. As a matter of fact, I'm very anxious to get to the point. What is it that you think you know?"

"Why would you ask me that? I only know what you told me," Alise said, and then she snapped her fingers as if she had just remembered something. "Oh, and I also know that there's something getting in the way of your story making sense, at least to me. Most people call it 'the truth'. Ever heard of it? I thought you were on a mission to set things right before God and everybody."

"I am. And that's the truth," Paula said, sitting back down in the chair at the head of the table. "Have a seat," she said gesturing to a chair at the other end of the table.

Alise sat in the chair and scooted it up until it touched Paula's chair. Then she leaned in towards Paula getting even closer to her. That was another thing Alise knew Paula hated, people getting into her personal space.

"Ok, then, tell me *this* truth because I can't figure it out: why do you have samples of Daddy's blood?"

Paula leaned back pushing Alise's chair away.

"Get out of my face! You could have asked that from across the room!"

"Well, I wanted to ask it up close and personal. I wanted to see the flecks in your eyes when you tried to lie your way out of answering that question."

"Oh, that's where you're wrong, honey. I have no intention on lying. Not to you, anyway."

Paula looked at Alise smugly "I saw you coming yesterday, from a mile away."

"What does that mean?"

"Oh, you'll find out soon enough, I promise you. But first let me answer your question. I got his blood years ago, right after he made out his will giving just about everything he owned to his biological children." Paula chucked. "Hell, he even gave the crumbs in the kitchen cabinets to those two girls. Leaving you and me with barely

182

anything, unless we could show that we were also his biological children, too.

"Which we couldn't, so why get his blood?"

"Hmmm, you have no vision."

"Well then, what was the plan Paula?" Alise sat back and crossed her arm. "What did you do, steal his blood while he was in the hospital?"

"I didn't have to steal it, he gave it to me. He told me to test everybody." Paula shrugged her shoulders and said, "He already knew what the results would be, but he just wanted to pacify me, I guess. He said that way his will wouldn't be contested when he named Callie and Marlisa as his biological daughters and beneficiaries."

"Only everybody wasn't tested. I know I wasn't, but I do remember that you asked me to get tested. You said something about getting proof of his *deserving* biological daughters. You were scheming then and I didn't want any part of it."

"And it would have worked, Alise! Girl, you should have just trusted me and I would have fixed things!"

"Fixed things? Everybody already knew we weren't his kids!"

"The lawyers didn't! It was some small firm out in California doing all the probate paperwork. None of y'all even saw the will except for me, so you didn't know exactly what it said. You just knew what I told you. How do you think I knew about all this testing and biological children stuff even before Daddy died? So it breaks down like this: the left hand didn't know what the right hand was doing. The lawyers didn't know anything but what was on paper including the "certified" test results they would get. And Callie and Marlisa would only know that we shared everything equally.

"With both parents dead and bogus test results, the money would have been a four way split – just the way it should have been in the first place. Who was going to question it? Certainly not Callie or Marlisa! Callie was too broken up about Daddy dying and Marlisa was too dumb. Even so, they wouldn't have cared a bit. Plus they *expected*

183

to share because we all grew up as sisters!

"But they would have known something was up if I got an equal share and you didn't. And you would have questioned it, too. Nope, I couldn't get mine unless we were both in it together. You blew it Alise, but now we have a second chance."

"I'm not a liar and a thief," Alise said flatly. "I didn't want any part of it then and I still don't! Let me ask you this," She said narrowing her eyes as she looked at Paula, "just how were you going to get those bogus test result for me and you?"

"Oh, that's easy. I would have just used samples from Callie and Marlisa's and then put *our* names on *their* blood."

"You know, I didn't bother listening to you that day when you called about getting tested. As a matter of fact, I think I hung up on you. If I had listened I would have know just how low you would stoop. To think all these years I gave you more credit than you deserved for just being a human being." Alise shook her head and looked at Paula with a mixture of pity and disgust. "You're sick, you know that?"

"Oh, don't give me that look. You and me got the same blood," Paula said leaning down in Alise's space this time. "We think on our feet. We learn how to get what we want and I want my share of the inheritance. When I saw Callie's CD in the record store, I knew I had to do something. It was a CD made with *my* money from *my* company and I wasn't even going to get a penny!"

Paula looked at Alise with distaste. "You're the one that made everything so hard. Things would have been set right a long time ago if you just didn't fight me on everything!"

She spat the words at Alise who immediately rose from her chair in anger. She spoke quickly and viciously looking Paula in the eyes.

"Why shouldn't I fight you? I'm good at it! You know what else I good at, Paula? Remembering! And I remember when you handed me that stack of custody papers there was a letter from Mama. I didn't really read it, but I remember that she wrote Daddy a letter!"

184

She reached in her pocket and pulled out her copy of the letter Paula had given them all just three days before.

"This letter! The part that's blanked out is telling Daddy it's *me*! The daughter that she's talking about in this letter is *me*! You turned everybody's life into a downward spiral because you hate that you're an Alexander!"

Alise threw the letter on the table and continued, "You got a lot of problems! But you know what? They're *your* problems! You're just a crazy fool and need some help! You might want to get yourself a therapist to talk to or maybe a Pastor!" Alise chucked "Just make sure the Pastor is nothing like you and actually knows who God is!"

Alise snatched her purse off of the table and looked at Paula. "The jig's up sista girl! We gonna run you outta town on a rail!"

Paula looked smugly at Alise and then pushed play on the projector. Alise heard her child's voice before she saw him on the large whiteboard. It was her youngest son, Jackson, in the middle of a drug transaction on the corner right in front of their house. Stunned she watched as he sold packets of marijuana and crack. Then she watched in horror as Jamal, sitting in her own garage smoked dope and over-saw Jackson making a deal for stolen bike parts.

The next shot took place in a liquor store. The person holding the video camera kept it trained on Jackson and her middle son Anthony as they each stole two bottles of vodka. Then the video showed what looked like a party in a place Alise did not recognize, but it was clear that they were all under age and drinking the stolen alcohol.

Alise watched stunned and then turned and glared at Paula, who wore a tiny smile as she looked back at Alise arrogantly and with hands on her hips.

"Oh, I got lots more to show you if you're interested. Your boys lead quite an active life right there under your nose. There are actually a couple of assaults and robberies on record here. If certain people saw this......."

Alise balled her fist and charged at Paula who scooted quickly to

185

the other side of the table. After almost tripping over the cord to the projector, Alise grabbed it and pulled the plug out of the wall causing it to topple loudly to the floor.

"Careful Alise, that was your copy in the machine. I hope the video isn't ruined because if I was you, and thank goodness I'm not, I would *really* want to see the rest of the video."

Paula then removed from her jacket pocket three more tiny cassettes.

"You might want to look at these too. They've done so much illegal activity it's like watching episodes of *Cops*. If this gets into the wrong hands, they surely would be on their way to a detention center or whatever you call jail for thugs in training. Oh, that's right, Jamal is over eighteen so he would go to big thug jail!"

"What do you call yourself doing?" Alise screamed. Paula could see Alise was seething, her chest raising and falling due to her heavy breathing. Paula could almost see smoke coming from her nostrils and she thought Alise looked like a bull. A very angry bull that would topple her if she got the chance. Nonchalantly, Paula took a few more steps around the table to put more distance between her and Alise.

"You were saying something about a jig being up or something?"

"I'm not playing with you, Paula! I said what do you call yourself doing making videos of my children?"

"I call myself getting insurance that you'll keep your mouth shut and not mess things up this time! I knew if anybody would figure things out, it would be you! You would figure out the letter even though I doctored it up and forged a new date. I knew it would be hard to fool you. You think like me and you know me very, very well. The problem is you underestimate me. But you know, if Callie hadn't pulled her disappearing act and just signed the damn papers, we wouldn't have had to have this little conference today!"

"Oh yes we would have! I knew you were up to something and I was going to find out!"

"Well, now that you know – now what?" Paula eyed Alise.

"Like I said, we run you outta town on a rail," Alise looked at Paula with steely resolve. "This little show of yours didn't change a thing."

"Oh, yes it did. If you don't cooperate with me, I'll give the cassettes to Terrance who, by the way, is the one that asked me to spy on the kids for him."

"What! You were in cahoots with Terrance to get to me? To get my boys in trouble?"

"Calm down! I wasn't in anything with Terrance." Paula made a face of repulsion. "I don't know how you put up with that joke of a man for all those years. He knew I was in town before anybody else did and he thought he would use the opportunity to have me spy for him. He asked me to get the goods on the kids and then give it to him. He wanted to blackmail you himself for the house. If you didn't sell, he would seek custody threatening you with the tapes. He figured you would rather sell the house than give up your boys to him or the police."

"Terrance has copies of the tapes?"

"No! For God's sake, no! Try to keep up Alise," Paula said impatiently. "I told Terrance I couldn't get anything on them. Why would I help him? Although, I should thank him since he did give me your Achilles heel." Paula cocked her head to the side and looked at her sister. "So what's it gonna to be Alise? Do you love your kids more than you hate me?"

She held out her hands, palms up, and motioned them as if they were part of a balance scale. "Do you protect your children or your sisters?"

Alise stared at Paula without saying anything. She would never let Paula win, but she couldn't think right now. She had to protect her children. If she went along with Paula now, it would buy her time to figure a way out of this mess without betraying Callie or loosing her children. She knew she had no choice but to do what Paula wanted, but she couldn't bring herself to give in.

187

"What about the DNA tests? Aren't they gonna show that both Callie and Marlisa are Daddy's?"

"Sure, one set will." Paula scoffed at the puzzled look on Alise's face and then said flippantly, "Oh, hell I might as well tell you. No need to keep you up at night wondering what I'm up to. Besides, it'll feel good to tell somebody and I know you can appreciate my true genius."

Paula sat on the edge of the table and said casually while inspecting her nails, "There will be two sets of test results for them." Paula looked up at Alise putting one manicured finger in the air. "One will be the correct results taken with their blood and the other set...." Paula held up a second finger.

"....will be the results from somebody else's blood," Alise said finishing Paula's sentence. "Why two sets?"

"So that I can have scientific evidence to back up my story. You see, I told Marlisa that Callie was the true biological daughter and I told Callie that it was Marlisa. They both think that they're the bad seed and since they don't even talk to each other there's no chance of them putting two and two together. I'll be able to give them both test results showing that they are *not* the biological daughter and true recipient of the inheritance and that the other sister is. You see? I'll do a mix-n-match for the results.

"It's clear that neither one wants to loose everything to the other, that's why Marlisa signed the papers immediately and Callie...well...I almost got her when I dangled Marlisa and Michael's ongoing relationship in front of her face. But now Alise, *you're* going to make sure she goes along with sharing everything equally."

"You're gonna actually show them the results? Don't you know it's about more than money to them? You're taking away their father! You're making them wonder who they really are.

"If I know Callie, she'll want to find out who her real father is and she'll start digging! She'll be chasing after a ghost, but she'll be digging up a lot of your dirt and she's not stupid. She already knows

188

something's not right! I wouldn't be surprised if she questioned the DNA results, double checking the samples they used to make sure they did the tests right. She'll find out there were two sets of results."

"That's why it's up to you to convince her to just sign the papers. And we'll make it a four way split, just so you're invested in this plan, plus it'll make Callie feel more comfortable. I hope you know it's in the best interest of your kids to discourage Callie from playing detective. As far as the results go, I don't have to ever show them to anybody. I didn't want them to take the test in the first place. I just want *my* share of the company because it was built using part of *my* inheritance money. Nobody looses, Alise."

"I'm telling you, Callie is gonna want to see the results with her own eyes."

"I'll put her off. Or maybe I'll show her the results I want her to see. She already believes that she's not the daughter. You just get her to sign the papers."

Alise folded her arms across her chest and looked at Paula stubbornly.

"This is the deal Alise," Paula said impatiently. "Tomorrow I'm going to get legal documents drawn up giving each one of us twenty-five percent. You *will* talk to Callie and call me to let me know she's going to sign those documents. If I don't hear from you by tomorrow night….let's see that'll be Tuesday night, then by Wednesday morning the cops will be on your doorstep looking for your delinquents. You can run me outta town if you want to, but believe me, I will not have any problem taking your boys down with me."

"She's not gonna sign the papers this week. There's Thanksgiving and the grand opening of the restaurant and I know Callie, she'll be happy for the distractions. She's not gonna want to be bothered with this mess right now."

"Fair enough. We can do it on Monday." Paula brightened saying, "As a matter of fact, we'll make it a big deal and have a signing ceremony! I'll order champagne and expensive finger food or something. Maybe cake for the staff! It'll be a great way to introduce us as new partners! But…," Paula's tone changed and became stern as she continued, "you still have to talk to Callie and I still need to hear from you no later than tomorrow night, otherwise your boys will be eating Thanksgiving dinner behind bars."

Alise locked eyes with Paula as she walked back towards the door and picked up her purse again.

Paula pointed to the mini cassettes still sitting on the conference table. "Don't forget your souvenirs."

"You're not gonna win," Alise said angrily as she snatched the cassettes up and shoved them in her purse. Paula watched Alise walk deliberately to the door before calling out to her. She waited until Alise turned so that they could make eye contact.

"Try to keep up, Alise. I've already won."

Alise sat watching the last of the three cassettes with tears running down her face. They were worse than she even expected. She was hurt, but the tears were strictly from anger. Anger that her children could even be a part of what she was seeing. They lived in a good neighborhood and went to good schools. She struggled hard to make sure that happened. And yes, they were without a male role model since Terrance was an absolute useless peek-a-boo father - now you see him, now you don't. But that was still no excuse.

They went looking for trouble and apparently found more than she ever imagined was available in this "good" neighborhood. She trusted them and fought for them and sacrificed for them and she was having a hard time believing what her own eyes were telling her. She was disappointed and tired and angry and so the tears came.

There were angry tears because of Terrance, who set this in motion for his own greed. If he knew about this, why didn't he reach out to his own flesh and blood to help, rather than use Paula to hurt? Some father he turned out to be, and yet, she picked him.

190

Angry tears because she had to choose between her sister and her children. But she knew before she left the conference room earlier that day that she really didn't have a choice. She had to keep her children safe, but she couldn't live with herself if she betrayed Callie. Here's another sister stabbing her in the back. She would never let Paula win, but for now she had to think about helping her boys. Paula would get what she wanted temporarily and only until she figured out how to stop her.

One thing Alise knew was that this was only the beginning of feeding Paula's greed. With Callie and Marlisa both thinking their inheritance was undeserved and jail being threatened for her boys, Alise knew Paula could eventually manipulate and blackmail her way to full ownership of the company. It was not like Paula to settle for only one forth, especially since Callie and Marlisa received a lot more money than what was used to invest in the business. She needed time and pacifying Paula would give her the time she needed to think of a way to set things right. Alise hated what she was about to do and hated that Paula held the upper hand. She picked up the phone to call Callie and the angry tears came again.

CHAPTER 23

Paula unlocked the front door of Marlisa's condo and walked into almost complete darkness. The only light was from the large fish tank against the far wall of the living room. Paula was a little puzzled since she had been the last to leave the condo and the curtains had been left open. Marlisa loved the view at night and bringing the brightness of the sun into the room during the day, so it was rare to have everything closed up like it was now. Paula began to feel uneasy since it was still light outside and the curtains were clearly closed now.

Putting her keys down on the credenza at the end of the hallway, Paula reached for the light switch when she heard Marlisa's voice.

"Don't touch the light," she said, her voice shaky and sounding weary.

"What's wrong?" Paula asked, alarmed now and looking around for intruders.

"You. You're what's wrong."

"*Okaaaay*," Paula said slowly.

It was clear that Marlisa wanted to have one of her episodes or pitiable tantrums. She was sniffing and her shaky voice was not from fear but from crying. Paula was not in the mood to even pretend to care. She had had a great afternoon and was feeling pretty good about things. Leave it to Marlisa to bring all of that to an end.

"Is there something I can do to help or would you rather be left alone?"

"Actually you can do both," Marlisa's voice was coming from the couch and Paula began to walk towards her when she stumbled over something that sent her tumbling to the floor. In the dark she felt the obstacle, and realizing it was her suitcase, she quickly stood up, focusing her eyes on the lump on the sofa.

"The something that you can do to help is to leave my home and leave me alone. You're already packed," Marlisa said.

"I don't have any place to go!"

"Hotel."

"I can't live in a hotel!"

"Apartment."

"I don't have the money for a nice place to live right now!"

"Too bad for you, huh?"

"I can't believe you're doing this to me! Your own sister!"

"You have two other sisters."

Paula thought about Callie and Alise. She would be about as welcome in their house as the plague, probably less so. She had to get back in Marlisa's good graces for at least a couple of weeks until she got settled.

"Look, Marlisa," Paula said sweetly, "I know this is a difficult time for you. It's a difficult time for everybody, but we can help each other through it."

"Help?" Marlisa sat up on the couch, "You have no idea what you've done, do you? You come here upsetting the balance of things and causing problems – big problems! So big, that Callie turned to Michael, who had been waiting for the first chance he could get to go crawling back into her good graces! Where do you think that leaves me, huh? Crying in the dark on my sofa, that's where. *He won't even return my calls!*" Marlisa burst into tears, falling backwards on the sofa. "I've …been….in love with…him…for twenty years!" she was sobbing so hard she could barely get the words out.

"I can help you! I can help you get him - get Michael!" Paula blurted out, running to the sofa

"How?" Marlisa sat up again up. Paula's mind was racing trying

193

to put together a plausible plan of action to tell Marlisa. Hopefully something good enough that Marlisa would allow her to stay.

"Well." Paula began, "You said you were in love with him, right?"

"Right."

"Does he know that?"

"Yeah, I told him even before he married Callie."

"What about after he was married?"

"Yeah," Marlisa said sniffing, but obviously intrigued with this line of questioning and what Paula would do with the information.

"I told him a few times, like the time we slept together."

"And what did he say?"

"Nothing or he said that he loved Callie, except the time we slept together. That time he said that he thought he could love me."

Paula smiled to herself in the dark. If she knew her sister at all then she knew Callie would not be pleased to learn Michael kept Marlisa's love for him a secret.

For Callie, their affair had dropped out of the clear blue sky. In a time of weakness, Michael had turned to someone else and her sister had also crossed a line. However, Paula was willing to bet Callie had no idea that love of any kind was involved.

Michael had known that Marlisa was in love with him, but neglected to tell Callie. All this time he allowed Marlisa to stay close to him, close enough to confess her love behind Callie's back more than once. He allowed Callie to welcome the woman that coveted her husband into her home. If memory served Paula correctly, Marlisa even lived with them while she was getting her condo redecorated. How many stolen glances were made in her own home, while Callie stood by ignorant of Marlisa's advances?

Paula was sure this piece of information would make Callie feel betrayed yet again. It would make her feel that Michael had kept a secret from his wife in order to protect Marlisa. Weak, innocent, misunderstood Marlisa, who was always in constant need of some-body's protection. This time it was Michael's protection. He even told her that he could love her during the time they had slept together! Paula's smile broadened. Callie would go completely off once she found out he said that! If used correctly, this information would make the insecure Callie turn on Michael again. Trust was important to her and she thought full disclosure was part of the package.

As usual, Paula wanted to get something out of it, but she thought she deserved more than just a temporary place to stay. No, if she helped Marlisa it would cost her a little bit more than that.

"Are you smiling?" Marlisa's eyes were adjusted to the dark, but she was still unsure if her eyes were deceiving her.

"Of course I am, because I'm brilliant," Paula replied and reached behind her to turn on the light. She was in control now.

"Whoa, you look a mess," she said looking at Marlisa..

"So what?" Marlisa said as she shrugged her shoulder and blinked her eyes against the light. Paula grabbed a tissue from the box on the sofa and threw it towards Marlisa.

"Girl, wipe your raccoon eyes. I can barely stand to look at you."

"So what did you come up with?" Marlisa asked wiping her smudged eye make-up off of her face.

"Well, if you follow my advice, I can help you cause another split between Callie and Michael, but then the rest will be up to you."

"Ok. How? What should I do?"

Paula stood up and began to pace, she first had to secure a place to live.

"I'll help you, if you help me."

Marlisa was silent and just looked at Paula.

"Marlisa, are you willing to help me or not?"

"What's it gonna cost me? My father? Oh, wait you already took him. What about my first-born? Will my first born do?"

"I'm sensing a little hostility here," Paula said flatly.

"What do you expect, Paula? Sisterly love? Hell, we didn't even miss you all these years. And now here you are taking from us. Take, take, take! What else do you want to take from me now?"

195

"I suppose I should be offended, but I'm not." Paula hesitated, trying to decide which way to play it. Should she let some of her true colors show or should she play the loving sister and Pastor? She decided on the latter. She may not be *completely* fooling Marlisa anymore, but it wouldn't do any good to make a confirmed enemy. If she was going into business with Callie and Alise, she couldn't have Marlisa totally against her too. She had to be smart to get what she wanted and right now, Paula wanted to find out how much Michael means to Marlisa.

"I'm sorry for everything, Marlisa. Really I am and that's one reason that I want to help you. You've been the only one to show me any kindness or respect since I've been here."

Paula sat next to Marlisa and gently rested a hand over Marlisa's hand. Her voice soothing and sincere as she continued, "That's why I told you that Callie is Daddy's real daughter, but I have no intention on showing her those test results. You've put time and effort in this business too and I don't think you should lose it. Callie left you holding the bag for months while she had a nervous breakdown or something."

"Michael helped me through that time," Marlisa said tearing up again.

"Well, now you have me to help with the business." Paula looked at Marlisa for a response but none came. "And like I said, I think I can help with Michael, too," she added.

Marlisa perked up. "Ok, how?"

"Well, as far as helping with Michael, I think I can pull off a huge break up between him and Callie. That's gonna give you room to operate, but you have to do exactly as I say."

"Ok. I'm willing to do whatever it takes."

"As far as helping with the business, I'm going need something from you."

"What?" Marlisa asked. Paula could see that she physically tensed up as she stared pensively at her.

196

"Come Monday, we will sign new papers dividing the business equally between the four of us."

"Four?"

"Yeah, I talked to Alise and we think sharing equally is best, but that brought up a concern for me. Callie and Alise are so close that they will always work together. It will always be the two of them against you or against me. And even if *we* work together then that will just mean we would always be deadlocked. So, I'm hoping that I can add a provision in the business agreement that the *individual* with the highest percentage of ownership be allowed to cast the deciding vote. If we vow to work together and you give me five percent of yours, then we can always beat them."

"Why don't you give me five percent of yours?" Marlisa said eyeing Paula.

"You don't trust me?"

"Why should I?"

"Because I'm on your side, Marlisa! Even though Callie's the real daughter, I still thought you should get something. I mean, if I showed Callie the test results she would make sure you lost more than just your share of the business. Twenty percent is still more than the big nothing that Callie would make sure you got. For once, Callie wouldn't get what she wanted. I would see to it."

Paula looked at Marlisa hoping the veiled threat didn't escape her. No matter how she sugar coated it, the point was to make Marlisa remember that she had no claim on the business at all – as far as she knew.

"I would see to it that you got Michael, too. That would mean I would become an enemy of Callie's forever. She would kick me out of the business too, if she found out she was the rightful owner."

Marlisa closed her eyes and Paula saw tears running down her cheek.

"I don't care about the company, just Michael. If I don't get him," Marlisa's voice quivered, "then I'll put all the cards on the table and tell Callie she's the biological daughter."

"Ok," Paula said trying to hide her apprehension, but she wasn't about to let this little set back derail her plans.

"One more thing, I need a place to say for about two more weeks. After that, I'll have my own place to call home."

"Go to a hotel."

"Marlisa, I honestly can't afford it right now."

Marlisa sighed and replied, "Two weeks only. I'll pay for your hotel room and help you with a few expenses, but after that, you're on your own."

"Fair enough," Paula said gathering her things. Marlisa rummaged in her purse and handed Paula a credit card.

"Paula, if I don't get Michael I'm gonna tell Callie everything, so don't get too comfortable unless you really have a plan."

"I heard you the first time, Marlisa. I'll call you with the details," Paula said, dragging her luggage out the door. The door slammed behind her and she just stood in the hall trying to get control of her thoughts and her emotions.

Admittedly, she was more than a little perturbed that Marlisa was being so demanding. Believing she was not the rightful owner of the company should have paralyzed Marlisa with fear, but in a strange way it has made her fearless. If Marlisa went to Callie with her version of the truth, then the house of cards she built so carefully would come tumbling down. Indeed, all the cards would then be on the table.

She felt nervous for the first time because she was not sure she could deliver Michael, even if she was successful with splitting him and Callie up for good. He didn't want Marlisa or else he wouldn't have waited twenty years. Hopefully, Marlisa will be satisfied with *believing* she could get him. But for her to believe it, Callie would have to be out of the picture.

Paula was fairly confident that she could make enough trouble in their paradise to give Marlisa hope. And the more hope she gave Marlisa, the more of her percentage of the business she would ask for.

198

Paula was prepared to use Marlisa's unhealthy obsession with her sister's husband for her own selfish reasons, but she had to admit she didn't believe Callie would ever be completely out of the picture.

She wished that Marlisa would give up and find her own man; there were plenty of them out there. Personally, she wished Michael and Callie the best. She didn't believe in true love but, if she did, Michael and Callie had it and they deserved to be happy. However, Paula was ready to escort them all the way to divorce court and even beyond that if it meant getting what she wanted.

CHAPTER 24

Marlisa drove around the block once more to get her nerve up. She thought about the importance of her visit to the quaint little house on the outskirts of Charlotte, North Carolina. Finally she parked, and after checking the house number once more against the address on the piece of paper she held tightly in her hand, she got out of the car. The house was the kind of house you would see in a Norman Rockwell painting. It was the picture perfect, small country home that was just full of love and family and hope.

That's why Marlisa was sure she had the wrong address. She had found it in Paula's things as she packed them in anticipation of kicking her out. It was included on a note offering help and declaring belief and support of Pastor Paula. The note was signed Annie Jones and it had a phone number. Marlisa had promptly called the number and after speaking briefly, Annie had agreed to meet with her. At first, Annie had been reluctant, but upon Marlisa revealing her relationship with Paula, she was all too eager. Any sister of Pastor Paula was welcome in her house, no matter what anyone else in town thought.

Marlisa had thought after making her alliance with Paula that she should find out a little more about her older sister. As a little girl, she hardly remembered anything about Paula, but after becoming an adult, she knew enough about her sister to make trusting her impossible. The entire Pastor Paula routine was an act and she certainly didn't believe Paula was acting out of any moral obligation. Paula had an agenda and it looked like it was to get as much money out of her and Callie as

200

they were willing to give. Marlisa really didn't care about the company, so if Paula wanted to get more of her shares in exchange for helping her with Michael, then so be it. Callie did a good job running it and if what Paula said was true, then it didn't belong to her anyway.

No, what Marlisa was looking for was something that would give her the upper hand. Right now, Alise and Callie were definitely on the same side. Paula was right about that. She was also right about the fact that it was better if the two of them worked together against the dynamic duo.

However, Marlisa knows that once the papers are signed and Paula begins to feel secure within the company, she will eventually dismiss her like yesterday's news. Not even the threat of turning over CM Music Productions completely to Callie will undo the hooks she'll have in the company and only God knows what else by then. It will take a stick of dynamite to get her out of their lives once she gets a taste of the money and no threat will be able to stop her then. What Marlisa needed was a new angle to make sure Paula stays the reluctant ally and help her get Michael. After contacting Annie, she thought she may have found it.

Marlisa knocked on the door and waited patiently, looking at her surroundings. There was a long porch swing and flower boxes lined up along side the railing of the porch. Apparently Annie had children because toys, mostly dolls, inhabited the corner of the porch along with a small Little Tike plastic table and chair set. Marlisa could almost feel the warmth of the home as she looked around. There were actually shutters on the windows. How did Paula wind up here? She was gone for so long and no one even knew where she was or what she was doing. No one, that is, until now.

The door opened and a smiling older woman holding a toddler on her hip unlocked the screen door and beckoned Marlisa inside.

"Come in, come in! I was just fixing to put Emma down for a nap. I'm Annie and you must be Marlisa," the woman said, shifting the baby from one hip to the other.

201

"Yes, I am. Thank you for inviting me to your home. It's lovely by the way."

"Oh, it ain't that much, but it's home, right Emma?" Annie said, smiling at the baby in her arms.

Emma looked at Annie and blinked a few times before burying her head into Annie's shoulder. Her long eyelashes were wet with tears and clearly she wasn't in the mood for company or conversation.

"Come right on in and pull up a chair. I'm just gonna see if she'll lay down without a fight. Be right back."

Marlisa sat down on the couch and could hear Annie fussing in the back room with the baby. When Annie reemerged she handed Marlisa an ice tea and sat down across from her in an overstuffed armchair.

"Well, what can I do for you, Marlisa? I know you had questions about your sister."

"Yes, I just thought it was time for me to get to know her. When she left us, I had no idea what was really going on in her life."

"I understand," Annie said sympathetically. "Getting to know your family is important. Sometimes, by the time you figure out you don't know them as well as you thought, it's too late. Little Emma is my grandbaby. Her mother, my daughter, overdosed when Emma was just two weeks old."

"I'm sorry to hear that," Marlisa said, watching as Annie sank further into the big armchair. She looked so small now. Marlisa's heart went out to her.

"You know what hurts me the most? It's that I couldn't even rightly help her. I didn't even know she was on drugs. I couldn't rightly help her because I didn't even know."

"I'm sorry," Marlisa, not knowing what else to say, repeated herself. This time it came out just above a whisper.

"Oh, I can see I'm making you uncomfortable," Annie said looking up at Marlisa. "The good thing about it is Pastor Paula helped me through every bit of it."

"She did?"

202

"Yes, ma'am. I met her at church. The Divine Church of Christ."

"She was a Pastor there?"

"Oh, no, no. She was just a parishioner, but she was already ordained. They didn't think she was right as a leader in the church."

They got that right, Marlisa thought.

"But she wanted to get a home church started and we did that right here in this house."

"You left the Divine Church of Christ?"

"Yep, me and several others. It was like a splinter group, I suppose. We just didn't like some of God awful things going on at the big church, like the music director was a..."

Annie leaned forward and looked around the room as if to check to see who was listening. Marlisa looked around the empty room as well, although she wasn't exactly sure what she was looking for. Then after a pause, Annie finished her sentence in a whisper, "…a homosexual."

Marlisa tried hard not to smile. She just nodded her head in understanding.

"And," Annie continued, "the pastor was having an affair with Mary Lucas." Annie nodded her head matter-of-factly as she scowled. "We had had enough. Pastor Paula was leading us in service every week here and we were getting along fine. When my daughter died, I needed so much help that Pastor Paula moved in."

"That sounds like the Paula I know," Marlisa said aloud, but more to herself than to Annie.

"Yes, she sure was gracious like that," Annie agreed, nodding her head in approval.

Gracious? Salacious is more like it, Marlisa thought to herself, careful not to verbalize her thoughts this time.

"Well, we were growing, there was about fifty or sixty of us, so Pastor Paula decided that it was time we had a church of our very own. We were going to build one. We just had to raise the funds."

I think I know where this is going, Marlisa thought.

"So we began to raise the money and Pastor Paula got an investor who would match all of our funds as long as we used his construction company."

"Hmmm," Marlisa said already thinking ahead.

"So, we started to go all out raising money. We had so many bake sales and cake sales and fish fries on the county line where we got a lot of tourists, that I couldn't keep count.

"And then Ralph Thompson sold his property near Raleigh and gave us some of the money. All in all, we raised one hundred and seventy thousand dollars! Add that to what the investor would give and we voted to start the building process. And then, before we knew it, the money was all gone."

"Who was in charge of the money?" Marlisa asked already knowing the answer.

"Why, Pastor Paula of course. But she sent it all to the investors who must have skipped out on us because we never heard from him again."

"Did you ever speak with him?"

"No, just Pastor Paula. But I know she wrote the check to him because I had to co-sign on the check."

"What was his name?"

"Gregory Gray."

Gregory Gray. Why does that name sound familiar? Marlisa thought.

"Well, he cashed it all right. Pastor Paula was very upset and intent on tracking the money down. Everybody was mad. Nobody could understand how she could lead us into trouble like this. They were saying things like, 'if she couldn't be trusted to get us a building, how could she be trusted to get us to heaven?' Pastor Paula took sick after that. She went back up north to be with her sisters for awhile."

That's news to me, Marlisa thought.

"She had taken care of her sisters when they were younger because of her mama was always being sick."

That's news to me.

204

"Well, what am I telling you for? You know better than me! She went to live with one of your sisters for awhile, Alise I think."

That's really news to me! Marlisa shouted in her thoughts. She didn't realize that her reaction was causing her eyes to bulge out until she noticed the look on Annie's face.

"I'm just finding out so much and it's a bit overwhelming. Tell me, did she every recover the money?"

"No, she managed to track it from Gregory Gray's account to a third party, but after that she couldn't get any more information."

Annie snapped her fingers and stood up suddenly. "As a mater of fact, I still have the papers she showed me from Gregory Gray's account. Somehow she got it to prove to everybody that he had the money and that she was just as surprised as everybody else that he walked away from his rightly duties with us. I'll be right back."

Annie rushed up the stairs as Marlisa sat back on the couch. So, Paula gave the money to this Gregory Gray (*why is that name so familiar?*) and he emptied his account and ran. That's Paula's story. Marlisa knew there was more to it than that. Possibly Gregory was in on it with Paula and gave her a share, but somehow Marlisa didn't think so. Paula would never have trusted someone else to be in charge of the money. Marlisa sat thinking of what could have really happened when Annie reappeared holding a few papers and a stack of postcards.

"Here are the statements," Annie said, handing Marlisa the papers, "and here are the postcards for the grand opening of our church. Pastor Paula never got a chance to see them before she, you know, left us."

Marlisa looked at the bank printouts. Sure enough there was a copy of the check written to Gregory Grey and his endorsement on the back. Also, there was a copy of his bank statement showing the money going in his account and immediately back out via a bank wire. Marlisa noticed the last four digits of a social security number at the top of the statement. She would have to do some digging but she was sure nothing was as it seemed.

205

Then she looked at the postcard, which was advertising the new church and was apparently going to be sent out to the community. It had Paula's face on it with an invitation to come and experience the fellowship at the brand new church. Marlisa grabbed a handful of the postcards and looked up at Annie.

"May I keep these?"

"Yes, of course. Keep everything. If you can find Mr. Gregory Gray and get our money back that would go a long way in clearing Pastor Paula's name. I'm sure she would appreciate it."

"I'm sure," Marlisa said dryly. Upon seeing the puzzled look on Annie's face at her response, Marlisa added quickly, "I'm sorry, it's just so much to take in."

"I always wanted to know how the service went. I wanted to come but Alise didn't give me any details when she wrote me."

"I'm sorry, I don't follow."

"Oh, the letter from your sister is there, too," Annie said, pointing to the papers in Marlisa's hand. "I tried to reach her but there was no return address and she didn't sign her last name. Was it a nice service? I mean as nice as one could expect from a funeral?"

Funeral? Marlisa almost fell out of her seat. She kept her head down and shuffled through the papers to hide the surprise that must be showing on her face. When she found the letter she began to read it, dumbfounded. What is Paula not capable of if she would fake her own death?

Marlisa almost laughed as she read the letter. It was full of lovely comments about Paula from all the sisters. She really laid it on thick. Apparently, she never recovered from pneumonia, but according to Alise she practically died of a broken heart from letting everyone down at the new church. Marlisa covered her face and shook her head in amusement but Annie, who thought she was upset, misinterpreted it. Annie quickly sat next to Marlisa on the couch and patted her hand in sympathy. Without giving herself away, Marlisa asked if she could get a copy of the letter.

"Keep it dear. I think it will do you more good than me."

"You have no idea," Marlisa answered, still sitting with her face covered.

Finally, when she regained her composure, she gathered her things and Annie walked her to the door. Marlisa's mind was racing trying to get all the pieces together. Once back inside the privacy of her car, she quickly made two phone calls, one to Gregory Gray's bank and the other to Alise.

"Alise, this is Marlisa. I don't want to keep you on the phone, but I just have a quick question."

"What do you want?"

Marlisa winced. Sometimes it still hurt to feel the resentment from someone she still loved. Alise was just as angry with her as Callie was because of everything that had happened.

"A name came up today. Gregory Gray. It sounds so familiar but I can't place it. Do you know who that is?"

"Was. Who that *was*. He was Paula's fiancé but he was killed in a car accident a long time ago. Why?"

"Paula was supposed to get married to him?"

"Yeah, why?"

"No real reason. His name just came up and I couldn't place it."

"Ok, fine. Bye."

Alise hung up before Marlisa could respond. Ordinarily, she would have been upset for a while over this rejection, but Marlisa was too preoccupied with putting the pieces of Paula's puzzle together.

Unfortunately, the second call to the bank gave her no information at all except to confirm the account was closed. A name from a dead fiancé, a fake death, missing money and a forged letter. It didn't make sense unless you knew Paula. Marlisa would get a private detective to connect all the dots with proof, but right now she knew enough. Paula had scammed the good people of that town out of one hundred and seventy thousand dollars. The success of Paula's plan depended on everyone being so complacent that they wouldn't do any follow up or

207

research to uncover the fraud. It was easier to believe that the person they trusted had *unintentionally* made a bad decision and lost their money, rather than to believe she had scammed them. They accepted her death just like they accepted all of her other lies.

Marlisa drummed her fingers on the steering wheel as she drove back onto the interstate. Apparently, Paula was no stranger to forging letters. Marlisa thought about the letter from their mother that Paula offered as proof of a paternity problem. A little digging around would probably unearth another thinly disguised scheme for money. Again, the key to success being a lot of trust with little follow up. Marlisa was now determined to get the proof she needed by investigating Paula thoroughly. Marlisa wondered what else Paula had been up to in her long absence.

Who else have you scammed Pastor Paula? What other criminal activity is in your sordid past?

Although Marlisa wanted to eventually force Paula out of town, she was not sure if she could send her own sister to jail. Not yet anyway.

But first things first. She needed Paula's help to run interference between Callie and Michael. So once she got the details of Paula's scams, she'll have the power and that's all she really cared about now. Alise and Callie had both turned their backs on her. And with the man she loves, the man she has sacrificed her family for, slipping through her fingers, Marlisa was desperate. If it weren't for Paula being forced to stand in her corner, she would have no one at all.

Again, it came down to getting the proof. The only thing she could prove now is that Paula lied about her death. Marlisa chuckled as she thought of Alise's reaction to those wonderful words she had supposedly written about Paula. Of course, Alise couldn't know about the letter just yet. Nobody could, not just yet.

Marlisa believed Paula probably first thought of the scam as she began to see the money grow in the bank. Her greedy, itchy fingers just couldn't stay put, so she thought of a quick and easy way to steal it all. She won't have much cover once Marlisa gets the bank information. If she was sloppy with such a big heist, Marlisa was sure she would have all the evidence she needed and it would point directly to the thieving Pastor Paula.

"Oh, you just wait Paula. You just wait."

CHAPTER 25

Callie looked at the white, partially shriveled bird with a mixture of panic and amusement. It was Thanksgiving morning and after cooking her turkey for nearly four hours, it looked more like something she found in the middle of the road rather than something she should place in the middle of her dinner table. How could she ruin a turkey? All she was supposed to do was cover it in foil and put it in the oven. In all the years she could remember Thanksgiving, she realized she had never cooked the turkey. She was either dining as a guest at a relative's house or here at home where Michael prepared the turkey and ham while she did dessert and sides.

Callie touched the bottom of a turkey leg where the meat was so dried out it was receding from the end of the bone. Well, maybe nobody will miss turkey this year. The kids always said if they had to choose between having turkey or ham, they would choose ham. It was Callie who felt Thanksgiving meant turkey, so they always had both. Now, she blanched looking at the stark white, scaly carcass. This is why people were vegetarians. She had to be the worst cook in the world to ruin a turkey.

Even though it was Thanksgiving Day, Callie thought that maybe she could still buy a pre-cooked turkey from somewhere. It was worth a try. Callie turned from the stove about to go in search of the yellow pages when Maya bounded into the kitchen.

"Hey, Mom! Oooh, what's that? Turkey!" she said excitedly.

"Uh, yeah. I guess you still can call it a turkey," Callie answered, looking at the white bird.

"Yummy! When you gonna cook it?"

Callie chuckled, remembering getting up at the crack of dawn preparing the turkey for its four hour appointment with her oven, just to have it still look raw.

"You really want to eat turkey this year?" Callie asked, still grinning.

"Oh, yeah! I can't wait! Is Aunt Alise coming over?"

"Yeah," Callie said pensively. "I'm gonna give her a call right now. Maybe I can get help with the turkey."

"What kind of help do you need?" Maya asked, puzzled. "All you have to do is put it in the oven to cook it. Even I know that," she added in a matter-of-fact tone.

Callie watched her daughter skipping out of the kitchen and wondered where she got the energy. Maya was always so vibrant that when she left the room Callie somehow felt out of breath and happily winded. She looked at the turkey, which had to be cooked even if it wasn't brown. She believed she could salvage it as she picked up the phone to call Alise.

"I'm going to get straight to the point," Callie said as soon as Alise answered. "I cooked my turkey for almost four hours, but it's still white and the ends of its little legs are so dried out that they look like potato chips."

"Did you let it cook without the foil?"

"What do you mean? Michael always covers it in foil and just lets it cook."

"Right," Alise said, "then at some point you're supposed to take the foil off so that it can brown. You should also baste it often to keep it from dying out, especially now that some parts are...well... crunchy."

"Oh, ok. I'll do that then," Callie said, now hopeful that she wouldn't be crowned the worst cook in the world.

"You never cooked a turkey before?"

211

"No. Michael always did."

"I don't know whether to say you're pitiful for being ignorant on what to do or lucky for never having to know what to do. Michael's a good man to always help with the dinner. All Terrance offered to do was eat and belch. Oh, yeah, and fart. I know you can barely contain your jealousy," Alise said dryly. "I was such a lucky woman."

"Speaking of Michael,-"

"I thought we were talking about Terrance, my Prince Charming."

"No, we were talking about Michael, my Prince Charming who is coming to dinner today."

Alise was so silent Callie thought they might have been disconnected.

"Hello? Alise?"

"I'm here. Are you and Michael getting back together?"

"I think we might be," Callie said, holding her breath waiting for a response.

"Oh, thank goodness!" Alise exclaimed, "I now have hope for the entire world of love! So I got through to you, huh? Damn, I'm good!"

"Well, I guess you sort of did."

Callie hunched her shoulders and leaned up against the counter.

"I'm willing to try to get past, well...our past. I want to go slowly because of the kids, but today will be a first step for us. Back together as a family- a very fragile family."

"Oh, this is exciting! It's gonna be like old times again!"

"I hope so," Callie said seriously.

"Well, since I'm gonna be at the love fest, I want turkey. A good delicious turkey, so get back to work on your bird!"

"Ok," Callie said, smiling broadly before hanging up.

"Need help?" Michael asked, walking into the kitchen. He was carrying two bottles of wine that he put on the counter and then went in search of a wine glass. He uncorked one of the bottles and after filling the glass, he handed it to Callie.

"Tradition dictates that you drink wine and get a little tipsy before

212

making the deserts. I do the turkey and the ham and, since you hate to cook, I usually do the sides."

"That's not true!" Callie protested. "I do the sides!"

"You must be drunk already if you can't remember how things work on Thanksgiving."

"Michael!" Callie said, laughing. "I can't believe you're trying to get credit for cooking that you don't even do! Who does the stuffing every year, huh? And who does the mashed potatoes?"

"Ok, ok I'll give you those. But – hey, what happened to the turkey?"

Callie looked at Michael's face as he looked at the white bird and burst into laughter. She then quickly relayed the situation including Maya's question on when she would cook the bird which had Michael bent over with laughter.

"You didn't take the foil off to brown it?" Michael asked, laughing.

"I never did this before!"

"You're a lousy cook!"

"I never pretended to be anything else."

"It's a good thing love is blind," Michael said, looking down at the unappealing turkey, "and prefer ham," he added patting his flat stomach. "Otherwise you'd never get any action." He bent down and kissed her tenderly on the lips.

"Why don't you go sit down and drink your wine? I can finish up with the turkey," he offered.

"Oh, no, no, no! I started this at the crack of dawn and I'm gonna finish it. I'm on the home stretch now, anyway. We *will* have a delicious and appetizing turkey to eat, otherwise I'll never live this down!"

"Ok, but when you serve us what looks like road kill, just remember I offered."

"Alright smarty, out of my kitchen, for now anyway. Why don't you go hang out with the kids for a little while?" Callie suggested,

213

sipping on her wine.

"Can you be trusted alone with all that wine?"

Callie looked at the two bottles on the counter and remembered all the wine she consumed while trying to drown her sorrows. She winced now even thinking about the pain she was trying to forget. Michael had no idea.

"This," she gestured towards the bottles, "is child's play."

Michael kissed her on the forehead and left the kitchen while Callie stood looking at her wine glass. She still had to fight the daily temptation to find comfort in a wine bottle like she did for all those many lost months. She put the glass down in a corner of the kitchen counter and then turned her attention to the turkey.

"I will not be defeated!" she said, opening the oven door. Grabbing potholders, she placed the turkey back in the oven. Her eyes drifted back to the wine glass sitting in the corner.

"Oh, what the hell," she said, reaching for it. "It's Thanksgiving!"

Alise arrived earlier than usual with her boys and another cousin, Shauna, for Thanksgiving dinner. Usually Callie and Michael would take the kids to visit aunts and uncles and make it a big family re-union, but Callie wanted to have a more personal reunion of sorts. It was a pleasant and cozy gathering and seemed to be just what every-one wanted. Callie and Michael made sure they had fixed everyone's favorites and there was more than enough food to go around.

The turkey was the talk of the dinner table. It had browned beautifully and since Callie was basting it every few minutes it ended up not being dried out at all, but juicy and tasty. Maya even exclaimed that it tasted better than the usual Thanksgiving turkey and laughed when Michael pretended to sulk.

All in all, the evening was one of the best that Callie could remember. She had her family back, even if it was just for one night. As the evening drew to a close, Callie turned her attention to the next big event - the grand opening. Alise had planned to be at the restaurant first thing in the morning and Callie wanted to have one last rehearsal that was set for early afternoon.

At first, the idea of having a restaurant opening the day after Thanksgiving seemed to be ridiculous to Callie, but Stephen had no doubts. Callie wasn't sure she liked it, but he made her realize that just because *she wanted* to stay at home, nice and cozy with family, didn't mean that everyone did. People celebrated the holidays differently and there was a whole host of people who loved being out and about. He had pointed out how crowded Disney World was during the holidays, even on Christmas day, and again asked for her trust, which she reluctantly gave. But now that it was standing room only, she had to admit Stephen could be trusted about making money, if nothing else.

Callie smiled thinking about Stephen and their challenging relationship. In just about every discussion they had, he went from friend to foe or vise versa in just a few short sentences. However, their weekend in Florida had been very nice and he seemed like someone worth getting to know better. He was sweet and funny and kind - definitely friend status the entire time they were out of town.

"What are you smiling about?" Michael asked, looking up from the television. The football game had just ended and his team had won. "You're happy that Dallas won, too?" he teased, knowing she disliked his favorite team.

"Ugh! You know this is 'Skins territory," Callie said, still smiling.

"Oh, she's smiling 'cause she's tipsy. You know Callie, she's a happy drunk- at first," Alise said, sipping on her own glass of wine.

"I'm not drunk!"

"Then she'll either turn mean or weepy," Alise added.

"I'm not drunk! And I'm never a mean drunk!"

"Oh, wait a minute, that's me," Alise laughed.

"Either way, she's all yours, Alise," Michael said grabbing Callie's hands and pulling her up from the couch. "I gotta go."

215

Then looking at Callie he added, "I told my mother I would stop by for dessert."

"Isn't it a little late for that?"

"If I don't come by she's going to have a heart attack and I don't want that to be on my head. Besides, Shannon texted me to let me know she was going to hang out there until I came. So they're expecting me."

"You know, I can't stand your sister," Alise said before draining her glass of wine.

"That much I know, Alise. I'm just not sure why."

"Because when I first met her we were at your rehearsal dinner and she couldn't go outside without that little parasol of hers. I asked her what she needed it for and she said she used it because she didn't want to "get black." What is that supposed to mean, "*get black*"? She was *born* black!" Alise poured herself another glass of wine becoming more animated as she continue speaking.

"Too many damn folks got it twisted! Light-skinned ain't another race, you're not unblack. Not in America!

"There's a very simple question everybody can ask to get the facts straight on how this thing works. Here's the question: If slavery times broke out right now, where would you be? Where would you be? All I know is that Shannon, parasol and all, would be right in the kitchen next to me and you Michael, right?" Alise was pointing her finger at Michael. "That'll clear things up for her, right Michael? Right?" She asked loudly.

"Right," he said, clearly amused by Alise's wine induced conversation.

"Sorry, Callie," Alise held up her hands in resignation, "but you'd be in the field."

"I thought I would be on the porch."

"*Well…* " Alise said slowly as she made a face and squinted upwards.

"In the yard?" Michael suggested, shrugging his shoulder. Alise

216

nodded her head in agreement and grinned at Callie.

"Ok, I'll take that. As long as I know where I stand just in case slavery breaks out again. You can never be too prepared."

They all laughed and Michael nudged Callie as Alise drained her glass again.

"She's just nervous because of tomorrow," she whispered in his ear. He turned his face towards hers and smelt her hair. Honeysuckle. Her hair smelt like honeysuckle, just like he remembered.

"Walk me to the door."

"Did you say good-byes to the kids?"

"Yeah, Maya wanted me to stay and tuck her in, but she warned me that she didn't plan on going to bed until after one am."

Michael and Callie laughed. Maya's bedtime was always extended on non-school nights, usually until ten-thirty. It was obvious that she had other plans this time. Michael put his arms around Callie and kissed her gently on the lips.

"The turkey really was tasty," he whispered. "Very, very tasty," he added giving her another soft kiss.

"Helloooo! There are other people in the room!"

Michael and Callie both looked at Alise who had covered her eyes and continued speaking in a teasing manner.

"There are people in the room who don't want to lose the contents of their delicious Thanksgiving dinner because of the sickening display of their relatives. Not to mention, I got eyes and don't want to go blind either!"

"Alise, I bet nobody ever called you subtle," Michael said to Alise who still had her eyes covered and now was making a face as if she was about to throw up.

"Well, I came for dinner, not dinner and a show," she said dryly. "But if I did come for dinner and a show, you guys are boring and I want my money back."

"Alright, alright, I'm walking him to the door and I'll be right back," Callie replied.

Michael and Callie walked out the front door and stood on the porch. Michael had put on his coat on the way to the door, but Callie stood shivering in her turtleneck.

"C' mere," he said, pulling her into an embrace and wrapping his coat, which had hung open, around her body.

"Feels like that sleeping bag thing we tried once," Callie said smiling up at Michael.

"If memory serves me, it was twice."

Callie grinned embarrassed and then felt silly for feeling embarrassed. It was still so new to her.

"I love you," Michael said and then lowered his lips to hers and gave her a passionate kiss. Callie returned the kiss with just as much passion. She felt her insides turn to jelly and her knees grow weak and she wanted more. They kissed again and the only thing she could think of was how much she loved him and missed him.

"One more kiss like that and I'm not sure if I'll be able to leave tonight," Michael said as he squeezed her closer to him.

"One more kiss like that and I'm not sure if I'll *let* you leave tonight."

They stood holding each other in silence with Michael nuzzling gently on her neck. Callie didn't want to let go, but she finally pulled away.

"You better go."

"I'll call you tomorrow."

"Tomorrow will be a little hectic. Grand opening, remember?"

"How could I forget? I'll be there front and center. Now you go inside before you catch a cold and then you'll sound like a bullfrog. Run everybody out of the place. Well, everybody except me." Michael said smiling.

He watched Callie open the door to go inside. She gave one final wave before stepping in the house and closing the door.

Michael stood for a moment longer staring at the door. He didn't believe he could ever be happier than he was at that very moment. It

218

was only a first step to getting his marriage on track and he knew there was work to be done, but he was still ecstatic. He knew Callie was still very hurt and a little afraid to let her guard down, but he was prepared to go above and beyond to get her trust back. Michael, already thinking of when he would see Callie again, got in his car and backed slowly out of the driveway and started down the street.

He was so preoccupied with happy thoughts of reconciliation that he never saw Marlisa, who stood just behind a large hedge at the end of the driveway shivering in the cold. She was dressed for the weather but had been standing outside her sister's house for quite some time trying to see in the windows, hoping for a glimpse of Michael. He would not take her calls, so she had stooped to following him in hopes of an "accidental" meeting.

Now, she realized as she wiped tears from her eyes, that she had been reduced to stalking. She had parked her car a block away and had walked to her sister's house to wait in the cold behind hedges and to peek in windows. And for what? To see Callie use Michael like her personal lap dog to push away or cuddle up with when the mood strikes? A month ago she hated him but now she's kissing him.

Marlisa was devastated by the display of affection she had just witnessed between Callie and Michael, but she willed herself to keep it together. She turned and ran the entire block to her car. Once she had the car started and felt the heat began to thaw her fingers, she reached for her cell phone. She dialed the number angrily and when Paula picked up, Marlisa yelled into the phone.

"I want them broken up now! Do you hear me? I'm coming over right now!"

Paula looked at a sleeping Winston lying next to her in bed and sighed. He would have to leave before Marlisa arrived. It was just as well - he had bored her to tears tonight.

"Alright," she said calmly to Marlisa who was becoming more emotional by the minute, "We need to talk about this anyway. If you do *exactly* as I say, we can split them up by tomorrow night."

219

CHAPTER 26

Marlisa stood in her office with the door cracked looking down the hall. From her vantage point she could clearly see past the receptionist desk and to the door of Callie's office. She could also just barely see who was entering or leaving the elevator. She stood in the dark waiting for Michael to come to her rescue. Paula had been sure he would and she had just called to confirm he was on the way.

It was all part of Paula's plan to get Callie, Michael and Marlisa together at just the right time. Paula had first called Callie with the news that Marlisa had completely lost it. She told her that Marlisa had admitted to destroying a lot of important company documents. Paula also told Callie that Marlisa had purposefully waited until everyone had left the office for the holiday, so that she could go through all the details of Callie's CD distribution and sales without Marvin looking over her shoulder. She convinced Callie that Marlisa was intent on sabotage and that she should at least go to the office to take a look at things.

Paula knew Callie would go nuts when she heard about Marlisa's antics and that was step number one to the manipulation game - know how to push what buttons. As soon as she was sure Callie was on the way, she had called Marlisa.

"Hello," Marlisa had whispered into the phone.

"It's me. She's on her way and she is pissed off at your behind so make sure you stay out of her way. You need to hide just in case she wants to take a look around your office."

220

"Where am I supposed to hide?"

"Don't you have a bathroom in there?"

"Well, yeah I -"

"Then hide in the shower! She'll be looking for papers not shampoo!" Paula sighed deeply.

She didn't have patience for Marlisa even on a good day, which this was not. None of these theatrics would even be necessary if she would just leave Callie's husband alone. She was so desperate it was sickening! However, Paula reminded herself, it was Marlisa's desperation that would eventually relieve her of most of her share of the company. But even though Paula knew she would benefit from Marlisa's obsession, it was still hard to watch.

"Ok," Paula continued, "did you toss papers around Callie's office and leave her door open?"

"Yeah, now what?"

"Now I made sure Michael is on his way. I told him what we talked about and what we agreed on."

"What did we agree on?"

Paula sighed deeply again. You would think Marlisa just learned English yesterday.

"That you're gonna kill yourself and that he's the only one you'll talk to."

"I never agreed to that!"

"Why do you think I gave you the sleeping pills? Don't go to 'nutville' now! You know you agreed that I could tell him any story, including suicide, if it would make him come to you!"

"I never actually said yes to that because I don't want him to think that I'm crazy!"

"But you *are* crazy! You standing there in an empty office whispering in a cell phone scheming to get you sister's husband! That makes you crazy as hell, girl!"

"But I don't want him to be with me because he feels sorry for me."

221

"You want him to be with you because he loves you, right?"

"Right."

"Well, that ain't gonna happen," Paula said impatiently. "He doesn't love you, but if you want to have a chance with him without Callie interfering, then you need to listen to me! Or we can just forget about the entire plan if you want to."

"Then you can just forget about your extra five percent and everything else because I'll tell Callie everything when she gets here today!"

"Fine! You know what? You do what you need to do! And I hope Callie and Michael live happily ever after! Bye!"

"Wait! Okay, okay! I'll go along with it," Marlisa reluctantly agreed. "But just for the record, I would never kill myself."

"You're never gonna need to as long as you have people lining up to do it for you."

"I'm not kidding Paula. I don't want anybody thinking that I would kill myself because I wouldn't!"

Who cares? Paula thought to herself and for the third time let out an exasperating sigh.

"I know you wouldn't, but this is the only reason I could think of to get Michael over there quickly and without running it by Callie first."

"I know but – Oh, here she comes! Here she comes! I gotta go!"

"Remember to put your phone on vibrate! I'll call you later! Bye!"

Now Marlisa stood watching with her eyes darting from the light under Callie's closed door, to the doors of the elevator. She needed to make sure Michael didn't notice that Callie was in her office and it was important that Callie didn't come out until after the drama began. Timing was everything, but since she could see Michael exiting the elevator, she would soon know how this would all play out.

Marlisa could feel her heart racing as she ran to turn on her desk light and uncap the bottle of sleeping pills. She sat on the floor beside her desk and poured the pills out on the floor in front of her just as

Michael came barging into the room.

"What are you doing?" Michael said rushing over to Marlisa. He grabbed her by the wrist and yanked her up to her feet. "Did you take anything?" he asked, examining her eyes.

"Why are you here?"

"Paula called me," he said, looking at the few pills left on the floor.

"Did you take anything?" he repeated.

"Oh, so you come when Paula calls. You talk to her. But me, you can't seem to remember that I'm alive. So why be alive, Michael?"

"Now you're just talking crazy."

"Am I, Michael? You know that I love you!" Marlisa screamed, "But somehow you just magically forget that or remember it when it suits your needs!"

"Marlisa, I'm calling 911," he said, reaching for the phone.

Marlisa grabbed the phone from the desk and threw it up against the wall. She knew she was supposed to make a scene to draw Callie to her office, but Marlisa had already forgotten about her sister. She was no longer acting out for the sake of the plan. She really wanted answers from Michael. She couldn't believe how he was treating her when all she ever did was love him.

"You just tossed me aside without a word. How could you do that? You were always there for me and then all of a sudden you're gone. *You won't even talk to me*! I've given up everything for you and you won't even talk to me!"

"What have you given up for me, Marlisa?"

"Everything! My sister! My family!"

"I never asked you to do that! You did exactly what you wanted to do! I never asked you for anything!"

"But you knew – no, you *know* that I love you! You used me because you knew I would do anything for you! You took me to bed and then you threw me away!"

"Marlisa, that's a lie and you know it! What happened between us was a mistake, one that I don't intend to repeat or to maintain. But it

223

doesn't matter anyway! I'm sorry, Marlisa, but you're a big girl and you should be able to take care of yourself. I need to piece together my own life and in my life, my wife comes first!"

"Oh, so there's no room for me? Not even as a friend?" Marlisa said with so much hurt that Michael softened just for a moment.

"No, Marlisa. I'm sorry, but I only have room for my wife. I love my wife."

"But you said that you could love me too, remember?" Marlisa said weakly. She walked up to Michael and tried to put her arms around him. "That day when we made love you said you thought you could love me."

"I didn't mean like that, Marlisa," Michael said, pushing her arms away from him.

"There's no other way you could have meant it!" Marlisa began to pound on Michael's chest yelling, "I told you I loved you and you took me to bed! I told you I loved you even before you married Callie and you acted liked we had a chance!"

"I never encouraged you!" Michael said, deflecting her blows.

"You never said no, Michael! Why didn't you say 'go away Marlisa? We can't be together?'" Marlisa shouted while still flailing her arms and hitting Michael anywhere she could.

"To avoid this!"

"You never pushed me away!"

"Well, I'm doing it now!"

"Then why did you take me to bed!" she screamed. Michael grabbed her tightly by the wrists to stop her attack.

"Because you were there!"

"You bastard!" The voice came from behind them.

Michael and Marlisa both turned to see Callie standing in the doorway. Her hair was in a curly upswept hairdo and her make-up was flawless. She was dressed for opening night in a beautiful low cut white silk gown and as Michael looked at her he thought she looked like a goddess. Just for a moment the only thing he could think of was how beautiful she looked. But then he saw the pain and the anger in her eyes, a look that had become so familiar over the many months since they split up. He let go of Marlisa and walked towards Callie.

"I didn't mean it the way it sounded," he said.

"Oh, I think you meant it exactly like it sounded. You went to bed with her because she was there. Because you *could*. She's in love with you and you've known since before we were married. You and Marlisa had this …this…secret relationship all these years and now you want to end it. Did I miss anything? Am I finally caught up to speed now? Because apparently I missed a whole lot of stuff going on right under my nose."

"We didn't have any secret relationship. It wasn't like that."

"Then tell me how it was, Michael! You knew she was in love with you and wanted you for herself, yet you allowed me to remain in the dark while you two played this little game. That's a *secret*, Michael! You knew and I didn't!"

"It wasn't important. Otherwise I would have told you."

"Like you told me about your affair? Oh wait, it seems that I found out about that on my own. Well, *practically* on my own since Marlisa, insisting on helping out her poor, trusting, ignorant sister, set me up to walk in on you two!"

"Callie, I only tried-" Marlisa began.

"Shut up or I swear to God I'll kill you this time!" Callie screamed glaring at Marlisa who took a step backwards and unconsciously touched her hand to her throat. Satisfied by Marlisa's silence, Callie turned her attention back on Michael.

"How long have you two been getting together behind my back? Since before we were married?"

"It only happened once," Michael responded.

"Once and she's in love with you? For twenty years she's been in love with you, but nothing at all happened until last year? Is that what I'm supposed to believe?"

"Yes, and that's the truth! *It only happened once!* Callie I'm in

225

love with *you!*"

"And *she's* in love with *you*! And all this time she's been hanging around, you want me to believe that you never did *anything* to make her think you two had something going on? Never gave her any indication at all that you two had a relationship, maybe even a future?"

"Callie, *I swear* I never led her to believe we could be anything but friends and in-laws. We never even *talked* about anything else."

"Then *why* did you sleep with her? *Why* is she in love with you? And *why* is she standing here begging you to take her back?"

Callie turned and walked down the hall towards her office. By the time she reached the receptionist's desk Michael had caught up with her. Grabbing her arm turned her to face him.

"In answer to your questions: *first*, I don't know exactly why I slept with her, but I've regretted it for every second since! *Second*, I have no idea what's going on in your sister's head. I'm only here because I received a phone call that she was going to kill herself! And finally, whatever relationship she thinks we had or will have has only been in her sick imagination!"

Just then the doors to the elevator opened and Michael and Callie both turned to see who would step off of it. Marlisa had quietly joined them from her office and all three stood staring at Stephen, who was startled by his audience.

"Oh, hey. I ...um... hope I'm not interrupting anything. I just came to pick up Callie. Remember, Callie? You asked for a car to be sent and I thought I would just come along."

Stephen, clearly feeling uncomfortable with the three still staring, reached out and pushed the elevator button. "But I can just ...uh...go and wait in the car."

"No, I'm coming. I just have to get my purse," Callie said to Stephen, trying to regain her composure.

"I'll get it. It's in the office, right?"

Callie nodded and watched Stephen walk down the hall, then she turned back to look at Michael.

226

"I just don't know what to believe anymore," she said tearing up.

"If you've never believed any other words I've ever said, please believe this; I love you and no one else. My heart has always been with you."

"Really, Michael? Even when you were having sex with my sister?"

"It was just the one time and, regardless of how she's acting, it didn't mean anything."

Callie's eyes flared again. "And you think that makes you *better* than her? No, Michael, it doesn't! It makes you *worse*! At least she betrayed me because you meant something to her. She's in love with you, for *God's sake!* And she was, and still is, obviously prepared to give up everything, including her pride, if it means she can be with you!

"And why did you betray me, Michael? What earth shattering reason do you have for doing what you did to our family? You dogged me out so that you could have *meaningless sex with my sister* and there's not another God damn reason why!"

"Are we gonna have to argue about this for the rest of our lives?" Michael said and sighed deeply. He threw up his hands in exasperation before putting them on his hips. "Will this ever be over?"

"Yeah," Callie looked at Michael and began backing away from him. "It's over right now."

She walked over to where Stephen now stood and stepped onto the waiting elevator. When the doors closed she closed her eyes and then felt Stephen's arm gently embrace her shoulders. She opened her eyes and sadly looked up at him.

"I can't cry," she said in a shaky, weak voice. "I have to sing tonight."

Marlisa walked over to Michael, who sat slumped on the edge of the reception's desk, and put a hand on his shoulders in an attempt to comfort him.

227

"It'll be ok," she said, rubbing his shoulder and back, "We'll get through this. We'll get through it together."

Michael, looking down at the carpet, shook his head from side to side. Smiling wryly he chuckled in complete disbelief.

"What?" Marlisa asked innocently, her lips curving in the beginning of a smile.

Michael grabbed her hand from his shoulder and then looked Marlisa in her eyes and held her gaze.

"There's something you need to know. No matter what happens between Callie and me, I want to be clear on this, no mix ups or misunderstandings."

"What?" she asked again, this time breathless from his nearness.

Michael leaned in towards her and she felt her heart flutter. He was close enough to kiss and she felt weak in anticipation as she stared in his eyes.

"I...don't...want... you," he said and then stood, walked to the elevator and got on without a backwards glance.

Marlisa watched Michael walk away from her and blinked back the sting of tears in her eyes. His words echoed in her ears and were so painful she found it difficult to breathe. Closing her eyes she took deep breaths, filling her lungs before slowly exhaling. Feeling calm and in control again, she opened her eyes and stared at the closed doors of the elevator.

"It worked," she whispered.

CHAPTER 27

Callie sat in the dressing room listening to Stephen's animated ramblings of the success of opening night. The show had been great, the food had been great and he was sure the reviews from the critics he invited would also be great. He was so focused on the activities of the night, he barely noticed that both Callie and Alise were lost in their own thoughts, which had nothing to do with the restaurant. It wasn't until Marvin stood in the doorway with one long stemmed rose and a note that Stephen quieted.

"For the star," he said and held out the rose and note towards Callie.

Callie managed a small smile and got up and reached for them.

"From Michael," he added.

Callie stopped short but then gingerly took them out of Marvin's hand. Hesitating only for a moment, she dropped them into a nearby trashcan.

"I need a drink," she said, walking back towards the dressing room doorway where Marvin still stood.

"You coming?" she looked at Alise and then Stephen.

"You ok, Callie?" Alise asked as if seeing her sister for the first time that night.

"Funny, I was going to ask you the same thing," Callie said looking at Alise, who diverted her eyes to the wall behind Callie.

She couldn't tell her what was going on with Paula and her blackmail scheme, or that she was stealing the company Callie had

229

worked so hard to build. She couldn't let Paula get away with what she was doing, but she had to admit she was backed into a corner that she didn't know how to get out of right now.

"I just have a few things to sort out, that's all," Alise said. "But you know what? Drinking probably won't help, but on the other hand I can't see how it'll hurt. I'm in."

Alise got up and joined Callie at the door where they both stood looking at Stephen.

"Didn't even have to ask," Stephen said smiling.

"Well, nobody asked me!" Marvin said.

Callie and Alise laughed. "You know you're always welcome!"

"I wouldn't drink with ya'll now even if you begged me. Besides, I gotta go. You do realize it's goin' on three in the morning, don't you?"

"Well, we're getting ready to partake in one of the fringe benefits of owning your own place – there is no last call," Alise said and then walked past Marvin down the narrow hallway towards the front bar.

Marvin kissed Callie's cheek, shook Stephen's hand and then yelled goodnight to Alise who was still walking down the hall. Alise, without looking back or slowing down, waved her hand high in the air signaling good-bye. After Marvin left out the back entrance, Stephen turned to Callie and looked at her contritely.

"I just realized I've been kind of a jerk. After what happened with you and Michael, I really should have been more sensitive. Here I am yammering on about how great business is going as if that was the only thing that mattered, and all the while you're hurting. I put it out of my mind to focus on tonight, but I didn't forget about your feelings. I'm really sorry about everything that's happened. You certainly didn't deserve it."

Callie smiled, suddenly realizing she could tell when he was being honest just by the thickness of his southern accent. When he was being guarded you could barely hear it and that was when he was thinking as a businessman. Totally out for his own profit, and that meant everything he said was tied to his personal agenda.

Then there were the times when he poured it on so thick that Callie knew without listening to the exact words that everything he said should be taken with a grain of salt. His main goal was to be extremely charming, as if the accent alone made him irresistible. And Callie had to admit, he could be *very* charismatic when he wanted to and the accent didn't hurt, either.

However, there were times, like now, when he didn't speak with a practiced voice or with the intention of delighting his audience. That was when Callie knew he was speaking solely from the heart. He was being sincere and suddenly she felt touched by his sweetness.

"Apology accepted and completely unnecessary."

They stood in silence together in the narrow hallway until Alise yelled for them from the front.

"I believe she's started without us," Stephen said laughing.

"Don't worry, I can catch up."

Callie walked quickly ahead of Stephen and joined Alise at a booth in the corner. She had lit the candle, which sat in the middle of the table and had brought over several bottles of a variety of alcohol.

"Oh, I see you're serious about this!" Callie said sitting down and sliding to the middle of the booth in order to make room for Stephen.

"Well, this is a celebration, isn't it?" Stephen asked.

"I suppose it is," Alise said lifting a full glass to her lips and taking a sip before adding, "Putting this together took a lot of hard work and money."

"Yeah, I suppose it is, too. A celebration of one big happy partnership," Callie said eyeing both Stephen and Alise. "Wouldn't you guys agree?"

"Ok, you can stop shooting daggers at me with your eyes now," Stephen told Callie.

"Those are her high beams," Alise said taking another sip from her glass. Callie shot a look at Alise.

"Don't you be high beaming me, girl!"

231

"She knows about our arrangement and the little set up we did to pull the wool over her eyes."

"Oh, look how late it is! I gotta go!" Alise grabbed her purse and stood to leave.

"Alise!" Stephen and Callie both said at the same time.

"Might as well face the music, Alise. I already have. A word of advice, it's best to keep all glasses of liquid out of her hands."

Callie rolled her eyes, but couldn't help but laugh as Stephen relayed the story of their fight to Alise. Soon all three were laughing and having a good time. The conversation flowed easily as Alise and Callie shared their own childhood fights and adventures growing up, while Stephen listened eagerly adding his own brand of wit with frequent comments. The time went by quickly and when Alise looked at her watch, she was surprised that it was now nearly five am.

"Oh, my goodness, I've got to go! For real this time! I have to be here for the lunch crew!" She exclaimed gathering her things.

"Where are my keys?"

"Whoa, slow down," Stephen said pulling his cell phone from his pocket, "you're not driving anywhere. My driver will take you home. He's in the parking garage waiting. I'll call him."

"You mean to tell me you let that man sit there all evening just waiting on you to call him? That's messed up!" Callie said with a lopsided grin.

"No, that's his job. All he does is drive, and not even that much since I like to drive myself."

"That's still messed up."

"He's compensated very well, believe me," Stephen said dialing the phone.

"Ok, big money grip!" Alise said grinning.

"What did you call me?"

Alise and Callie both laughed as Stephen spoke briefly into the phone.

"I think it's time we *all* call it a night," Stephen said rising. "You

232

two wait out front and I'll lock up."

He picked up his bottle of beer that was still half full. He had enjoyed himself but only had the one beer. He had wanted to keep an eye on both Callie and Alise, who were both clearly drinking to forget. They were trying to ease some kind of pain, something he knew a little about.

He had spent a lot of time with his hand around a bottle trying to forget that he was never going to be good enough in the eyes of his parents. Neither one of them seemed to want him while he was growing up and once he was grown, his father didn't believe he had what it took to take over the business. He should be thankful that his father had so little confidence in him since that was still the driving force behind his every move in business. He was determined not to fail and with each successful venture, it was like putting another nail in dear old Dad's coffin.

Stephen thought about how Callie had held it together all night. She was now eager to forget her emotional hurt, but he wasn't quite sure what was going on with Alise. This should be one of the happiest days of her life, having her dream realized, but her happiness was muted by something she wasn't ready to share.

Callie stopped before stepping out the door and looked at Stephen and Alise.

"Wait, I have to do something," she said and walked slowly down the hall towards the dressing room.

Alise and Stephen looked at each other and Alise shrugged her shoulders before walking out the door to the waiting car. Stephen quickly cleaned up the table where they had sat, but he kept glancing in the direction of the hallway for Callie's reappearance. He was still quite concerned for her.

Callie stepped into the dressing room and stood over the small trashcan. She reached down and took out the rose and the note, keeping watch that no one had followed her. She held the note, trying to decide whether to throw it back in or to read it. In the end she

233

thought she would decide later and stuffed it in her small purse. Holding the rose, she broke off the long stem and stuffed it in her purse, also. Then turning off the light, she hurried back down the hallway feeling foolish.

She didn't want to know what the note said or to keep the rose, but at the same time she needed to have the items. It was as though she couldn't help herself, but she didn't want anyone to know how weak she was when it came to Michael. She should have already walked away from him, but each time she took even one step away, it seemed too painful to take another and so she retreated.

She rushed back down to the entrance to where Stephan stood waiting for her. He let her out and, after locking the door behind him, joined Alise and Callie in the Escalade. Alise had made a drink from the bar and was sipping it slowly when Stephen got in.

"Well, hell don't look at me like that Stevie-boy, I'm not driving."

"You're gonna pay for that in the morning," he said.

"News flash, it's already morning, so what's one more drink gonna do?"

"You have no idea how many times I've said those exact words," he told her grinning.

Alise continued to sip on her drink and talk about anything and everything that popped in her head. Finally, the car rolled up in front of her house.

"Ok, this is me," she said attempting to get out of the car.

"Make sure you take some Excedrin before you go to sleep to fight off that headache you're gonna have," Callie said.

"Girl, I know the drill. I prob'ly taught you," Alise replied, pushing herself off the seat.

Stephen jumped out his side and helped her out of the car and up the walkway. When she was safely inside the house, he returned to the car where the silence was deafening since Alise was no longer there with her loud and lively conversation. As the car pulled away, Callie sat in deep thought, clutching her purse tightly to her chest.

"You must be exhausted," Stephen said while watching her. "You'll be home in no time."

"I don't want to go home. Not tonight."

"Well, where do you want to go?"

"I want to go home with you."

"Well, I ….don't know…..I mean I'm staying in a hotel."

"Then that's where I want to go. I can't go home. Michael is there."

"How do you know? What's he doing there?"

"I don't mean physically. I mean, no matter where I am in the house it feels like he's about to walk into the room at any moment. I can even smell him. I know it sounds crazy but I …," Callie began to get upset again.

"No, no, no. You don't sound crazy. I know what you mean. Listen, I have a very large suite that I'd be happy to share tonight."

Callie gave a small smile and looked out the window as they drove along.

"You're not gonna try to take advantage of me are you?" she asked, still looking out of the window.

"Well, why else would I invite a drunk woman back to my room?"

Callie smiled broadly and stole a quick look at Stephen.

"I'm not drunk. I'm just a little tipsy. But I'm not so tipsy that I can't put you in a sleeper hold. That's a wrestling move, you know."

"Oooh, I *love* wrestling. Especially in my hotel room with a *drunk* woman who *thinks* she's tipsy."

"Ok, don't take me seriously, but that was a threat, Stephen. One that I have carried out before," Callie said trying to look serious but only barely managing to suppress her smile.

"A threat, really? I thought inviting me to wrestle was just your way of getting me all excited. 'Cause I was about to let you know you really didn't have to work that hard."

Stephen sat across from Callie and grinned, "I'm easy," he added.

Callie couldn't help but laugh as she looked at him. There was that

235

smile that could always get Callie so flustered that she would become too embarrassed to look at him. But tonight she didn't turn away. Instead, she moved to the seat next to him and took his hand.

"You're very sweet."

He put his arm around her and pulled her close.

"Actually," he whispered into her hair, "I'm extremely sweet. Not to mention an all around fantastic guy."

Callie laughed and then they rode in silence until they reached his hotel.

CHAPTER 28

Callie stretched across the big bed and opened her eyes. That was not her ceiling. She quickly looked at the clock on the nightstand next to the bed. That was not her clock. She sat up suddenly and looked around the room. Of course, this was not her bedroom. She fluffed the pillows and slowly leaned back against them. She was in Stephen's hotel room and it was nearly one o'clock in the afternoon.

Callie got up from the bed to get her purse that was sitting on the chair next to the window. She took out her cell phone and dialed her home number. Vanessa answered on the third ring.

"Mom, where are you?"

"Everything ok there?"

"Yeah, everything's ok here. Where are you?"

"I just had something to do, that's all. I'll be home soon. If you need anything before I get home, call your father. Ok,bye."

Callie hung up before Vanessa could finish giving her the third degree. She knew her daughter meant well, but right now she didn't want to talk and she liked the freedom this disappearing act had given her. Callie looked down at the clothes she had slept in. She vaguely recognized the large tee shirt that belonged to Stephen. The dress she had worn the night before lay across the chaise lounge in the corner of room. Callie gently stroked the shirt she wore while piecing together the details of the previous night. Stephen had practically carried her into the bedroom and helped her lay down on the bed.

"We gotta get you out of that dress," he said standing next to the bed.

"I thought you weren't gonna take advantage of me."

"It's tempting," Stephen said smiling and looking down at Callie, "but I'm a man of my word. What I meant to say was, let's get you something more comfortable to sleep in."

He walked to the armoire, opened a drawer and grabbed a plain white tee shirt.

"One hundred percent cotton," he said shaking it out and walking back to the bed where Callie was now sitting.

"The bathroom's in there. I'll have the front desk bring up some toiletries for you, so you should have everything you need."

Stephen handed her the shirt and pointed out the bedroom door. "I'll be out there if you need anything else right now."

"I do need something else," Callie said smiling and standing up from the bed.

"Can you unzip me?"

"Oh…okay," Stephen said hesitantly as Callie turned her back to him.

Slowly he unzipped her dress, taking note of how tantalizingly low the zipper went. Quickly, Stephen turned and stepped away from Callie, announcing once again that he would be in the other room if she needed anything.

"I need something else, Stephen," Callie said softly. Stephen turned around and a small sigh escaped his lips. Callie was standing in black, hip hugging, tiny, lacy underwear and a matching bra, which barely covered her ample breast. Still wearing her high heels, she stood smiling at him wearing a matching black garter belt to holdup her silk stocking.

She stepped close to Stephen and before he could react she was kissing him. She felt his arms go around her as he passionately returned the kiss. Feeling the softness of his lips and the warmth of his tongue made her tingle as she caressed his chest and began unbuttoning his shirt. A soft groan escaped his lips before he gently pushed her away.

"No, no, no not like this," he said breathlessly, taking a step back.

"Not like what?" Callie asked. The straps had fallen from her lacy bra, completely baring her shoulders. Even though her hair was a bit disheveled and her lipstick had been kissed off, Stephen had never seen her look sexier. She was now looking at him with such innocent round eyes that Stephen, feeling more drawn to her, had to turn away.

"Like this," he gestured around the room. "You're here because you're running away from facing Michael. You've been drinking to forget him and to forget the hurt. The last thing I want to do is make things worse."

"Stephen," Callie whispered, taking a step towards him.

"Listen Callie, I'm you're friend first. And although you are a beautiful, sexy and desirable woman, tonight is not the night. When we.....if we ever go further than friends, I want to make sure it's because you see me. I don't want to feel like it's about being with anybody except Michael. You have to want me as much as I want you. I want us to be special. No regrets. I care about you too much"

Stephen kissed her on the forehead and walked to the bedroom door.

"I never thought I would be throwing myself at you tonight," Callie said sitting back down on the bed.

Stephen turned and leaned against the doorjamb. "And I never thought I would be turning you down tonight," he replied smiling at Callie.

"I have to admit that was the sweetest, most romantic turn down a girl could ever hope for. You're quite the gentleman, Stephen Russell." Callie bent down to pick up the tee shirt that had somehow ended up on the floor.

"Gentleman my ass, girl," he said grinning, "you better lock this door."

He winked at her before closing the door behind him.

239

Callie sat smiling as she thought about Stephen and the events of the previous night. He could always make her smile no matter what the situation. She opened her small purse to put her cell phone back when she noticed Michael's note. She could smell the scent of the rose, whose petals had all fallen off and were crushed inside the bottom of her purse.

Callie slowly took the note out and read it. Then she re-read it, hearing the melody that went to the words she had written for Michael so very long ago. They were the words she had sang to him on the night he asked her to marry him. And now, apparently he wanted to remind her that those words still mattered to him.

You and I, we've been written across the sky
We've been lifted up in glory
That's not the end of our story
Oh, no we're just beginning
There'll be a happy ending
Because you and I, we've become one
Thank you for loving me so much

At the end of the verse he had added his own words.

You are my soul mate. You are my love. You are my life.
Love Always, Michael

Callie sat in the chair and looked out the window thinking about Michael. She didn't know how to face him. Did he lie when he said that he was with Marlisa just the one time? And did that one time do so much damage that they couldn't rebuild their relationship? It had seemed that he was being completely honest when he asked for her forgiveness. Callie had to admit she had been close to forgiving him just two days ago. She knew it would have been easier for her if it wasn't her sister that he cheated with, but she also knew that no matter who it was, trusting him again wouldn't be easy.

But now, Callie had something more to think about. Did he lie to Marlisa and lead her to believe that they had something special? If so, that meant things were worse than she imagined. If he purposely misled Marlisa, then she had no idea who she was married to. The man she knew would have never toyed with Marlisa's feelings like that, but then again the man she knew would have never slept with her, either. However, there's still a difference in a one-time lapse in judgment as opposed to years of deceit.

The most incredible thing was that Marlisa had been after her husband since before they were married and she had had no idea! Her little sister that she had loved and adored had wanted her husband since the very beginning. And Michael knew! But did he ever have another weak moment?

Callie thought she would have sensed it, sensed that something was wrong. But shouldn't she have sensed what her sister was up to? It was too confusing and right now she just needed to think or rather *not* think. What she needed was food.

Callie jumped up from her chair and went to the bedroom door. She grabbed the doorknob, ready to swing open the door when she looked down at her outfit. The shirt was not long enough to comfortably cover her, not to mention the thinness of the material. Callie suddenly felt a little too modest to speak with Stephen about room service dressed only in his shirt. She smiled to herself thinking it was a little too late to feel embarrassed after last night. Nevertheless, she went to the closet and found his bathrobe to put on.

Just as she opened the door, Stephen was approaching with an armload of boxes.

"Hey, sleepyhead! I come bearing gifts."

He held out the packages to Callie.

"I realized you probably didn't want to go home in an evening gown, so I picked up a few things for you at the boutique downstairs,"

"The boutique? Oh, I'm impressed," Callie said, accepting the gifts.

"I guessed at your size. I hope you don't mind."

"Only if you picked large," Callie murmured, laying the packages on the bed. She opened them one by one by to examine the outfits.

He had chosen several sweaters and two pairs of jeans and they were all the right size.

"You're the first man I ever met that knew a little something about clothing sizes for a women. And you did pretty good."

Callie looked at him and smiled broadly. "Thanks. I'm impressed for the second time"

"Ok, I can't take this pressure," Stephen said.

"What?" Callie laughed. "What are you talking about?"

"Don't be so impressed. I looked at the inside of your gown 'cause I didn't have a clue. Then the lady downstairs helped me."

"Wait a minute. That means you had to come in here while I was sleeping to get to my gown." Callie eyed Stephen suspiciously. "You watched me sleeping didn't you?"

"No I -"

"You gotta little freak in you, don't you?" Callie asked teasingly, slowly walking towards him. Stephen began to walk backwards towards the bedroom door.

"A little freaky-freak don't hurt nobody," Callie said smiling, still walking towards him. "I kinda *like that*."

"Are you trying to take advantage of me?" Stephen asked stopping in the doorway.

"Maybe I am, cowboy," Callie said seductively.

"Well, I'm tired of fighting you," Stephen looked at Callie and sighed dishearteningly. "You've worn me down."

Callie put her hand on his chest and pushed him backwards.

"Get out," she said laughing and shut the door.

"You say get out now," Stephen yelled through the door, "but

242

you're gonna want me tonight, baby!"

Callie chuckled as she walked towards the bathroom to take a shower. She shook her head from side to side, grinning and still thinking of Stephen as she turned on the shower. He really could bring a smile to her face.

CHAPTER 29

After dressing and eating the room service meal Stephan had ordered for them, Callie quickly gathered her things from the bedroom to meet Stephen at the elevator. It was late afternoon and she had to get her hair and make up done for tonight's show. She was booked from Friday to Sunday night, and then Alise was bringing in other local talent. Hopefully, in the not so distant future, they would be able to bring in national musical acts, but for now they had to be careful with the money just to get in the "black".

Callie rushed to the elevator and gave Stephen the armload she was carrying, consisting mostly of the new clothes he had just purchased for her.

"Oh, I forgot my gown," she said just as the door to the room slammed shut behind her. Stephen fished in his pocket for the room key and handed it to Callie.

"Why don't you go on," she said as the elevator doors opened. "I'll meet you downstairs."

"You want to embarrass me for as long as you can, don't you?" Stephen stood wearily holding her things. "You sure you don't want me to hold your purse, too?"

Callie put her hands on her hips and watched Stephen step into the elevator. She stood waiting to make eye contact with him but he never turned around. He just stood facing the back of the elevator and sighing loudly as the doors closed.

"That man is going to drive me nuts," she whispered to herself before giving in to the small smile that tugged at her lips. Then returning to the room door, she inserted the key and entered the large suite again.

Callie retrieved her gown, grabbed an apple from the fruit basket on the hall entrance table and went out the door to wait patiently for the elevator again. She had no idea that at the other end of the hall Paula stood watching her.

It was no accident that she had taken a room on the same floor as Stephen. Paula always followed the money, and since he had an interest in her sister's venture he could prove to be useful. A chance meeting in the elevator, a nightcap in the bar, frequent dinner companions and soon bed. Once they had that type of intimate relationship, Paula knew she would be in control. Manipulation was an art that Paula had mastered long ago.

But what was Callie doing coming out of Stephen's room carrying the outfit she wore last night? Paula knew Callie didn't make it home last night since she had received a call from Vanessa asking about her mother's whereabouts. She also knew, and in great detail since Marlisa had immediately filled her in, about the fight with Michael. But did Callie turn to Stephen?

Paula shrugged her shoulders and searched her bag for her own key as Callie stepped onto the elevator. She had no doubt that she would get what she wanted with Stephen, Callie's involvement just made it more interesting. Besides, this little tidbit of information would definitely come in handy.

Quickly she let herself into her hotel room and tossed her purse on the loveseat. A gift had just fallen into her lap. As Paula sat dialing the phone, she smiled and acknowledged she was indeed a genius.

"Hi, Michael. This is Paula," she said when he answered.

"Hey, Paula. What's up?"

"Well, I was just a little concerned for my sisters. This new

245

development has begun to take its toll on everyone."

"Yeah, it seems that way. Is Marlisa ok?"

"Yeah, I think she's going to be alright. She's going through a lot, but right now I'm worried about Callie. Vanessa called. Did she make it home last night?"

"Make it home? What are you talking about?"

"Vanessa didn't call you?" Paula asked innocently, but with the right amount of alarm in her voice. She had to work at sounding sincere since she was grinning broadly.

"She called me earlier a little concerned, but she called back to say everything was alright." Michael said pensively.

He didn't have any idea of Callie's whereabouts, just as she suspected. Now it was time to give Michael enough information to get him concerned that Callie was ready to move on. As far as Paula knew that may actually be true, but that was beside the point. She wanted to keep their relationship off balance and nothing does that better than the involvement of a third party.

"Well, I'm glad to hear that. I shouldn't be too surprised since this isn't the first disappearing act she has pulled recently. She just went away for the whole weekend with somebody." Paula paused but got no response from the other end. "But it seems like there's no need to worry. So, I guess I'll talk to you later, Michael. Bye."

Hanging up, she then called Marlisa's number. She needed to appease Marlisa until she could secure her place in the company.

"Hello, Marlisa. Guess who Callie was with last night?"

"Who?" she asked anxiously.

This was too easy. She could practically feel another five percent of the company slipping from the sweaty, little palms of Marlisa's desperate hands.

CHAPTER 30

Alise stood looking at herself in the mirror. She had to take a minute to clear her head, so she locked herself in the small bathroom right next to her office and splashed cold water on her face. It was getting more and more difficult to concentrate because of the impossible position she found herself in. Betray her children or betray her sister and best friend. She needed to do something soon to put things back in balance. Right now there was no way she could control where the videos of her children would end up if she shined a light on what Paula was up to, but she couldn't let her take Callie's company, either.

Alise realized she was finding it more and more difficult to even look Callie in the eye nowadays, which is exactly why she was locked in the bathroom. She had heard Callie coming towards her office and she couldn't bear to face her.

Alise grabbed a paper towel and patted her face being careful not to remove her eye make up or lipstick. This was night two of her very own restaurant and it had gotten such great reviews that she had more reservations than she could handle. This type of success was almost unheard of and Alise knew Stephen and his connections had a lot to do with it. It also helped tremendously that the food was delicious and Callie, a celebrity of sorts, was singing. She wanted to expand Callie's dates but she couldn't bring herself to even talk about it with her sister. How could she ask her sister to help build the business that she always dreamed of, while she in turn was helping Paula destroy

Callie's business and Callie's dreams?

"Alise, are you in there?" Callie asked, banging loudly on the door.

Alise, initially startled by Callie's knock steadied herself before answering in the most casual voice she could muster.

"Yeah, Callie. I'll be out in minute."

"What are you doing in there?"

"What, you want a play by play?"

"Ugh, you're so nasty!"

"*Me?* You're the one begging to know what's going on behind a closed bathroom door."

Alise opened the door to see Callie dressed for the night's performance.

"You look good, but I been meaning to ask you – do you even own a dress that don't show your cleavage?"

"No. Do they make dresses like that?" Callie asked innocently.

"I guess not," Alise said. Then staring at Callie's chest she added. "Them things are growing."

Callie chuckled as Alise walked past her and back into the office.

"Look, I'm hungry," Callie said following Alise into the office. "Can you get one of your chef guys to make me something?"

Alise looked at Callie in disbelief.

"Just go to the kitchen and fix yourself a plate. This is your restaurant too."

"I know, but I don't want to be in the kitchen," Callie said making a face. "I might back into something and knock it over or slip with these shoes." Callie lifted her gown to show her expensive high heels.

"You just trying to be a Prima Donna," Alise replied, putting her hands on her hips.

"No, I'm not!" Callie said laughing. "I slipped the last time I went in there."

"Yeah, right."

"No, for real! I just didn't want to-"

"Save it!" Alise held up her palm to Callie to silence her. "I'll get

248

the diva her food."

Alise walked out of the office and returned just a few minutes later. "Mike's gonna bring us a tray. I'm kinda hungry too," she said flopping down on the couch.

"You look tired," Callie said, watching her sister intently.

"I *am* tired. I had a late night remember?" Alise made a face and grinned at Callie.

"No, it's something more than that. You look like you're tired all the way to the *bone*. You've been having sleepless nights again which of course means something's bothering you. What is it? The boys? Or is Terrance acting a fool over the house again?"

"Stop psychoanalyzing me."

"Stop avoiding the question. What's going on with you?"

"Nothing, Callie," Alise stood up and walked behind her desk to sit in the chair. "Just drop it *pleeeeese*."

"Ok, I'll drop it. For now. Mmmmm, the food's here!" Callie sat upright and took her tray. "Thanks, Mike."

"Thank you, Mike," Alise said, taking her tray.

Callie waited until they were alone again before broaching the subject for a second time.

"Just remember Alise, I'm here for you just like you've always been there for me. It seems like you're the only one I can truly trust."

Callie looked at Alise and smiled and Alise wanted to put a dagger in her own heart.

"Well," Callie continued, "except for that little gag you pulled with Stephen about the partnership. That set you back a few points," she said grinning. Alise smiled and they ate in silence for a while each lost in their own thoughts.

"Well, as sisters go," Alise cleared her voice, careful to keep it steady, "you can't trust Marlisa, and she's proven that beyond a shadow of a doubt. She's still trying to get Michael, you know. And you certainly can't trust Paula. She's worse than Marlisa because she doesn't want to take your man she wants to take your *life*, your very

249

soul. She started with taking your father and next she's gonna try to take your business."

"I know. I went from owning half a business to owning one quarter. But at least with you in my corner, I'll still feel like I still own half. I'm just going to have to fight Marlisa and Paula on everything *I* want to do 'cause Paula is going to want to call the shots and Marlisa is just going to side with Paula. They haven't seen each other in years and now they're as thick as thieves."

"Thieves! That's the right word to describe them!"

"Well, I could think of a few more," Callie announced and they both laughed.

"I don't think I should finish this," Callie said dropping her fork and standing up. "I don't want to be too full and bloated before going on tonight. I'll see you later. I have to go warm up."

"Ok, Miss Diva. Just leave your garbage for me to clean up," Alise said teasingly.

"That goes without saying."

Callie lifted her nose in the air and sashayed out of the room.

Alise sat there long after Callie had left contemplating the idea Callie had unknowingly given her. It could work. It wouldn't fix things, but it would halt Paula's march towards a complete take over of the production company without endangering her boys. After that, she would have to figure out a way to completely oust Paula, but at least for the time being, she would have thrown Paula off of her game.

Alise picked up the phone and dialed Paula's cell phone.

"Yes?" Paula answered on the third ring.

"I got a proposition for you."

"Oh, I can hardly wait," Paula said dryly.

"I'll go along with everything for now if you agree to give me an additional two percent."

"And if I don't?"

"Then I'm gonna have to come clean. I'm not like you. I can't do people dirty and then smile in their face. I'm not promising I'll stay

250

quiet forever, but at least I'll feel that I've done what I could to help my sister."

"Oh, so you're trying to help me now?"

"What are you talking about?" Alise asked.

"You just said you want to do what you can to help your sister. I assumed you meant me"

"Meant you? I said *sister* not crazy demon seed. I can see how you might confuse the two since being a sister ain't nothing but a word to you."

Paula chuckled. "Yeah, you got me there."

"You know, if you only used your powers for good instead of evil, you might have been somebody."

"I am somebody, sweetie. I'm part owner of a very successful music production company. And when I'm done, Fortune 500 won't be nothing but a word!"

"Do I get the two percent or not?" Alise asked impatiently.

Paula thought about if for a moment before deciding to agree. Alise must have somehow figured out the one with the controlling interest would get the fifth vote if ever there was tie in major business decisions. She was certain Alise had not spoken with the lawyer to get the details of the paperwork they would all be signing on Monday, but somehow Alise must have figured out her angle. Maybe Alise would even suggest the fifth vote rule herself. Paula realized her baby sister understood her better than she thought. Must be in the blood.

Whether she found out or not was inconsequential. The point was that Alise was just trying to make her a less than equal partner and therefore, making it more difficult to gain control. But what she didn't know was that she already had control. Marlisa's five percent gave her the edge. Paula was sure Alise didn't know that otherwise she would have asked for more than the additional two percent. Paula thought about her choices. Even if she agreed she would still have control at twenty-eight percent compared to Alise's twenty-seven. Paula chucked again to herself. Poor Alise, for such a worthy

251

opponent, she was still always a step behind.

"You know what, Alise? I'm feeling generous. Take the two percent," Paula said smiling.

There's more where that came from, she thought. She was already planning how she would siphon more from Marlisa.

"Fine. I'll call the lawyer and have him change that part in our agreement."

"Go ahead. And by the way-"

Paula heard the click of Alise's hang up and threw her cell phone on the bed. She felt her anger rise at the audacity of Alise to dismiss her like she was not important. However, she calmed quickly by envisioning the look on her sister's face when she found out her plan didn't work.

"Always a step behind, dear sister," Paula said sitting on the bed and tapping her foot in delicious anticipation.

Alise immediately called the lawyer and explained what she and Paula had agreed on. However before hanging up, Alise asked that another separate agreement be drawn up and ready to sign on Monday, too. The lawyer promised everything would be in order and that he wouldn't bring in the new agreement until she requested it.

Alise hung up and clasped her hands nervously together.

This could work, she thought.

For the first time since Paula came to town, Alise felt that she would be able to sleep tonight. It wouldn't be peaceful, but at least it was something.

CHAPTER 31

Callie lingered by the exit door of *Josephine*'s pretending that she wasn't waiting around to talk to Stephen. Alise had quickly left after they closed, but not before ensuring that Stephen and Marvin would be okay locking up without her. She felt guilty for leaving the clean up work to others, but as she explained, she wasn't as young as she used to be. She couldn't handle two late nights in a row. She'd hardly gotten any rest between her previous late night departure and her early morning arrival back to the restaurant. Now she was paying for it, as she could hardly keep her eyes open. After hugging Callie and thanking her for a great performance, she was gone.

Stephen had declined Callie's offer of help, letting her know she was off the hook. For now she was the "talent in the joint" and he told her she should probably go home to get rest, too. Instead of leaving, Callie stood at the door trying to think of an excuse to hang around to be near Stephen. He was getting to her and she had to admit that she liked it.

"Everything ok, Callie?"

"What?"

Callie whirled around and was standing face to face with Stephen.

"You look like something's on your mind. Are you ok?"

"Oh, yeah. I was just thinking."

"About what?"

Callie hesitated and then decided to tell the truth.

"About you."

"*Really*" Stephen raised an eyebrow and smiled. "I knew it wouldn't be long. I saw you looking at my butt tonight."

Jokingly, he turned his back to her and leaning against the door, he looked at her from over his shoulder.

Callie laughed. "You are so full of yourself."

"Oh, yeah? Well, then what *were* you thinking?"

"I was thinking… I was thinking that maybe I was wrong about you. Maybe I can trust you."

Stephen became serious and moved close to Callie. Touching her softly on the chin he tilted her face up to look directly into his eyes. "You can. I wouldn't hurt you, Callie. Or Alise. But especially you."

"Ok," she said wanting to kiss him, but instead she turned to go.

"See you tomorrow," she said softly.

Stephen smiled and waved goodbye as Callie walked slowly out the door.

Callie was surprised to see Michael's Range Rover in her driveway when she arrived home. Immediately, she thought something had happened to one of the kids. Jumping out of her car she ran to the front door frantically searching for her keys. Just as she had given up and was intent on banging on the door, she heard the door of the SUV slam. Turning she saw it was Michael. She had been so focused on getting into the house that she didn't bother to check to see if he was still in his vehicle. She had run right past him.

"Oh, thank God! Is something wrong, Michael? Are the kids ok?"

"Yeah, they're fine."

"Where's Ashley?"

"At home."

Callie pointed back at the house. "She's inside?"

"My home. She's at my home."

Callie turned away from him surprised by how awkward she still felt hearing him call somewhere else home.

"Don't worry," he continued, "Maya and Vanessa are fine too. I checked on them earlier in the evening."

"Well, then. If everybody's ok, what are you doing sitting in the driveway at this hour? How long have you been here?"

Michael sighed deeply and turned away from her. He was too upset to look at her right now.

"Did you sleep with him?"

"Sleep with who?"

"Your new business partner. Did you sleep with him?"

Callie had gone from being alarmed, to being curious and now she was just irritated.

"Did you wait outside my door to ambush me and question me about something that's, frankly, none of your business? I thought something was wrong, Michael! You scared me half to death!"

Michael turned suddenly and quickly walked up close to Callie. "It's a simple question, Callie. Yes or no? Did you sleep with him last night?"

"Last night? Are you spying on me? Is that what you do now? Spying on me, stalking me all over town and then questioning me! You have lost your mind! I don't answer to you! You weren't interested in our proper sleeping arrangements before, why now?"

"Why are you yelling? You don't have to make this a drama for the whole neighborhood to hear!"

"*I'm* making it a drama? You're the one sitting in the car like Darth Vader!"

"I just want to know where we are in this relationship!"

Callie couldn't remember seeing Michael this mad before. But she was mad, too! He had no right to question her, especially like this! Here he was, demanding she soothe his male ego in the middle of the night, after she had worked all evening and just wanted to go to bed.

"Where we are in this relationship is questionable! You expect me to take everything you dish out and just forgive you! It's not that easy!"

"Oh, I already know it's not that easy, with your insecurities and now all of your hoop jumping! Why can't the fact that I love you be enough! I made a mistake and I'm willing to pay for it, but not forever Callie. Not forever!"

"Not forever? This is all your fault! Everything -"

"I already know everything is my fault! It's not like you're ever going to let me forget it, but that's the price I have to pay! And I'm ok with that because I love you! But I need to know if we have a chance! I need to know where we stand! Are you seeing other people? I think I have a right to know!"

"You don't have any rights, Michael! It's not about you now! It's about what's best for me and my girls! You were sneaking behind my back for twenty years-"

"It was not like that. It was *not* like that," Michael said dejectedly. He took a deep breath and willed himself to calm down.

"Look, I didn't come all this way, and sit in my car to wait for you just to have another argument. I just wanted to ask you one question that you apparently don't want to answer."

"I don't have to answer you."

"Because then you'd be in the same boat as me."

"It's not the same!"

"So you slept with him!"

"I said, I don't have to answer you!"

Callie pulled the keys out of her bag, glared at Michael and then pushed past him. Before she could get her key in the lock, Michael had snatched them from her hand. Then grabbing her arm he spun her around to face him. Callie was pressed up against the door as Michael leaned down close to her face.

"Did you fuck him?" he said through clenched teeth.

Callie pushed him back and slapped him across the face with all the force she could gather.

"I am *not* your whore! You don't get to talk to me like that! If you

256

think you can handle me any kind of way, you got the wrong sister!"

Michael, rubbing his face, took a few steps backwards while still eyeing Callie.

"Yeah, maybe I do have the wrong sister."

Dropping her keys, he turned and walk deliberately back to his SUV. Callie grabbed her keys and quickly went into the house, slamming the door behind her.

CHAPTER 32

Callie added the fresh strawberries and ice to the mixed fruit and milk already in the blender and selected 'Frappe' on the setting. Because of her perpetual lack of hunger, she had taken to drinking her breakfast rather than skipping it completely. Arguing with Michael in the dead of night, after a long evening on stage, did nothing to improve her appetite this morning, either.

In any event, she was still proud of how far she had come. Even though she had thought about drinking a glass or two of wine, she was able to easily dismiss the idea. And for the first time in a long time, she didn't cry herself to sleep. She was just too tired and too mad, plus she finally figured out that it didn't do her any good anyway.

However, she still longed for the good old days, when she and Michael would sit in bed early on Sunday mornings and just relax. They both read the paper, hardly talking at all but just enjoying their time together. Callie sighed, thinking about her husband, lover, father of her children and man of her dreams. If only they could turn back the clock. She filled her glass with her homemade smoothie and wondered what he was doing right at that very moment.

Michael rolled over in bed and put a hand over his eyes. He had a terrible headache. Payback for all the drinking he had done the night before. He was too wound up to sleep and he thought the liquor would help him achieve his dreamless night sleep. He didn't count on waking up so early in the morning or that his throbbing headache wouldn't let him slip back into unconsciousness.

He stumbled into the bathroom and after splashing cold water on his face, he brushed his teeth to get the horrible taste out of his mouth. He didn't normally drink and he didn't know how people could put themselves through this punishment over and over again.

Michael went into the kitchen and put on coffee. Hopefully, caffeine would help his headache and allow him to think clearly. He had messed up last night - big time. The problem was, he wasn't ready to admit that to Callie, not just yet. She owed him an explanation first. Here he was, bending over backwards to work on their relationship, while she had other plans.

What do you want, Callie? Michael thought.

If she ever spoke to him again after the way he behaved last night, maybe she'll answer that question. Michael sighed as he grabbed his coffee mug and walked towards the breakfast nook.

"Oh, my God. That is disgusting."

Ashley sat in her pajamas in the breakfast nook with a bowl of cereal looking at Michael with her nose turned up.

"What's disgusting?"

"You! Walking around, especially in the kitchen, without your shirt on!"

Michael looked down at himself and back at Ashley.

"So?"

He was wearing only his pajama bottoms and standing in his bare feet. He still had a flat stomach and a well defined chest and arms from working out on a regular basis. Marlisa was not the only women interested in the status of his split from Callie.

"*So?* I'm sitting here minding my business, eating Cheerios and watching Sponge Bob and then look up to see a half naked man in the kitchen. Now, it would be different if you were a hot, young guy or something, but you're not," Ashley said flatly, taking another spoonful of cereal. "You're my Dad and that makes it kinda disturbing," she said between crunches.

"Why would it be different if it was some hot, young guy? What

259

are you trying to say?"

"I am not gonna have *that* conversation with *you*. Oh, my God," Ashley said rolling her eyes. "I think I'm gonna finish eating in my room."

Ashley grabbed her cereal bowl and pushed past Michael as he shook his head in disbelief.

"The female brain. I don't even understand the young ones," he said aloud. Then, after reminding himself that she was supposed to be like that at sixteen, he grabbed the paper from the kitchen table and walked out the side door into his office.

He was surprised to see the message light flashing on the desk phone. He was positive he had cleared all the messages last night before going to see Callie. Who would have called him between then and now?

He hesitated before pushing the play button. Marlisa had taken to leaving messages on his private home office phone lately since he wouldn't answer her calls from his cell phone. He had also left strict orders at the office to only take messages when she called. She was never to be put through to speak directly with him, not that he had to tell Harriet. His secretary had already instituted that policy on her own.

So now to reach him, she was using his home office phone to leave messages. That's how he was alerted to Callie's whereabouts over the weekend. Vanessa and Paula had called him worried because no one knew why Callie didn't come home. Then Marlisa called to give him the dirty details. He had hoped it wasn't true. It was not like Callie to have everybody worried about her, while she's off playing around with some man. Michael scowled just thinking about it.

Then he turned his attention back to the phone and continued to frown but now in bewilderment. After listening to Marlisa's last phone message about Callie and Stephen, he had blocked all of her numbers. So, who called in the middle of the night on his private office phone?

Michael pushed the play button and braced himself. Marlisa could have used another phone to contact him. He didn't know how much more he could take of this sister drama.

"Uh...Michael...this is Callie. I'm still mad right now, but I wanted to let you know that even though you had no right to question me - I mean it! You had no right at all to try to handle me like you did tonight. But...well, I shouldn't have hit you. You deserved it! So in a way I should have....but...um ....it's no excuse for me getting...well, I'm sorry for slapping you. Everything else stands, though...maybe not the crack about the wrong sister...well, maybe you deserved that, I don't know...jury's still out on that....but I was wrong for hitting you. ...so, I'm sorry.....if it's any consolation, my hand still hurts... I got you good... ok, bye"

Michael stood looking at the phone smiling. She sounded schizophrenic, going from dark anger to apologetic to amusement by the end of the phone message.

She always owned up when she thought she had wronged someone. She always tried to do the right thing. This was not new, this was classic Callie. He checked the time of the call and realized it had come in while he was on his way home last night from their fight. She didn't hesitate to reach out to him.

Michael took a sip of his coffee and smiled again.

God, I love that woman.

CHAPTER 33

Alise paced around her bedroom in anticipation of the day's events. The weekend had gone very well at the restaurant and on that front she was very happy. Ecstatic in fact, but she couldn't afford to savor the opening weekend success. This was Monday morning and if things didn't go as planned to stop Paula from taking over Callie's business, then she would be true to her word. She would spill the whole, completely awful truth to Callie and Marlisa. And she was under no illusion that Paula wouldn't be true to her word and turn over the very damaging tapes of her boys in the mist of their illegal activities to the police.

Well, if it came to that, she would just have to deal with whatever came up and she knew she would have to do it alone. Terrance would be of no help whatsoever. She could never count on him and the boys had given up on needing their father a long time ago. No matter how much they wanted or needed him, he never responded unless there was something in it for him. This whole mess was all Terrance's fault and Alise couldn't wait for the day that she could confront him. But that would have to wait. She didn't need him finding out about the tapes and trying to blackmail her, too.

Alise was hoping that Jamal would just settle down on the west coast once he graduates college. He was toying with the idea because of the various job opportunities. Alise didn't like the idea of him being so far away, but distance might keep him away from the kind of legal trouble he could face in town if those tapes surfaced. The kind of legal trouble that could ruin his adult life before it really started.

Anthony was struggling in school and had been talking about joining the army. Alise had talked him out of it more than once. Now she wondered if that was the right thing to do. With the Iraq war going on, he would probably be sent overseas immediately. She couldn't bear wondering on a daily basis what was happening to her child. But she couldn't let him be arrested on some of the charges she saw on the video. He was beyond petty theft and smoking a little weed. He could be charged with more serious crimes and Alise would not be able to bear that either.

At least the army will teach him how to be a responsible man, something that his father never attempted to do. And something, Alise realized sadly, that she had failed to do. Not because she didn't try, but because as a woman and as a mother, she just didn't know how to show her son how to be a man.

And what about Jackson? What was in his future if he continued to be the teenager she saw on the video? Alise threw her hands up, indicating she didn't have all the answers. No, actually she didn't have *any* of the answers. Not yet anyway. The only thing she knew was that she wasn't going to let the streets get her sons. She wasn't going to let Terrence get them, either. Maybe she could get her hands on the tapes to destroy them. It was a long shot, but it was still possible.

Alise found solace in the fact that as soon as she destroyed all the tapes, she would let loose on Terrance in a way that he has never seen before. Alise promised herself she would not step one foot in the grave until she dealt with him about this. She could only pray that he wouldn't die before she had her say.

She chuckled, realizing how foreign it was to have a prayer for Terrance *not to die* inside her head. She grabbed her purse and sighed deeply. Time to go and do battle with Paula – again.

CHAPTER 34

Marlisa sat behind her desk tapping a pencil and staring into space. She was dreading the upcoming meeting with her sisters, especially Callie. Every time she saw Callie she wanted to do something to get back into her good graces, but all she saw in Callie's eyes was hurt and anger. Callie would never forgive her and why should she? What happened was no mistake or moment of weakness on her part. She wanted Callie to find her and Michael together. She wanted Callie to hate Michael so much that she would leave him.

But she also wanted Callie to forgive her and at some point accept that Michael had moved on. She wanted acceptance for her and Michael as a couple so that the three of them could be friends again. Michael would come around, she was sure of it, but she had to be careful with Callie. She may have lost her sister forever, but even after all this time it was still difficult to deal with that realization.

But she was sure that if Michael had known how much she loved him, he would never have married Callie. He was married to Callie by default. Marlisa didn't believe he read the letter she slipped under his door that night so long ago, professing her love for him.

They had a connection that couldn't be broken by anyone including Callie. He was a good man and she was a patient woman. So she waited. She knew he had wanted to stay faithful to Callie and she admired his devotion. Hopefully, he would be that devoted to her once they were together.

Marlisa knew she was right about everything when things got

difficult in his marriage and he turned to her. He had needed her and she had gladly been there for him. But now things were different and she could no longer wait patiently and quietly. She was willing to do whatever it took to be with Michael. If her sisters didn't know that already, today they would get a glimpse at how far she would go. To align herself with Paula said it all.

Paula. What a piece of work she is turning out to be. But she needed someone like Paula right now to help fight the most important battle of her life – getting Michael. Paula had already let her know what they needed to do to capitalize on Callie and Michael's latest fall out. Callie was interested in Alise's new business partner at the restaurant, so they were going to work that angle with Michael to weaken his confidence. One thing Michael never had to worry about was losing Callie to another man. If he believes that she will be able to move on without him, it could shake up his insecurities. Marlisa knew first hand what could happen if he gets to that point, so she would try to get close to Michael again. Continue to support him as Callie turns away from him. She wondered if Michael had listened to her phone message. Could there be fallout already? She smiled in anticipation.

Marlisa sighed heavily. She was still dreading the meeting. Today, everyone would know she gave up part of the company to Paula and it wouldn't take a genius to figure out it was in exchange for something very valuable to her. And right now it was no secret that the only valuable thing to her was Michael. Callie would hate her even more than she already did - if that was possible. But Marlisa had at some point made a decision. Michael was the love of her life and she was determined to have him. And even though she loved her sister, she loved Michael more. Besides, with everything she has done and was prepared to do, there was no turning back now, even if she wanted to.

CHAPTER 35

Paula pulled into the parking garage and let the motor run a few moments longer in order to hear the end of the song on her CD. It was a classical, instrumental piece that always seemed to soothe her. She never liked to listen to a song with words when she needed to think about things. She had long ago tossed her gospel music - too much hollering. She still had some around for show, being that she was still technically a pastor and all. But all of her sisters could see right through her, so there was no need to pretend. She is who she is. She still loved God but He was just a little slow on the rewards.

Paula turned off the car and checked her make-up in the mirror. Perfect.

What did you expect, Paula? she thought.

Everything was perfect. Today was the day she had been waiting for for quite a while. An equal share of this company was just her fair share and what she deserved. Having control was an added bonus.

Paula got out the car and straightened her skirt. She was dressed in a navy pinstripe suit with a white silk camie. She wanted to look nice on her first day on the job.

Now it was time to face her sisters: Superhero Alise, Heart-broken Callie and Moron Marlisa. Paula walked quickly towards the elevator. She couldn't wait to get the party started.

CHAPTER 36

Callie sat in her car that was still in the driveway. She had backed out of the garage but couldn't seem to find the energy to continue. She was dreading the events of the day. But why should today be any different? Every time she thought she had her life back on track, something would come up just to prove that she was in denial. She fought against crawling under the covers with a bottle of wine. It wouldn't settle any of the problems in her life, even if she was able to forget them for a little while.

Michael hadn't called since their fight and she had to admit she was a little disappointed. It was just as well, since she didn't know if she could bring herself to speak to him, anyway. For one thing, she had too many things to contemplate right now.

She was confused, but even more scared of what she might find out about his relationship with her sister. Right now she couldn't even figure out if she should care. If he led Marlisa on, she knew she couldn't stay married to a man like that. But if it was as he claimed, just the one horrible mistake, then maybe she should forgive him. They could just put everything behind them and start fresh.

Callie sighed deeply and adjusted the rear view mirror. She caught a glimpse of her eyes and turned away.

You can't look at yourself because then you'll have to admit the truth, Callie thought.

Part of the confusion surrounding her relationship with Michael was because of Stephen. She could have ended the confrontation with

Michael if she had just told him the truth. She hadn't cheated on him and slept with Stephen. But she wanted to – does that count? Callie didn't have her relationship with Stephen straight in her mind yet. All she knew was that she liked him; *really* liked him and she couldn't help wondering about him.

Michael had given her a free "sleep with someone else" card that she wasn't quite ready to give up. If she went back to Michael to work on their marriage, she would have to relinquish it. However, if she put off deciding anything *right now…*

Callie couldn't even imagine the new complications that would arise in her life once she opened that door with Stephen. For one thing, Michael would be devastated that she turned to another man. That was more than obvious by his reaction the other night. But the other, bigger problem was that if she slept with Stephen she just might like it – a lot. And then what?

Callie toyed with the idea that what she was feeling was more about payback with Michael than pleasure with Stephen. After all, he deserved to suffer the same way that she had, but Callie knew it was more to it than that. During the entire time she was overwhelmed with the pain of what he had done to her, she had never once thought about being with another man to get back at him. Kill him, yes. Take all his money, yes. Castrate him, yes. Cheat on him – never. She loved him too much and she still does! But every time she thinks of Michael a thought of Stephen is never far behind.

However, a man was the least of her worries today. Today she had to deal with a far more vicious species – sisters. Marlisa and Paula together in one room was more than what any decent human being should ever have to endure. Alise was right when she said the two of them wanted to take everything that's ever made her happy and defined her life. Now, because of them her father is a mystery, her marriage is in turmoil and her business is not hers to run like she did before. How could things get any worse?

Callie slowly backed out of the driveway. Whatever the day brings she'll just accept it for now. She was tired of fighting and feeling confused. She was both mentally and physically exhausted dealing with all the surprises her sisters had sprung on her while trying to keep her life from spinning out of control. Although, she promised herself she would conserve her energy and when the time was right, both Marlisa and Paula were going down.

CHAPTER 37

Alise walked into the conference room and was a little surprised by the festive arrangements. There were colorful balloons tied to the backs of several chairs and confetti scattered across the table. Sitting in the middle of the conference table was a huge chocolate cake that read *Congratulations Partners!* Next to it a bottle of champagne sat chilling in a bucket, alongside four flutes sitting on a silver-serving tray.

Alise surveyed the room and tried to control her emotions. She was teetering between feeling sick enough to throw up and feeling enough rage to choke Paula with her bare hands. It was obvious that no one but Paula was responsible for this fake show, because no one but Paula was even remotely happy about this so-called partnership.

"Alise! Good of you to make it!"

Alise turned to face Paula who was smiling broadly.

"I wouldn't have missed this show for the world," Alise replied dryly.

"I didn't think you would. That extra two percent must have been just the incentive you needed to get your big behind down here."

"My big behind? You know what's big Paula? My foot, which is itching to stomp your lying ass out of our lives."

Paula laughed, "You know Alise, you've always been entertaining. You should be in the movies. Oh, that reminds me, how are the boys?"

Alise eyed Paula and then smiled.

"Your day is coming," she said looking intently at her sister.

"Maybe. But it ain't today, is it?"

"What ain't today?" Marlisa asked walking into the room and taking her place at the far end of the table.

"What's all this?" Callie asked, following Marlisa into the room and looking around in disgust. "Who the hell thinks this is a happy occasion?" she added snatching the closest chair from under the table and plopping down onto the seat.

"This is a good day for all of us. To come together as a family," Paula said, sitting down at the head of the table.

Alise, Callie and Marlisa all rolled their eyes at Paula who smiled before pushing the intercom button on the phone and requesting that the receptionist send in the lawyer. Callie sat and stared at Paula who, after briefly trying to ignore her, turned to meet her gaze.

"You can turn off the high beams, Callie. I get it. You're pissed. This is not what you wanted but it's the best way to handle things."

"Says who?" Marlisa asked.

"Says me," Paula answered.

"You could have done the right thing and just walked away," Marlisa said.

Paula scoffed "I know *you* of all people did not just say that!"

"You know what," Callie said just as the lawyer walked in, "something is wrong here. I can feel it."

"You're right, Callie," Alise agreed and came around the table to sit next to her. Paula shot Alise a look.

"Let's just sign the papers and get everything over with, Alise," Paula said, "that way you can get home to check on your boys. Franklin," she said, looking at the only man in the room, "you can start now."

The lawyer took his cue and began riffling through the documents he held in his hands. He explained the details of each and showed exactly where they should all sign. Once he got to the breakdown of the percentage, Callie stood up.

"I'm not signing this! Marlisa, why did you give up five percent to

271

Paula?"

Marlisa looked at Paula who shrugged.

"Tell her. Don't tell her. Do whatever you want. I really couldn't care less, Marlisa."

"I ....uh.... just thought she could run things just as good as you, that's all."

"Wait a minute, wait a minute," Alise said looking at Marlisa. "You gave up part of your *successful* company in order to put it in the hands of an ex-pastor-"

"Current Pastor," Paula chimed in.

"-who couldn't even run her own church? Who has a string of failures long enough to go around the whole world-"

"Not the world, Alise."

"-twice?"

"Maybe just America, to be honest," Paula said smiling.

"You're really enjoying this, aren't you?" Callie said.

"Just a little. Everybody seems to be fighting the inevitable."

"What's the inevitable? That you and Alise - no offense Alise - have more of my company than I do?" Callie shouted.

"Each one of us has more to lose by not signing the papers!" Paula shouted back and stood up to face Callie. "The inevitable is knowing that and doing what's best for everybody!"

"I'm not signing these papers!" Callie repeated pushing the documents off the table before storming out of the room.

"Alise, you better get your sister!" Paula snapped. She gave Alise a knowing look before kneeling down to hurriedly gather the papers off the floor.

"That day that we were talking about before, is gonna be so sweet that I can almost taste it," Alise said standing up slowly.

"And that day that we were talking before, *ain't today, is it?*"

Alise turned and looked at Marlisa. "Does that five percent have anything to do with Michael?"

Marlisa looked away from both sisters and stared out of one of the

272

large glass windows.

"I thought so," Alise said, before walking out of the room to find Callie.

Alise walked quickly down the long hallway towards Callie's office but decided she had to "let loose" on Marlisa first. How dare she team up with Paula? Turning around, Alise stopped before entering back into the conference room. Looking through the glass double doors, she was witnessing what looked to be a very interesting exchange between Paula and Marlisa.

"What's this?" Paula asked after Marlisa slid a blank envelope in front of her. Marlisa remained silent but just pointed to the envelope and watched Paula carefully. Upon opening the envelope, Paula's shot Marlisa a look of surprise, which she quickly covered with a smile that remained frozen on face.

"I'll ask again. What's this, Marlisa?"

"Looks like an invitation to the grand opening of a church," Marlisa said. She leaned forward and pointed to the picture on the postcard. "You see, that's the new Pastor, which is you and that's-"

"You know what I mean," Paula snapped. "Why are you showing me this?"

"Because I know the good people of North Carolina would be happy to know that their pastor, who scammed them out of their hard earned money, is alive and well."

"You can't prove anything."

Paula leaned back in the chair confidently dismissing Marlisa. However, she nervously fiddled with the hem of her skirt.

"I can prove that you're not dead."

"So what? It was a misunderstanding."

"Misunderstanding? Is that the new word for forgery? Like in the letter where you signed Alise's name?"

"Ok, what do you want?" Paula quickly sat up and slapped her hand on the table. "Because this is clearly not about anything that happened in North Carolina. Do you want the shares to your company

273

back?"

"Maybe later." Marlisa smiled, looking Paula in the eyes. "But for now Paula, I don't care about this company. I don't care about you giving back the money or if you have to go to jail. Right now, the only thing I care about is Michael and you're gonna help me get him, whether you like it or not."

"I'm helping you already."

"Yeah, but after signing the papers today, it's going to be a lot harder to get you out of the business. After all, Callie and I are both voluntarily signing over our shares. I figure once you actually have what *you* want, you might not stay focused on our little deal. But I knew this," she tapped the postcard, "would get and keep your attention."

Paula held Marlisa's gaze and got a chill. She had never seen her sister like this before. Blackmailed by Marlisa? Who would have thought that could happen? Paula was impressed, but she needed to find out just how much Marlisa knew.

"You're blackmailing me?"

"I'm just asking for sisterly advice."

"Well, if you have evidence of a crime and you don't tell, then I'm pretty sure you can get in trouble. I mean, not that you can prove anything. Then again, if you can't prove anything, you really don't have a lot of leverage for blackmailing, do you?"

Marlisa grinned and continued to look directly in Paula's eyes. "I won't have any *firsthand* knowledge of a crime because I decided I wouldn't read the *evidence* that my private investigator digs up. I will honestly be able to answer any questions about your dirty work with 'I don't know'.

Besides, I don't want to know the details of your scam. I don't want to feel so sorry for the people you scammed that I turn you in or something. How does that benefit me? The whole point of blackmailing is to *not* use the information. All I ask is that you stick with our agreement to help keep Callie and Michael apart."

274

"You're doing all of this just to get Michael? You're willing to give up everything for him?"

"I've already given up everything for Michael. The problem is I don't have him, so I've given up everything for nothing. And that's just not going to do."

Paula was surprised by Marlisa's responses. Her little sister was really devious. She couldn't have been more proud.

"Ok." Paula shrugged her shoulders. "Ok, you'll get what you want and I'll get what I want by working on the same team."

"Really?"

Paula was stunned as Marlisa's personality morphed right before her very own eyes. Suddenly, the old Marlisa was back. There was no power behind her eyes anymore. Paula thought that maybe she had imagined it or perhaps Marlisa had just faked a good game. Or *maybe,* old Marlisa was the act. The helpless, clueless damsel in distress has always worked well for her. After all, that's how Michael fell into bed with her.

"You really have your game down, don't you?"

"What?" Marlisa looked at Paula befuddled.

"Quit the act, Marlisa. I've already seen the real you. You just blackmailed me to help steal your sister's husband, remember?"

Marlisa looked at her puzzled and Paula was now puzzled, too. The sharpness and clarity was gone from her eyes. In its place was …well, nothing. Marlisa batted those big, brown cow eyes at Paula, looking at her as if she was trying to remember her own name.

Paula was reminded of an old movie where a mentally handicapped man was given an experimental serum which transformed him into a genius. The problem was the effects of the serum were short term and toxic. Without continued treatment, he went back to being unable to tie his shoes. With continued treatment, he stayed a genius, but he was poisoning himself to a quick death. Unfortunately for Marlisa, Michael, or rather her obsession with Michael was her serum.

"Why are you looking at me like that?" Marlisa asked blinking fast. All she needed was a cowbell.

"Just thinking about a movie," Paula said absent mindedly. "And lunch," she added with a hint of a smile. "Suddenly, I want a hamburger."

However, Marlisa was no longer paying attention to her. She had stiffened and was looking through the glass doors. Following her gaze, Paula saw Alise watching them. Slowly her hand covered the envelope, which still lay on the table, and sliding it towards her, she dropped it into her lap. Then she mouthed the words "go" while pointing in the direction of Callie's office.

Alise backed away and walked slowly down the hallway, knowing she had witnessed something important and hopefully useful. Paula had reacted nervously to whatever was inside the envelope that Marlisa gave her. Clearly Marlisa was in control, which was startling since Marlisa was never in control. Alise would make it her business to find out exactly what was going on between them.

However, right now she had to fix an immediate problem which was to get Callie to cooperate. This would be one of the hardest things she's had to do since Paula came to town.

Alise walked into Callie's office and found her sitting behind her desk checking messages.

"Save your breath, Alise," Callie said without looking up. "I have my limits and apparently I've just reached one with this idiotic agreement."

Alise could see Callie's hands shaking as she busied herself with things on her desk.

"I know you're upset but-"

"I am not upset. I am mad!" Callie stood up and pointed her finger at Alise.

"I am mad that I let this go this far! This is *my* company. *I* worked to make it what it is today! Marlisa is here in name only! Everybody knows she has the business sense of a fruit fly! Hell, even Marlisa knows it! And I am not going to stand by and let her and Paula ruin

276

what I worked for and built up! I'm not going to do it Alise, so you can just save your breath!" Callie flopped herself angrily back down onto her chair.

"No, you know what Alise? Say what you've come to say. That way you can go back and tell them that you tried! But I'm not budging on this! I had it all wrong thinking that other people were responsible for my happiness! My mother, my father, Michael! No, nobody is responsible for what *I* get out of *my* life except for *me*!

"I should have fought back from the beginning instead of just lying down and playing dead because I was so wounded by Michael. Everybody's been controlling my life for me! And what did I do? I just let it happen! Well, that's over now. I'm not taking this any more, so just say what you have to say and leave!"

Alise calmly walked around the desk and sat on the edge of it. She grabbed one of Callie's hands, which was still shaking, and squeezed it.

"I think you should fight," she said quietly looking into Callie's eyes, "I'll be one hundred percent behind you, you know that but…."

"But what?"

"But right now, I just need you to trust me," Alise said feeling guilty even as the words came out of her mouth. She was one of those "people" controlling Callie's life.

"Trust you? What are you talking about, Alise?"

"I need you to sign the papers."

Alise spoke so quietly that Callie had to strain to hear her.

"I thought you said I should fight," Callie replied confused.

"This *is* one way to fight them. I can't explain everything now. I wish I could. But what I can try to do right now is to get you to sign the papers and trust me. Some things will be set right for you today. Other things," Alise let go of Callie's hand and stood up, "other things will be set right later. I promise you that."

Callie, puzzled by Alise's eerily calm demeanor and quiet voice, watched her sister as she walked to the office door and slowly turned to face her.

"But if you decide to fight back now and not sign the papers, I'll understand." And with that comment she was out the door closing it quietly behind her.

Callie rushed around her desk and out of her office catching Alise in the hallway. She blocked her sister's way and stood with hands on her hips.

"Ok, Alise. I don't know what's going on, but I trust you."

Alise hugged her, feeling an overwhelming sense of relief. Then she smiled and grabbed Callie by the arm, pulling her down the hall back towards the conference room.

"Good! Now just follow my lead and we can have some fun with this part!"

"Whoa! Wait a minute," Callie said, pulling away from Alise and stopping.

"What?" Alise asked stopping too.

"You just went from being all down in the dumps and mysterious to being so happy that you're practically jumping out of your skin. What is going on here?"

"I just wanted this to be your decision. I didn't want to talk you into anything. I'm just happy that you're gonna go along with me on this."

Callie looked at Alise and opened her mouth to say something but was cut off by Alise.

"Now don't try to psychoanalyze me or nothing."

"Don't worry, I won't. I already know you're crazy," Callie said walking around Alise and opening the door to the conference room.

"Everything ok?" Paula asked making eye contact with Alise.

"Let's just get on with this," Callie said sitting back in her place.

"Where do I sign?" she asked Franklin, who had just come back into the room.

Paula leaned back in her chair and looked smugly at Alise.

"What a good sister you are, Alise. Always putting other's needs

278

in front of your own."

Alise bristled at the comment knowing that Paula meant it to be sarcastic and cruel.

"Paula, you know most of the problems for the people in this room would be miraculously solved if you were to just...oh, I don't know...disappear."

"Is that a threat? Should I be scared, Alise?" Paula asked leaning towards Alise. "Because if it's a threat," she continued, "then I'd have to have you arrested and what kind of role model would you be for your boys if you wound up in jail?"

Paula looked at Alise in mock sincerity before turning to Franklin and dismissing him.

"Now that the legal stuff is out of the way we can have our first meeting as partners," Paula said. She took out a group of files from her briefcase which sat on the floor beside her chair.

Callie and Marlisa both groaned and squirmed in their chairs at the announcement for a company meeting. Neither of them had had to endure this in the past. Callie made most of the major decisions alone and with Marlisa's blessing.

"Well, I tell you what, let's put this to a vote," Paula said looking around the room. "After all, this is a partnership. All in favor of a meeting right now raise your hand. And remember my vote counts as two in case of a tie."

Paula had thought she would have to coerce Marlisa into voting with her against Callie and Alise, but she was surprised when Alise raised her hand instead.

"Well, well, well. It seems that Alise has something to say," Paula said folding her hands atop the stack of files that lay on the table in front of her.

"Go ahead, Alise, and start the meeting. I can't wait to hear what you've got to say."

Alise pushed the button on the intercom and asked the receptionist to send Franklin back into the conference room.

279

"What kind of grand standing are you up to Alise? The documents are *signed, sealed, delivered*," Paula sang the last part to the tune of the famous Stevie Wonder song and then smirked at Alise.

"Why are you acting so crazy, Paula? You're dressed in a suit and acting a fool. You're supposed to be the oldest sister and somebody that we all look up to. But instead, you're just destroying lives while snapping your fingers singing Stevie Wonder songs. What's *wrong* with you?"

"You know what, you're right, Alise. I'm sorry," Paula said seriously and looked around the room. "I'm just happy that we can all be together and work as a family because –oh, let me stop lying people! I should at least be honest with y'all. I am happy, no *thrilled* that I finally have my piece of the pie. I did this for you too, Alise, even though I know you don't believe me.

"The money used to build this business came from *my* inheritance, too. It came from *my* mother's life insurance money and *my* father, the only father I ever knew, life insurance and savings. It wasn't right that the two of you got everything and I got cut out. It wasn't right that Daddy loved you more than me. There," Paula spat the words, "I said it."

"You make it sound like it's our fault. Like you hate us for it," Marlisa said in a weak childlike voice.

"Maybe it is your fault. And yeah, maybe I do hate you for it," Paula answered dryly.

Alise looked at Callie and Marlisa who were both staring at Paula in disbelief. Alise had heard it all before, but this was new for the two of them. They had all seen their sister go from happiness to hatred in just a few short sentences.

Alise felt somehow relieved that Callie and Marlisa could get a glimpse of the Paula she had known for years. The real Paula had reared her ugly head. Maybe now they could figure out that she would lie to them about their father and couldn't be trusted to handle the DNA test.

280

Alise was hopeful that things could work themselves out without her having to sacrifice her boys. She knew Callie was smart, but still very overwhelmed from the turmoil in her life. The old Callie would have been suspicious from the beginning, but now she seemed so lost that her emotions didn't allow her to think clearly. However, today Callie seemed stronger. She already knew something was not quite right so maybe, after seeing the real Paula, she would figure out that there was more to her story.

Alise realized that while she was hopeful, she was also fearful at the same time. While she hoped this revelation of who Paula really was would open their eyes, she was also afraid that another family rejection would make them both want to bury their heads. They had both just been told their mother had lied to them their whole lives and that their father is currently unknown. What Paula just confessed to them was another emotional slap in the face that they didn't deserve and that they might not be able to handle.

But Callie said she wanted to fight back and Alise was prepared to do everything in her power to make sure Callie didn't surrender. Even though Alise knew that Callie was smart, she knew that Paula was smart, too. Not to mention, a lot more deceitful than Callie will give her credit for.

Alise already believed she would somehow use this moment of truth and turn it into a cry for help. This hurtful confession, one that she would later be ashamed of, will almost certainly be used to host a pity party with Marlisa and Callie as the invited guests. Paula was gifted at manipulation and scheming and more than likely she would be up to any challenge Callie or Marlisa sent her way. So Alise knew she couldn't put her guard down and rely on this one episode to trip up Paula.

Although she had to admit that deep down she didn't *want* the two sisters to put two and two together. It was purely selfish on her part, but Alise knew that if they uncovered Paula's scheme, that would mean she would not be able to personally take down Paula in defeat.

Any other resolution would mean that Paula was the victor in the battle of wits between the two of them, and Alise refused to let her win.

"Not so happy now, huh Paula?"

"No, I'm still happy Alise," Paula answered matter-of-factly, recalling that on some level, she had control of each of her sisters, "because I'm the smartest one in this room. But you are a close second. No offense Callie, but me and Alise have been playing this game a long time."

"What about me?" Marlisa asked.

Paula rolled her eyes and shook her head from side to side sighing.

"Ok, Marlisa, you're smart too," she said in a mocking tone.

"What's that supposed to mean?" Marlisa asked, extremely offended.

"It means what it means, Marlisa."

"Are you trying to say I'm stupid?" Marlisa snapped, standing up from her chair. "People in North Carolina don't think I'm so stupid."

"You're stupid for talking about North Carolina right now," Paula snapped back without missing a beat. "Besides, I didn't call you stupid."

"Yes, you did," Alise chimed in. "We all heard you. Wait a minute, North Carolina?"

"I just want to make the point that your choices are questionable," Paula said, ignoring Alise.

"What choices?" Marlisa asked innocently. Paula tried hard to contain her irritation, but Marlisa was trying her patience.

"Well, you're going after your sister's husband, a man who is clearly in love with his wife and who clearly *does not want you*!"

"He slept with me, didn't he?"

"Careful," Callie warned eyeing Marlisa.

"Girl you got a lot of nerve, I'll give you that," Paula said to Marlisa, giving Callie a quick look.

"And so do *you*!" Alise countered.

282

"You're right Alise, I do. But I'm not spending my life trying to take somebody's man and then sitting across the table from her looking her right in her face. Callie ought to choke you right now for that!"

"I don't need you on my side. You hate me remember? And all because *my father* loved *me*," Callie said frowning at Paula.

"You sure he's your daddy?"

"Oh, hell no!" Alise said pushing back from the table. "We ain't gonna go there unless you really want me to!"

"Get your butt off your back, Alise. You too, Callie. And if it makes you feel any better I'm not on your side, I'm just stating a fact. Marlisa probably drugged Michael to get him into bed with her in the first place. Callie, you are obviously the winner of that man's heart. You should just forgive him and get on with your life."

"She doesn't need your sisterly advice," Marlisa said, still standing.

"And I don't need your sisterly two cents," Callie snapped staring at Marlisa intently.

"Ok, everybody should just calm down." Paula said as she began pouring champagne in the glass flutes. "This is our first meeting and it's about to be a free-for-all."

"Don't nobody tell me to calm down! I don't have to calm down if I don't want to!" Marlisa yelled looking at each of her sisters.

"Marlisa you better sit your butt down before I choke you myself!" Alise said, angrily.

"Oh, surprise, surprise," Marlisa said, "Alise is on Callie's side!"

"When it comes to sleeping with Callie's husband, she should be on her side!"

"Shut up Paula! Don't tell me whose side I should be on!" Alise shouted now directing her anger at Paula.

"Oh, Alise, please. This is ridiculous! All of ya'll are just being too dramatic! I don't even know what started this argument in the first place."

"What started this argument," Alise said "is the fact that we can't stand each other!"

"Well, for once I agree with Paula," Marlisa said, looking directly at Callie.

"Don't be agreeing with me making me look bad."

"- this *is* ridiculous," Marlisa continued, "and I'm not wasting any more of my time hating on nobody!"

"You don't have a reason to be hating on nobody! You're the one crying after people husbands!" Alise replied angrily, letting her experience of dealing with the "other woman" come out.

"Not people – *yours*," Paula said pointing at Callie before taking a sip of her champagne.

"I don't need to hear nothing *none of ya'll* have to say. I'm leaving!" Marlisa grabbed her purse.

"You don't get to run out on this," Callie said standing up.

"Oh, yeah?"

"Yeah. You take one step towards that door and see if I don't come across that table and choke the life out of you."

"What's with ya'll and all the choking'?" Marlisa asked, throwing her hands in the air.

"You're about to find out! So if I were you I'd stand still, 'cause *you know* she's quick across a table," Paula said grinning, enjoying the entire confrontation.

"Oh, Lord I'm having a déjà vu. Everybody just wait a minute," Alise said throwing up her hands with one palm facing Marlisa and the other facing Callie. "Just freeze both of you!"

The women all fell silent, just as Franklin entered the conference room. He stood uneasily in the uncomfortable silence.

"You couldn't have better timing, Franklin," Alise said calmly, looking from one sister to the other.

"Can we all just sit down and be quiet now?" she asked.

"I'm already sitting down, Alise," Paula said taking another sip of champagne, clearly amused.

284

"I'm glad you're having a good time, Paula. But you just hold that thought. Franklin, you have everything?"

"Everything is in order. Just like you asked."

"I don't know what you think you're up to, but I'm not signing nothing else. You can't take anything away from me," Paula said suddenly becoming serious.

"You see, that's just how you think, Paula. It's always take, take, take with you isn't it?"

"It's the American way."

Callie, Marlisa and Alise all took their seats and Franklin laid out the paperwork in front of Alise and Callie. Paula fell silent as she watched Alise and Callie sign several documents. She noticed that Callie looked a bit confused and hesitated for just an instant. That told Paula that Alise was the one who had put this new show together and Callie was just following along as usual.

Paula admittedly felt a bit nervous but she was more curious than anything. After Franklin left with the newly signed papers, Alise picked up a champagne flute and stood up. Callie grabbed a glass and stood up, too.

"Now we can celebrate," Alise said smiling.

"What's going on?" Marlisa asked.

"I'm sure Alise is just about to fill us in," Paula answered setting her glass down.

"Here's to our new partnership," Alise said lifting her glass and taking a sip.

"What are you talking about? What were those other papers that -"

"Be quiet, Marlisa," Paula snapped while locking eyes with Alise.

"Don't tell me to be quiet 'cause I'm tired of everybody trying to order me around! Be quiet, Marlisa! Sit down, Marlisa! Sign this, Marlisa! I am not a child and I am tired of everybody talking down to me!"

Paula sighed heavily and rolled her eyes turning her attention to Marlisa.

"Don't you have a man stealing class to go to or something? You know you can't afford to miss even one class because *clearly* you're failing."

Callie snickered and looked at Marlisa. "You have to admit, she's a bitch but she's funny."

Marlisa sat back in her seat and folded her arms. The other sisters knew this to be her pouting pose. They often saw it after she would have a tantrum when she was little. And just like when she little, they all quickly ignored her.

Ironically, it had always been Callie that broke rank and would go to her to make sure she was okay. All she needed was a little attention and she would be happy as a lark. Callie looked at her now remembering the sister she had adored and felt her heart aching from the loss. She knew they could never go back to the way they were and she had accepted that a long time ago. But it was these unexpected flashes of memories which she couldn't control that would always send her for a loop. She briefly closed her eyes and steadied herself before turning her attention back to Alise.

"Go on Alise," Paula implored while smiled slyly. "I know this has got to be good. What did you and Callie just do?"

"We just changed the partnership agreement."

"You can't change what we already signed. I still have twenty eight percent."

"True. I didn't change that."

Alise could see the relief in Paula's face and felt a surge in satisfaction knowing that she wouldn't be relieved for long.

"But I *did* change *my* percentage. I just gave Callie twenty-six percent. Add that to her twenty-five percent and well, you do the math."

Marlisa threw her head back and howled with laughter. Clapping her hands, she stood up and then grabbed a glass.

"All that loud talking and backstabbing for control and you got shut down! Yep, I think it *is* time to celebrate!" Marlisa lifted her flute up high, grinning at Paula.

"I don't know what you have to celebrate. You just went from owning half of a company to only owning twenty percent. The lowest one here." Paula reminded her.

"Correction. I have the lowest percentage here," Alise said. "I had twenty-seven percent, remember? I kept one percent but I did give Callie power of attorney to use my percentage and proceeds anyway she wants. I really only have it in name only."

"In name only? What's the point?" Marlisa asked puzzled.

"That's easy," Paula said eyes narrowing, "she wanted to keep ownership in order to have access to company information. She wants to be able to keep an eye on things going on around here."

"Things or people. But you get the point," Alise said looking at Paula.

"I always did say you were a worthy opponent, Alise," Paula said. Then smiling knowingly she added, "but the game is not over."

"Oh, no where near. You're still here, aren't you?" Alise asked before taking another sip of champagne.

Callie looked between the two of them, knowing there was a deeper meaning to all of this, but also knowing neither one would be willing to explain it. Alise said she would explain it all one day so Callie would not push - for now. She had given her word that she would trust her sister and she would not go back on it. But she needed answers soon and one way or the other she would get them.

Callie let herself feel thankful and happy. Alise was right about setting things right today. She now had complete control of the company, which actually put her in a better position than when she shared it equally with Marlisa.

She would immediately put out a memo to all staff that neither Marlisa nor Paula had the power to make business decision on behalf of the company. Contracts from now on were only to be signed by her and any changes to policy must be approved by her as well. By the time she was finished, they wouldn't even be able to order a set of

287

pens.

The next task she was going to do was to make the two of them share an office. They were going to hate it. Callie smiled at the thought. This arrangement could make coming into the office a great source of personal entertainment. Hopefully it will make both Marlisa and Paula steer clear of the office altogether. Neither one was needed anyway.

Callie felt a sense of relief for the first time in a long time, but she also felt a little apprehension. There were things going on between her sisters behind her back, secrets that directly affected her. Callie decided she was going to find out about one of those secrets right now.

"That's an interesting observation that Paula made Marlisa. I mean, you only have twenty percent, that's *less than one fourth*, and you seem completely satisfied. Why is that?"

"Because I'm not as stupid as y'all think I am. I didn't just spend, spend, spend but I invested my money too. I have somebody working really hard to keep my portfolio profitable. I don't actually need the income from this company to keep me in the lifestyle that I've become accustomed to and I certainly don't need to power trip about being in charge. So twenty percent is just fine with me."

"I'm not talking about the money or the power, Marlisa. I'm talking about having less than the twenty-five percent that we all started with. That five percent that just floated around this table belonged to you and I want to know why you let it go.

Supposedly, you thought Paula could do a good job running things, but that little happy dance you just did was like an alcoholic at an open bar. You didn't give away your share to put Paula in charge because you thought it was a good idea and you certainly didn't do it for nothing. So why'd you do it? What did you get for it?"

Marlisa looked at Callie stunned by the question. She wasn't ready for the question and she certainly wasn't ready to tell the truth. Callie had no idea how devoted she was to Michael and Marlisa knew that that could work in her favor. Right now, Callie thought that Michael may have used or misled her somehow all these years. That speculation kept a wedge between them, a wedge that Marlisa could easily exploit. It would be in her best interest not to let on that she was anything more than a harmless, lovesick fool. She didn't want to let Callie know she *really was* plotting to get her out of the way so that she could have Michael.

Marlisa also felt a deep sense of sadness because she didn't want to hurt Callie any more than necessary. It was just destiny that she and Michael end up together, but since Callie didn't understand, she would be terribly hurt. Even through all that has happened, deep down she still loved her. This revelation would cut deep and Marlisa wasn't quite ready to do that to her sister.

"You know what?" Paula stood up and grabbed her glass, "this is time to celebrate. Are you going to tell her Marlisa, or should I?"

Marlisa stared wide-eyed at Paula before letting her eyes drift back to Callie.

"I'll take her silence as a thumb up. I got the extra percent of the business because I blackmailed her."

"What!" Marlisa looked incredulously at Paula.

"She had it in her mind that you and Michael were getting back together and she wanted to do something to get you at each other's throats again. She made sure that you, her and Michael were at the office together so you could overhear how he knew that she was in love with him. She thought you would freak out - something about 'trust issues'. I found out that it was a set up and that I was used as a pawn."

"You're lying!"

"I don't have to lie! The truth of the matter is that you used me to get them there for your little trap and I found out about it!"

"I didn't use you! You volunteered!"

"So it's true? You lied about killing yourself just to get Michael there?" Alise asked.

"It was Paula's idea. I didn't -"

Marlisa stopped suddenly because of the cold splash of champagne across her face.

"Another round, Alise," Callie said, looking intently at Marlisa as she extended her empty glass towards Alise.

"It wasn't my idea!" Marlisa insisted, wiping her face with the back of her hand.

"Callie, I don't believe Paula's role in this was as innocent as she's making out."

"It doesn't matter, Alise. Marlisa went along with it because she wants my husband."

"You're right, I did," Marlisa admitted in complete control of her composure.

She knew they had expected her to run crying from the room or become hysterical but she realized she was playing with the big kids now. Paula added an entirely new dimension to everything. She would have to play it smarter now and that meant to trust no one and always do her homework.

She looked at Paula wanting to smile. She couldn't wait to start using all the dirt the private investigator would dig up on her. It wouldn't end with just getting Michael. She would make sure Paula was out of their lives forever.

"Things have gotten out of control and I don't know what I can do about it."

"You can leave him alone. You can leave us alone!"

"You're getting a divorce!"

"He's still the father of my children! I'm still your sister! That makes it wrong! But you don't see that because you're so selfish and lonely that it's pathetic!"

"Amen!" Paula said, raising her glass in a toast. "I'll drink to that!"

"Nobody seems to understand that I'm sorry for the trouble I've caused, but I don't know how to fix it!" Marlisa knew changing her approach was the first step to playing it smart.

She had to work on her relationship with Callie because although

290

she stood between her and Michael, she was also the only link between them as well. Without Callie, Marlisa couldn't even get within ten feet of Michael. He wouldn't even talk to her. And since she couldn't count on being invited to the family Christmas dinner, she could only interact with Callie in the office. Marlisa would use their working relationship to get closer. She would become a mature, hard worker that Callie could count on to get things down. She knew the bond they shared could never be the same as it was before, but she could make their relationship better, friendlier.

She would get Paula to work hard on Michael, while she would turn her attention on Callie. She would become the little sister that needed protection again, reminding Callie that Michael may have taken advantage of her. If Callie was unsure of Michael, then the rift between them would always be there and Marlisa fully intended to take advantage of it. But of course she had to get close to Michael, too. And the closer she got to Callie, the closer she would get to Michael.

"Callie, from the bottom of my heart, I am sorry. I was just…just confused about everything. I don't like where we are now. I miss my sister."

"You never apologized before," Callie said surprised.

"She never apologized before?" Paula asked in disbelief.

"I always wanted to but I was afraid you wouldn't think I meant it."

"I don't think she means it now, Callie," Alise said.

"I *do* mean it, Callie. It took me awhile to get it, but I know how wrong I've been. I've lost a lot this past year starting with you. Can you forgive me?"

The room was quiet while all eyes were on Callie. She stood silently looking at Marlisa, wanting to have her sister back, but she couldn't do it. She couldn't forgive Marlisa, at least not now. One apology was not going to do it.

That bitch is good Paula thought as she watched Marlisa. *Callie is softening, just a little.*

291

Suddenly, Paula grabbed the champagne bottle and filled everyone's glass to the top.

"Ok, that's not going anywhere. New subject. I would like to propose a toast," she said raising her glass in the air, "To the new partnership."

Marlisa, Callie and Alise all stood looking at Paula without raising their glass.

"What? What's the matter?" Paula asked.

"I ain't drinking to that! I am not happy about being your partner," Alise said frowning.

"Ok, then. How about," Paula raised her glass again, "To peace in the family."

"Peace? With you in the picture?" Alise crossed her arms. "I ain't drinking to that, either!"

"Ok," Paula said frowning as she tried to quickly think of something else, "how about 'To honesty'." Paula raised her glass and then chuckled adding, "Oh, who am I kidding! With this group? I won't drink to that myself!"

"Drink to it? You can't even say it with a straight face," Callie said slightly amused.

"Ok, I got one," Marlisa said lifting her glass, "How about 'to clearing the air.'"

"How about 'to clearing your desk'," Callie said dryly.

Paula chuckled again. Alise couldn't help herself and finally smiled.

"Alright then, how about 'to finding happiness'," Marlisa proposed, again raising her glass.

"How about 'to finding your way to the door'," Callie said, trying to keep a straight face while Paula and Alise laughed. Even Marlisa had to smile.

"How about 'to being able to sleep tonight'," Alise offered looking at Paula.

"That's no good for me. I sleep good every night. But how about 'to winners'," Paula said. "I know a little something about that," she added, grinning at Alise.

"Are you kidding? How can I drink to that when the room is *half* filled with losers," Callie smiled and looked between Paula and Marlisa. All the women laughed looking around the room at each other.

"Ok, how about 'to sisters'," Marlisa said raising her glass.

"How about 'to having too many sisters'," Callie said lifting her glass towards the middle of the table.

"Here! Here!' Alise said raising her glass to meet Callie's.

"Now I'll drink to that!" Paula raised her glass too.

"Amen!" Marlisa brought the last flute to meet the others.

Callie looked at each of her sisters participating in the toast as they touched glasses and sipped their champagne. Secrets, lies, promises, hurt, betrayal and love is what they all brought to the relationship. Is this how it was with all sisters? Callie didn't know how other sisters in other families got along, but she couldn't believe any family could be worse than the group in the room with her at that moment. Callie took another sip of champagne and then laughed as another insult hurled across the room.

These women, her sisters, were a part of her life that she now had to face daily. Even though it seemed impossible, she realized that she loved them all. It was different for each one, but there was still an inexplicable bond. They were her family. This was her life. When dealing with her sisters she understood that she still had some secrets to uncover and relationships to define and that sometimes, no *most* of the time, it would be all out war. It was odd, but she felt a glimmer of hope, a feeling she had lost over the last year.

Callie smiled in spite of herself because she knew at that very moment that she was going to be okay. Things would be different, but then again she was different. For the first time that she could remember, she didn't have every little detail in her life well thought out and planned ahead of time. It felt strange, but she was realizing that sometimes it's good to just live in the moment.

Now, with her sisters in the middle of her life, she had no choice but to take things day by day. She didn't know what chaos her sisters would bring with them, but she felt energized rather than afraid. She didn't know what was going to happen with Michael or Stephen, but the challenge of facing everything, including the unknown, head on was actually a little exciting.

She had her company back and she decided she would accept her new relationship with Michael - even if they didn't get back together. She hoped they could be a couple again. However, it was important that they forge a new relationship, discovering each other all over again. It was unrealistic to think they could somehow pick up where they left off.

Already she had spent too many nights wishing for the past and afraid to face the future. Not anymore. She had to look forward with confidence instead of looking backwards for comfort. Callie suddenly felt at peace. She couldn't explain it, but somehow she knew she would survive whatever life threw her way. She wouldn't be perfect, but she wouldn't break, either. She would survive by accepting the good, releasing the bad and crossing her fingers for luck with everything in between.

And if she knew her sisters, if she knew anything about the women gathered around the conference table, she knew this – she was going to need a heck of a lot more than luck.

Don't miss the upcoming sequel!
"Too Many Secrets"

Made in the USA
Lexington, KY
02 November 2011